GLOWING PRAISE FOR
White Girl Problems

"Made me laugh a lot and cry a little. It's about time someone drew our attention to the devastating reality: white girl problems are all around us . . . absolutely hysterical."

—Susan Sarandon

"A snarky, satirical diary/memoir of how the poor-little-rich-girl goes from the lap of luxury to rehab after a $246,893.50 shopping spree meltdown at Barneys. . . . A confessed train wreck, [Babe] giddily invites you to stare. And just when you think you might finally need to look away, there's the impossibly startling— and hilarious—faux insight that keeps you hooked."

—*Publishers Weekly*

"A pop-culture send-up with a troubled material girl anti-heroine . . . wickedly funny."

—*Kirkus Reviews*

"Amusing and laugh-out-loud funny."

—*NewNowNext*

"Do you ever go to the mall, buy one too many shirts, and then realize you're $11 million in debt? . . . If you love Hollywood and love to laugh, *White Girl Problems* is the page-turner for you."

—Examiner.com

Psychos

A WHITE GIRL PROBLEMS BOOK

XO

Babe Walker

G

GALLERY BOOKS

New York   London   Toronto   Sydney   New Delhi

G

Gallery Books
A Division of Simon & Schuster, Inc.
1230 Avenue of the Americas
New York, NY 10020

First Gallery Books trade paperback edition April 2014

GALLERY BOOKS and colophon are registered trademarks of Simon & Schuster, Inc.

For information about special discounts for bulk purchases, please contact Simon & Schuster Special Sales at 1-866-506-1949 or business@simonandschuster.com.

The Simon & Schuster Speakers Bureau can bring authors to your live event. For more information or to book an event contact the Simon & Schuster Speakers Bureau at 1-866-248-3049 or visit our website at www.simonspeakers.com.

Interior design by Jaime Putorti

Manufactured in the United States of America

10 9 8 7 6 5 4 3 2

Library of Congress Cataloging-in-Publication Data

Walker, Babe.
Psychos : a white girl problems book / Babe Walker. — First Gallery Books trade paperback edition.
pages cm
1. Young women—Fiction. 2. Women, White—Fiction. 3. Self-realization in women—Fiction. 4. Humorous fiction. I. Title.
PS3623.A3588P89 2014
13'.6—dc23   2013033580

ISBN 978-1-4767-3415-6
ISBN 978-1-4767-3416-3 (ebook)

Dedicated to the strongest
person I know: me

La terre est couverte de gens qui ne méritent pas qu'on leur parle.

(The earth swarms with people who are not worth talking to.)

—Voltaire

contents

Psychos

one

FLOAT IN THE LIGHT.

When I first got to rehab, I was morbidly obese. Not physically, but emotionally. I was angry at myself, angry at the world, and angry at my phone. But four months of rehabilitation for a (possible) shopping addiction and an (alleged) alcohol/drug addiction had brought me to a much more peaceful place.

Achieving inner (and outer) peace had been no picnic. Rehab basically sucked for the first three months. People passive-aggressively punished me for being pretty, I ate 100 percent more white foods than I would have liked, and I shoveled way too much horse shit, literally. Like, actual shit that came out of a horse, with an actual shovel. But then something changed. I couldn't tell you why, but the last month at Cirque Lodge was magical; it was like the fog cleared and I suddenly understood why I'd made so many bad decisions in my life. I gave in to my own healing process. I wrote apology letters and made amends with some loved ones whom I'd slandered in the past, told a nurse with bad skin that she was smart, met my birth mother for the first time, taught myself sign language, and accepted that the real reason people hate each other is because they hate themselves.

I was unchained. It was like having a midlife crisis, except instead of being a sad, saggy forty-six-year-old with a botched face-lift, I was twenty-five and ten pounds lighter, thanks to a stomach virus and the medication I took to treat it. I was in the best shape of my life. I was a New Babe Walker, a glowier Babe, a Babe with goals and aspirations. As I looked out over the sprawling Utah mountains on my last day of treatment, I realized I was my own soul mate. I was ready to marry myself and take myself on a honeymoon to The Rest of My Life. In that moment of beauty and reflection, I could've never foreseen what was soon to come.

When Jackson, my rehab counselor, walked me out of Cirque and helped me load my fourteen suitcases (Goyard) into two idling black Escalades, I felt what can only be described as heartache. This was it. I was actually leaving the place that had been my sanctuary of cigarettes and fur for the last four months of my life. I felt like a delicate butterfly emerging from a chrysalis. The winds were strong, but I knew I had to be stronger.

"So this is good-bye, I guess," I said, giving Jackson's arm a gentle squeeze. I would have hugged him, but I'm allergic to raw lamb's wool. "Thanks for helping me find me."

"Babe, I was but an eagle soaring overhead, lovingly watching you scale the canyons of despair and the peaks of hope on your journey back to your true self."

"Well, you're the best eagle-man I've ever known. I won't miss your almond breath, but I'll miss your spirit."

"And I'll certainly miss your liveliness and your honesty, Babe. You can always call me if you feel like you're slipping back into old habits."

"Got it. I'll text you when I get home and wanna do coke or buy an entire spring collection."

"Alright. May your path be one of serenity and sincerity."

"And may your path lead you to a Sephora, where you'll discover that French shampoo I've been telling you about. Bye, Jackson."

"Walk in love and light, Babe. Let the universe deliver."

A single tear rolled down my cheek as the Escalade drove away from Cirque, Jackson getting smaller and smaller as I watched him wave through the back window, but I wiped it away with a sense of pride. I had set out to do something and I'd finished it. That felt good. I put my headphones on and listened to a playlist I'd curated of Tibetan monks chanting life-affirming statements, all the way to the airport.

In a few short hours, I'd landed safely at LAX and was in another Escalade (white this time) on the way to my dad's house in Bel Air. Apparently rehab had worked, because I didn't raise my voice once during the entire trip back home. A first for me. Thankfully, the flight was only mildly annoying. Some ogre tried to steal my window seat, but moved when I delivered an icy but kind stare instead of speaking directly to him. Then, when

I was retrieving my luggage at the baggage claim, I mistakenly counted thirteen suitcases instead of fourteen, which would have been a disaster for Old Babe, but New Babe was all about grace under pressure and re-counting. The whole moment was defused quickly with a few breathing exercises. Such a tough scenario, because baggage handlers can be *so* flippant some-times—it's like they don't care about anyone's needs but their own. But I guess everyone has a story.

Standing in the foyer of my dad's house, I inhaled the aroma of Tom Ford Tobacco Vanille candles—the quintessential smell of home.

"Welcome back, love!" my dad shouted from the top of the stairs. "You look bloody radiant."

"Dad!" I exclaimed, climbing the staircase to hug him.

"Let me look at you. My God, I know five actresses and one pop star who would kill their firstborn if it meant having your glow," he said as he kissed my forehead. "How are you, my sweet?"

"I'm good! I'm so glad to be home," I said, looking around. "Did you get my email about moving out?"

During my last week at Cirque, I'd decided that the first order of business as "independent me" was getting a place of my own, so I'd informed all family members as well as the staff that I'd be relocating to our guest house. It's important to have your own space post-rehab, where you can be still, reflect on life, and not get distracted by any personal family chefs you used to fuck or pets you don't like.

"Of course, darling. Everything was moved this afternoon. Your new home awaits. I must say, I'll miss you. This house won't be nearly as loud or messy without you."

"I'll miss you too, Dad, but it's for the best. Think of me as a delicate lotus flower. In order to bloom, my leaves have to float on the surface of the pond, but my roots will always reside here."

Overcome by the power of my inner recognition, he grasped the banister for support.

"You sound like Keith Richards after he detoxed in 1977. I'm—I'm glad to have you home. Get settled—dinner is at eight."

The main house on my dad's property is a post-Gothic, ivy-covered precious gem. It's huge but it's cozy, and it's cute but it's cluttered. Great for Old Babe, but too much for New Babe. New Babe needed warmth, light, and space, which is why the guest house made perfect sense. It was originally a three-bedroom that belonged to our neighbors, until a dispute over a weeping willow in the backyard got ugly and my dad decided to buy their house out from under them so they'd leave us alone forever. Then we gutted it and turned it into a huge one-bedroom, complete with an enormous walk-in closet, state-of-the-art bathroom, solarium, and sauna/steam situation. Think French Moroccan meets Tibetan minimalism meets Mary McDonald.

I lost my virginity in this guest house, so it was a sentimental space for me. It had, however, been off-limits after a teeny incident during which the solarium burned down when I let my friend use it for her fledgling nail polish company, which turned out to be a cover for her boyfriend's meth lab. So it was also a dark place for me. Lightness and darkness. Now that the solarium had been rebuilt, I had been rebirthed as New Babe, and my dad trusted me again, it was time for me to make the guest house my own. Little did I know, my safe space would soon be violated.

After I'd watched Mabinty, my Jamaican bff/confidante/housekeeper, unpack my suitcases and smudge the guest house, I had a low-key welcome-home dinner with my dad, Lizbeth (my dad's annoyingly beautiful, upsettingly tall, slightly too young, and far too nice girlfriend), Mabinty, Mabinty's new bangs, and Mabinty's new boyfriend, Carl (a fifty-eight-year-old white version of Randy Jackson . . . unclear). The lighting in the dining room was perfect, and the food was super fresh and low-cal. My dad made a typical dad toast to kick things off.

"When Babe called me to say that she was off to some rehab in Utah, I thought, Oh, here we bloody go. My daughter's addicted to heroin. But then it turned out that she just had a bit of a shopping problem and I was relieved. Then, when Babe called again to tell me she was staying an extra three months at rehab, I knew it must've been heroin all along. As it turns out, she just wanted to put in the extra work. Proud of you, Babe."

"Actually, I was addicted to coke," I interjected, then waited a beat. "Just kidding."

Everyone laughed.

"I hear that, girl!" shouted Carl. Mabinty affectionately patted Carl's back.

"My brother's struggled with addiction for years," Lizbeth chimed in, "but he's not nearly as driven as you are to get his life together, Babe. It's amazing how well you're doing."

"Thanks, Lizbeth. Addiction is no joke. But I was never addicted to drugs. I was addicted to shopping, and that made me feel so good that I wanted to celebrate by taking drugs.

What we resist enslaves us, but what we embrace, we become," I explained calmly.

My dad went on. "It's all very impressive, Babe. You know when enough is enough, you know who you are, and we're so happy to have you back in our lives. Cheers!"

We all took a sip of sparkling water with lemon. Everyone was making a big deal of not drinking alcohol even though I said I didn't care, and I could tell by the end of dinner they were all jonesing for a cocktail. Lizbeth, especially. She kept asking me if I was "okay" and putting her hand on my arm. Old Babe would have stared at her until she stopped talking, but New Babe was absolutely better than okay. I just used some emotional realignment techniques to center myself, smiled, and kept reassuring Lizbeth that I was "great." This whole song-and-dance routine went on for half an hour, and by the end of dinner I was so exhausted that I decided to call it an early night and retreat back to the guest house to unpack my vintage archives, which had just arrived that evening from storage.

I must have fallen asleep inside one of my wardrobe boxes, because I awoke the following morning to a hard slap on the face from my bestie, Genevieve, who was kneeling next to me holding an iced coffee. Roman, my best gay, stood next to Gen.

They looked pissed.

"Babe, get up," Gen commanded.

"You're thinner," remarked Roman.

That got my attention. I rubbed my swollen eyes and threw my hair up into a high pony.

"What time is it?" I asked.

"I have no idea. Ten a.m.?"

"Who let you in?"

"Mabinty. Why don't you want to hang out?" Roman asked.

"No, no, I do," I said as my eyes finally unblurred. "Wow, you both look really slutty, but in a prude way."

"I genuinely appreciate you noticing," Gen responded. "So, how did rehab work out for you in the end? Was it worth it? You look great, but you missed an amazing winter season."

"She didn't miss anything. Stop fucking with her. We were lost without you, Babe. You're a bitch for not calling us the second you got out."

"Yeah. Dish."

"Okay," I sighed as I climbed out of the box, "I fucked this really hot guy named Paul."

"Obviously." Gen smiled.

"Met my mom and her lesbian lover."

"You have a mom?"

"Yes. I'll explain later. It was kind of insane."

"Love it."

"Had an amazing rehab dog."

"Woof."

"Who unfortunately met an untimely death."

"Woooooof."

"Had a terrific rehab masseuse. Learned a lot from her."

"Love."

"She also met an untimely death . . . unrelated."

"So much death. So dark."

"I know. Addressed some of my underlying abandonment/ eating/drug/shopping issues."

"Work. Okay, get dressed. We're taking us to brunch."

"Guys, just because I went to rehab doesn't mean I eat brunch now."

"I know, that was a joke. We're going to Malibu. You don't have to eat."

"Okay, give me thirty."

Two hours later, we all piled into Gen's new Tesla Model S and headed off to Malibu. You leave town for four months and cars become slightly more expensive, electric, and have a huge iPad display thingy in the front dash? Unclear.

"How excited are you about Roman's new single?" Gen squeaked.

"*Quoi?*" I squeaked back.

"You haven't heard it? Romie, you didn't send her the song? It's everywhere, and it's everything!"

I was confused. Roman didn't sing. He refused to even enter a karaoke bar.

Gen continued. "Right after you left town he started recording some tracks with this DJ he knows." She beamed. "It's in the Top Ten on iTunes—"

"It's called 'Pièce de Résis-dance,'" said Roman. "Stupid name, I know, wasn't my idea, and it's pretty much—"

"THE club song of the year. I'm so proud. We're obviously going to listen to it immediately." Gen started messing with the dashboard/iPad thing.

The song was heinous, but I could already tell I'd love it after a few more listens or a few hits of a joint.

"Wait—Roman, this is actually good." I smiled.

"Thanks. I mean, it's whatever. Also . . . Gen just found out last week that she's being made senior vice president at her firm," he announced.

I was annoyed that the focus wasn't 100 percent on me and my struggles, because I'm pretty sure I was the one who just got back from rehab, but I just smiled and nodded. Neither of their successes was surprising. Roman was a club promoter, he knew every DJ in town, and was one of the best-looking gays in LA, if not LA and New York. And Gen had been working in real estate ever since her parents put her on Adderall at age ten.

"Congrats. I'm so happy for you both. Isn't it nice that we've all come so far in the past few months?" I continued. "Roman is a YouTube celeb, Gen got a promotion at work, and I've been emotionally promoted to a higher level of existence and understanding about life." I knew that was kind of rude, but I'd just reemerged into the world and was finding it hard to be genuinely interested in someone else's moment.

We drove around for a while, smoked cigarettes, watched people brunch, and went to Gen's parents' newly renovated Malibu house, where she and Roman revealed their plan to throw me a proper welcome-home party.

I accepted their offer because rejecting it would have made me look like a cunt, and I may be a cunt, but I sure as fuck didn't want to look like one. Especially not fresh out of rehab. Post-rehab, you want people to think that you're better but not completely healed of your special sickness, whatever it may be. If you act like you're totes fine and nothing happened, then people will think you're insane and you will have zero sex. Trust. I may have only been in rehab for four short months, which is nothing by LA standards, but I knew my shit.

Anyway, the next day they both came over to sketch out the broad strokes. After careful consideration, we decided to have a small dinner party in lieu of a massive blowout. They didn't want me to, but I insisted on helping and went ahead with curating the guest list, floral theme, and scent story. Roman smoked a joint, Gen got annoyed at him for being stoned, and then Roman showed us the people he was "seeing" on Grindr.

I spent the next morning aggressively texting/inviting/guilting my desired ten-person guest list to come to the party. They all eventually agreed, thank God. I then went about locating and booking rare tropical birds to make up for the party's otherwise lack of wildlife. No post-rehab bash is complete without a few representatives from the animal kingdom. They elegantly remind us that we're all animals on this earth, constantly evolving yet eternally caged. At Cirque they told us that having animals in our lives would keep us grounded, and that caring for another living thing releases oxytocin in our brains and that's, like, as powerful as doing a line of blow or something. I didn't totally get it, but I was going with it. So the party needed birds.

Planning this event was proving difficult. Gen was "too busy at work" to return my texts, so I couldn't even get an approximate pool depth for my exotic fish guy, which meant there would be no platinum arowanas (google them) spicing up the otherwise boring backyard. Also, my orchid dealer was too busy planning Demi Moore's new boyfriend's bris to handle putting together centerpieces for my intimate soiree. Hydrangeas would have to suffice.

On the day of the party, I found solace in a kale lollipop for lunch, went for a quick jog down and then back up my drive-way, showered, and then napped for twenty-five minutes. When I felt rested enough to be nice to my hair and makeup people, they came over.

Mabinty and I were sitting in my bathroom while Hair gave me a blowout and Makeup worked on dulling my forehead shine. I would usually learn their names, but I was under a lot of stress that night. I really didn't appreciate the fact that I was going to have to eat in front of people again to fully display my recovery. Oh, and yes, I have forehead shine. I'm human, get off me.

"So," I said to Mabinty, "when I walk in, should I just go straight to the head of the dinner table and begin the toast I wrote to myself? Whoa, easy with the powder up there."

"Sorry, Babe," whimpered Makeup.

"You're forgiven." I turned back to Mabinty. "Or should I greet people and act as if the party's not all about me? Like, be totally casual? I'm glad it's going to be intimate, but that almost makes it more awkward to navigate."

"Yuh gwan be fine. Don' overtink nutin' tonight. Be yuh-self, that's what yuh friends be missin' the past few months. So, give dem Babe Walker. Don't worry what dey tink," advised Mabinty, the wise one.

"Oh. Okay, I'll just completely disregard what anyone thinks about me. That's really easy to do, Mabs."

"Yuh bein' a bitch."

"Mi know," I muttered, closing my eyes and rubbing my temples in an attempt to center my thoughts.

"If yuh dun know by now, we rootin' for ya, gyal. Yuh need a smooth transition back into yuh life here in LA."

"Mi know," I said.

God, I'd missed my sweet, cunty Mabinty.

"But yuh gwan be fine. Bettah than fine. Yuh'll be great again. While yuh were away, mi started meditatin' like yuh always told me to do."

"Mabs! Bless!" I turned to Hair. "I've been telling her to get her zen game together since I was eight. So stubborn, this one." Hair just nodded. "What time is it?" I asked.

"Seven fifteen," said Makeup, glancing down at some kind of plastic Michael Kors watch, I'm sure.

"Fuck. Okay, we're done here. I need to get dressed. Cocktails started at six, so people are probably showing up there now."

I'd sketched out a few looks (like I always do, as mirrors are not to be trusted) and decided on my party outfit: a vintage Pucci jumpsuit, a vintage Judith Leiber Buddha Bag, and purple Prada platforms. I slowly walked toward the front door of Gen's parents' Malibu manse feeling powerful yet likable, expecting to simply float into a manageably small and chic gathering; I stepped through the front door only to be confronted by a very, very harsh reality. It was packed. Hundreds of people. Strangers. It smelled like sugar and beer, which was alarming because I'd designed a lavender/old library scent with my aromist specifically for the event.

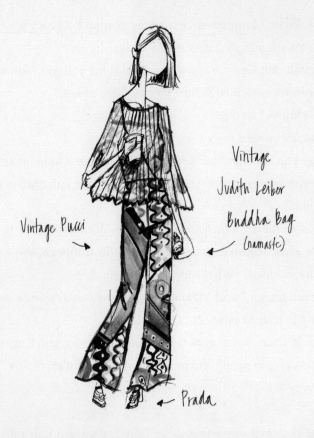

Vintage
Judith Leiber
Buddha Bag
(namaste)

Vintage Pucci →

← Prada

Genevieve and Roman had apparently invited all of Malibu, half of the Lakers, and anyone who'd ever slept with James Franco. In a word, it was *merde*. I'm talking magenta balloons, WELCOME HOME banners, plastic cups, teenagers, and a keg.

My body must've gone into shock. If that Laker hadn't been there to catch my fall, I would have broken my nose from fainting, again. I found the closest unoccupied room and stood in silence with my eyes tightly shut, trying to calm myself. *I am peace. I am me. Me is peace. I am peace. I am me. Me is peace. I am peace. I am—*

BAM! The door swung open so hard that it almost flew off of its hinges.

Standing before me was a very drunk Genevieve and some girl I didn't recognize, whose presence at that particular moment baffled me because she was also wearing vintage Pucci and a lot of foundation.

After I struggled to stomach Gen's inappropriately formal, one-shouldered Christian Siriano gown, I released the following words from my trembling lips:

"Why are you doing this to me?"

"Um. Are you kidding? Look around," she slurred, motioning with her Solo cup filled almost to the brim with vodka cranberry. "This is way more fabulous than your party plan."

"What?! No, it's not!"

"And this vibe is so much more you."

"So much more me???" I yelled at her.

"You love when I invite the Lakers! Oh, and the bird guy had to take the birds home. I tried to get him to stay so you could at least see them, but you were so late and he said rap music was too scary for them. So, he left." All of this was said so flippantly, as if she had no idea that I was hysterically crying on the inside.

It was at this exact moment that I realized being away for four months had had a real effect on me. Before rehab, I would've loved a party like this. But I wasn't going to tell Gen that. "You obviously don't know me anymore. Excuse me, I have a party to hate." I looked at the girl standing next to Gen. "I don't really know who you are, but I'd appreciate it if I never found out."

With that, I attempted to walk past her and into my party, but she tried to hug me.

"You don't know me, Babe, but I hope that you find the strength to—"

"Excuse me?" I lashed out at her.

"You're in a dark place. I've been there."

"You don't know me, weirdo. Don't pretend that our mutual appreciation for Pucci gives you the right to tell me where I am."

I stormed off, allowing the crowd to swallow me before she had a chance to respond.

The saddest part was that no one there knew who I was. I was standing in a house full of people boozing, coke-ing, smiling, and avoiding Charlie Sheen, yet no one was rushing toward me to tell me that I looked really happy, or that LA blows without me. What was the point of this party, anyway? I didn't want to drink, and I couldn't shop, and I couldn't slap anyone, and there were no hot guys there. The longer I stood watching everyone, the tighter I balled my fists, and the more I wanted to scream.

Float in the light, I am the light, light is light, we are light, ham sa, ham sa shanti—fuck this.

"Do you even know who I am?" I scrasked (scream-asked) a girl in an Alexander Wang dress from the bad season, grabbing her arm.

"Um?"

"Exactly. You should go. It's not safe here." I ushered her away from the crowd.

"But my bag. Wait, what? I just came with some friends . . ."

"You'll be fine."

And like that she was out the door.

I continued this evacuation procedure and was actually making good progress with one of the Jenner girls when someone grabbed my arm and pulled me backward.

"BABE, STOP." It was the strange girl who was with Gen earlier and she looked mad but also scared. Was I being scary? I was totally being scary.

"Who the FUCK are you?!" I shouted at her. I noted that, in extreme close-up, her skin was in really good shape, surprisingly enough.

Roman was standing behind her. "This is ridiculous. Babe, you need to stop, everything is fine," he commanded.

"Roman, you have to understand. I'm fragile and Genevieve is just doing this to annoy me." As if on cue, Genevieve then approached the three of us. "Right, Gen? You've been waiting months to fuck with me again. I get it."

"NO! I thought you would be happy that so many people showed up. But I guess you're right, I DON'T know you. Or at least I forgot what a cunt you can be."

"Wow." I was basically speechless. "And who is she?" I said, motioning to the random girl. "My replacement? Clearly you guys don't give a shit about me anymore."

"Babe," Roman said, trying to grab my hand, but I was already making my way toward the door. I stopped and looked at them with cold, dead eyes.

"The next time one of you gets home from rehab, I'll remember this."

On my way out I grabbed the first tall guy I saw by the hand and dragged him with me. He was oddly not bothered by my psycho behavior.

"Can you take me home? Please? This was supposed to be

my party, but the whole thing got totally out of hand. I hate all of these people. Except you. You're fine. But everyone else. I just . . . I was . . . I'm really fragile tonight. I just . . . I can't."

And then I totally lost consciousness, but I kept repeating those words: "I can't." Over and over and over. It was like a seizure fucked a blackout and gave birth to a litter of tourettes.

"I'll get you home. Just stop talking," I heard him say through the fog.

"Thank you. Um . . ."

"Jonathan."

"Jonathan. Thank you, Jonathan. I'm just really confused right now."

This catastrophic evening took a momentary turn for the better when I stepped into Jonathan's black Land Rover. Once we were in the car, I realized that he smelled amazing, his tan was amazing, he had huge amazing hands, and the top of his head was blessed with amazing surfer hair. Totally not my type, but also totally my type.

"So, did you have fun?" I said, looking out onto the empty highway.

"You mean before you dragged me out?"

"Sorry about that."

"It's okay. And yeah. I guess I was having fun. I'd never seen a Playboy Bunny naked, so that was cool."

"THERE WAS A FUCKING PLAYBOY BUN—" I stopped myself before my scream became crying. I managed to cool down quickly and squeeze out a whimpered: "Oh. Cool. Awesome."

Silence.

"So, who are you?"

"I'm Jon, remember?" he said, smiling.

"I remember your name. I mean, who are you? Besides a potential kidnapper-murderer."

"I surf, I work at a surf shop here in Malibu. I'm in a band, but we don't really play shows. I actually went to high school with you. I was a few years older than you guys."

"You guys?"

"You and Genevieve."

Then I put it together. This was Jonathan Larson. Gen's older cousin through marriage whom she has always wanted to fuck and probably will always want to marry. We used to send him anonymous boob-texts when we were sophomores.

"Oh yeah! You're that guy. I remember you now. You used to date that heavy girl from Spain."

"Flora. Yeah, she was actually at that party. She's engaged now."

"Wow. Good for her."

Silence.

Luckily we were pulling onto Sunset, so I was only a few minutes away from home and the end of this awkward taxi ride.

"So, is it weird to have the same name as the guy who wrote the Broadway musical *Rent*?" I asked.

"Sorry, not a big theater guy. What is that?"

"Oh. Hmmm, I don't know that I've ever met someone who didn't know what *Rent* was. This is my house, you can just let me out here." I grabbed my bag and exited the car. "Thanks for the ride."

"No prob. Uh . . . ?"

"Babe. Babe Walker."

"Right. How could I forget a weird name like that? Later, bro."

After that last sentence, all I could do was look in his general direction and wait for him to reach over and close my door from the inside. I made my way to the guest house, and tried to reconcile my anger with Gen and Roman by doing a yoga/meditation session in the steam room. I couldn't believe they'd thought that was an appropriate event to throw for someone who'd just gotten out of rehab. But considering how fucked up my life was going to get over the next few months, that shitty party would be the least of my worries.

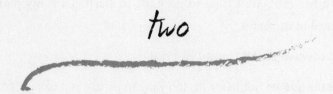

two

TRYING TO DO MORE
REGULAR-PEOPLE STUFF.

Genevieve 7:16AM What is your problem?

This was the text from Gen that I awoke to in the morning. I knew I'd have to deal with her being mad at me after I stormed out of the party, but I didn't like the idea of her being mad at me while I was supposed to be mad at her.

Babe 9:10AM What is your problem?

Genevieve 9:10AM What do you mean?

Genevieve 9:11AM I asked you.

Genevieve 9:15AM What is your fucking problem?

Babe 9:16AM Before answering that, I'd really like to know what your fucking problem is.

Genevieve 9:18AM My problem is that I'm not clear on what your huge problem is right now.

Babe 9:19AM I'm busy. brb

Under the impression that Gen and I could now move on from her mistake, I tried to go back to sleep. Then my phone buzzed in my hand.

Genevieve 9:25AM I fucked your dad.

Babe 9:26AM Not funny. It's too early to be that not funny. Call me later.

Genevieve 9:28AM I'm not trying to be funny.

Babe 9:28AM Genevieve

Genevieve 9:29AM Babe

Babe 9:30AM Genevieve

Genevieve 9:31AM Babe

Babe 9:32AM Gen

Genevieve 9:33AM Babs

Babe 9:35AM Don't call me that.

Babe 9:37AM Why are you doing this?

Babe 9:37AM It's fine. I'm not mad anymore kind of.

Genevieve 9:45AM Ok

Babe 9:46AM Ok what?

Genevieve 9:50AM Ok I slept with your dad while you were at rehab.

Babe 9:51AM You're fucking insane. Being this annoyed right now is giving me wrinkles, I can feel them sprouting.

Babe 9:54AM And besides, I fucked your cousin Jon last night after he drove me home. He's really nice.

Genevieve 9:54AM What?

Babe 9:55AM Kind of weird that he's your cousin, though.

Babe 9:56AM He had a huge dick. It was like losing my virginity all over again.

Genevieve 9:57AM Literally Babe, the DAY after you went to rehab, your dad emailed me and was like you should come over for tea darling and all this shit.

Babe 10:02AM My dad hasn't written one email in his life. Cheryl does them for him.

Babe 10:03AM Did you know Jon plays the bass?

Genevieve 10:04AM Your dad took me to Nobu.

Babe 10:05AM Jon asked me to come on tour with his band.

Genevieve 10:06AM The Nobu in Tribeca. In New York. New York City.

Babe 10:07AM I came six times, it was actually excessive.

Genevieve 10:08AM He fingered me in the restaurant.

Babe 10:08AM He wants to teach me how to surf.

Genevieve 10:08AM Out of all the old guys I've fucked, your dad is definitely the most limber.

Babe 10:08AM Between your younger brother and Jon, I pre-ferred your younger brother.

Genevieve 10:08AM We TRAVELED together.

Babe 10:08AM I'm PREGNANT.

Genevieve 10:10AM You're insane.

Babe 10:11AM We're family now.

Genevieve 10:12AM So are we.

Babe 10:12AM You're my cousin.

Genevieve 10:13AM I'm your mom.

Babe 10:13AM Bye.

Genevieve 10:14AM Ugh bye.

There's no way Gen and my dad ever even did so much as run into each other at The Grove while I was away, much less copulate. He would never and she would never. So I knew she had to be lying. But that didn't mean I was going to come clean about my lie anytime soon.

I fell back asleep and woke up at noon, feeling properly incubated and ready to grab life by the tits. I crawled out from under my igloo of pillows, flossed, brushed my teeth, and headed across the yard to the main house to pick up my hearty breakfast of green juice and an e-cigarette followed by a real cigarette. One of my post-rehab goals was to quit smoking. It's a process.

As I approached the kitchen I heard two very British men talking about the stock market or cars, I can't remember. One of the voices belonged to my dad, but the other was unidentifiable. I try not to enter rooms unless I know exactly who is inside, so I stood waiting for a bit, peering through the thin crack between the door and the wall.

My dad sat with Anonymous at the island, with a cup of tea and an empty cereal bowl in front of him. I could only catch glimpses of the other guy, but I could tell he was about my age and had good hair. I figured he was safe, so I opened the door and feigned surprise when I "saw" them sitting there.

"Oh, good morning," I said, walking toward the fridge.

Not only did this guy have great hair, but his smile was warm and oddly familiar. He was hot, in the most British way. Dirty blond locks, blue eyes, a solid nose. Chris Martin meets Eddie Redmayne meets Prince William. I immediately felt attracted to him, so I ignored him.

"Glad to see you're still getting your fiber, Dad."

He smiled and put his arm out, roping me into a side hug. "If it weren't for this one here, I'd probably have keeled over by now."

"Dad, please! Don't be dark." I kissed him on the cheek and went back to the fridge, maintaining my silent treatment toward the boyfriend in my kitchen.

Then, "Babe, you remember Charles Dean," my dad said. I had to make eye contact now, there was no way around it.

"Hiya, Babe," said Charles. "It's been a long time."

"Charles Dean. Charles Dean? As in fourteen-year-old Charlie Dean from London?" I asked.

"Well, a bit more like twenty-seven-year-old Charlie Dean who now lives in New York. But yeah, same guy."

I hadn't seen Charlie since I was eleven years old, but a flood of memories came rushing back when I realized who he was. His dad grew up with my dad and we've known each other since we were babies. Not only was he one of my first friends, he was my first kiss. I was eleven and there was no tongue, but it was still totally my first kiss.

"You're so much hotter now!" Oh fuck, I really didn't need to say that out loud.

"Well, thanks!" Charlie laughed. My dad was thankfully tuned out, looking at his BlackBerry. I could feel my face turning red. "Lest you forget, I was just thirteen years old when we had our fling," he said with a wink. "I've grown into my teeth since then."

"So random, you being here." I tried to play it cool after my minor word-vomit mishap.

"My girlfriend's here for work, she's an actress and she's doing a few episodes of *Californication*."

"Oh . . . so are you cool with your girlfriend being naked in front of millions of people? I mean, I'm assuming she has to at least show her boobs to be on that show, but I've never seen it, so I wouldn't really know."

"Well-done. She's playing a 'high-class escort,'" Charlie said, making air quotes with his hands.

"That's really cute," I lied, putting some celery stems into the juicer. I had virtually no relationship with Charlie and yet the second he said he had a girlfriend, I was annoyed. I told myself to relax, New Babe doesn't speak jealousy. "So, you're in town for a while?" I asked.

"Just a few days. Figured I'd take meetings with some West Coast clients if I was going to be in LA anyhow."

"Charlie's a big hedge fund guy now, aren't ya? Doing great for himself," my dad said with a huge grin. He'd always loved Charlie, I remembered that. I even recall thinking Charlie might've secretly been my brother, which was weird because we'd kissed that one time.

"I love the work, but it keeps me on a pretty strict schedule in New York, so just a short trip. And no offense, you all have a lovely house, but this town isn't for me. There's just so much—"

"Please," my dad interjected, "I never wanted to live in the face-lift capital of the world, but after almost thirty years, I've grown to love this fucked-up city."

"You have to be a truly open-minded person to live in a place like LA; I think that's why I prosper here," I said, pouring my juice into a glass and walking toward the door. "Hope your girl-friend becomes a big star. It was interesting seeing you, Charlie."

"Likewise, Babe. Do let me know if you're ever in New York. Get my number from your dad, I'd love to catch up properly."

"You got it," I said, almost out the door.

"Oh, I quite liked your book. I read the whole thing in one sitting on a flight to London."

I paused and turned back toward Charlie.

"*White Girl Problems*." Charlie smiled.

BTW: While in rehab, fueled by Adderall and Diet Coke, I'd penned a memoir over the course of forty-eight hours titled *White Girl Problems by Babe Walker*. It was basically my life's struggles put down on paper. When I was finished writing it, I sent it to my dad as part of a "growth exercise" that Jackson recommended. Long story short, my dad (who is an entertainment attorney in Hollywood) loved the memoir, thought it could be a huge hit, and got my blessing to send it out to a few book agents and publishers. There was a bidding war for the manuscript, I got a book deal with a major publisher, it was a

New York Times best seller, blah, blah, blah, the end, back to Charlie, juice, my kitchen.

"You read my book?"

"Yep. Loved it. I know I'm not your key demo, but I'd argue that we've had fairly similar upbringings. So, I'd like to think I get it," Charlie said.

"Thanks. Most people read it and don't think that I'm real, so it's nice to hear that you loved it."

With that, my green juice and I were on our way to the solarium, where I blessed my juice and had a quick meditation before heading to the Equinox on Sunset for a workout. Charlie's smile lingered in my brain.

Old Babe would never be caught dead in a gym, but New Babe was all about putting herself out there and interacting with the incredible, positive people found in sacred places like mosques and group spin classes. While at Cirque, I'd gotten into a workout routine where I'd basically do an hour of yoga, followed by an hour to an hour and a half of cardio (depending on my mood). My yoga practice was getting so solid that I could almost do a pinky-stand, which is major. Google it if you don't believe me. Endorphins were my cocaine and Lululemon pants were my rolled-up hundred-dollar bills.

I was on minute 173 of an 180-minute elliptical sesh, nearing the end of my meditation, when my mind started to wander . . . *Jackson told me to "let the universe deliver," but what does that mean, exactly?* I thought to myself. *What does the universe have in store for me, besides mental clarity and spiritual fulfillment? Will I get a job? If so, where? Do I want a job? Not really. Probably best to wait on the whole job thing for now. Charlie*

*was cute. Will I ever fall in love again? Am I even ready to fall
in love? The last person I loved made me insane. God, I miss
Robert sometimes. He smelled so good and had the best teeth.
And he was funny. I mean, not as funny as me, but I don't really
think I'd want to date someone funnier than me. I wonder what
Robert's doing right now? I wonder if he hates me. He definitely
hates me. But I'm okay with that.* Ohm.

Just as I was pumping out the last few strides of my workout, I took three deep cleansing breaths, closed my eyes for a
moment, and when I opened them again, I saw one of the most
shocking sights of my entire life: Robert was standing about ten
feet away from me doing bicep curls. The same Robert who had
broken my heart into a thousand pieces only two short years
ago. Or had I broken his heart? Either way, I couldn't believe
it. These things don't just happen, right? I took a sip of my oxi-
dized, electrolyte-infused bottled water, wiped a layer of shine
from my forehead, and casually walked over to where Robert
was standing.

"I can't remember, has the restraining order been lifted?" I
smiled. "If not, then I think I have five seconds to move one
hundred and fifty feet away from you. But if it has, then . . . hey."

"Hi, Babe," said Robert in a gravelly tone.

God, he was so fucking sexy. "Hello, Robert."

"I thought you didn't do gyms?" He smiled, putting down
the thirty-five-pound weights he was holding and standing up
to talk to me.

Jesus, his arms were beautiful.

"I'm trying to do more regular-people stuff these days," I
explained, adding, "Also, Fabio works out here, which I love."

"Yeah, it's hilarious."

"You're hilarious." I gave him a coy smile, not flirtatious enough to seem like I was hitting on him and just solicitous enough to be fishing.

"You're pretty funny yourself. Nice yoga pants—namaste."

"Namaste, Robert. Namaste."

I had no idea what else to say next. So I plastered a huge, confident smile on my face and started slowly backing away from him.

"Wait, where are you going? We should catch up. You want to get lunch later?"

"Sure, I'd like that."

The universe delivers.

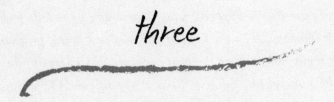

three

FULL. BODY. CHILLS.

Last Season on *The Babe and Robert Chronicles*

*I*t *was the winter of 2011. On a brisk and clear January morning, while at Barneys on Madison Avenue in New York City, Robert noticed Babe as she was buying herself a well-deserved little present (Céline purse). Robert was beautiful in all the ways a man should be. He was 6'4", a successful sports agent with a focus on the NBA, and he was immediately attracted to Babe's energy. How could he not be? She's a force of nature and her hair looked especially shiny that day.*

After discovering that he had a great sense of humor, a passion for designer menswear (in a straight way), and a massive but manageable penis, Babe was smitten. These two love kittens were on the path to romance. They dated for a few months, fell

*in love, and no one could stop them from the wedded bliss that
awaited.*

*But that never happened, because Babe morphed into the
worst possible version of herself, known only as "Babette," and
scared Robert away forever. Babette is a psycho who completely
takes over Babe's life/personality/iPhone when she falls in love
with someone. She's the kind of girl who will fake a pregnancy,
text a guy ninety-seven times in one night, wear Uggs to dinner,
make a bucket list, and put "eat at thirty different Olive Garden
locations" as number three on said list. As soon as Babette reared
her ugly little head, Robert panicked (rightfully so) and broke
things off, but Babette couldn't let go, hence the restraining order.*

*W*ithout question I had single-handedly fucked up the
perfect, promising romance I'd had with Robert the first time
around, but in the back of my mind I'd always maintained a
sneaking suspicion that there was something driving me, cosmically, to him and to our inevitable happy ending. This was it.
Rehab, my current body weight, the positive astrological cli-
mate, global warming, the lighting at Equinox—all of the stars
were aligning.

I rushed home with one mission: putting together a master-
piece of an outfit to wear for my rendezvous with Robert. The
hardest part about being in recovery from a shopping addiction
is the "rule" that you're not "supposed" to "buy new things." My
previous life was based around buying clothes and then finding
events that were worthy of their exposure. I once outbid Anne
Hathaway on a vintage Oscar de la Renta ball gown and wore

it to her engagement party the following week. Fashion used to be my raison d'être, *ma vie, ma mère*. But like all obsessions, it got dark, I lost control, and after hitting rock bottom at Barneys (my sanctuary), I had to be shown the light with some actual therapy—easier said than done. Yes, I'd gone through shopping withdrawals in Utah. I had nightmares about Kim Kardashian wearing Givenchy, and I may have attacked Jackson in a blackout rage when I discovered there was no Internet access, which meant no Net-A-Porter.

When I was at rehab, my look was very mountain-chic. Think Moncler, Michael Kors plaids, *Nanook of the North* furs, turtlenecks. But everyone else at rehab dressed like they were in an episode of *Dawson's Creek,* so it was easy not to think about S/S '13 Lanvin, and all the sample sales around the world that I was missing.

New Babe was resourceful. I'd promised myself that I would only go shopping in my closet for the next six months. Despite having at least seven hundred pieces of clothing that still had their tags and a vintage collection, putting together the perfect look was still going to be one of the more harrowing challenges I'd face post-rehab. I mean, I got out of Cirque right as Lagerfeld debuted Chanel's Fall 2012 collection, which was conceptualized entirely around crystals, so you can imagine how hard it was going to be not to buy six pairs of the embellished Mary Janes.

I ran my hand over last season's dresses, thinking about what look I was going for. Robert would smell desperation from a mile away (he's really observant, for a straight person), so I didn't want to come across like I was trying too hard. I needed an ensemble that embodied a willingness to accept and understand my past and its foibles, yet represented an even greater willingness to move forward and renew. It had to remind Robert of all of the amazing, wonderful, and magical things about our time together, without triggering any reminders that I had become a maniacal chupacabra at the end. This would be our first post-restraining-order encounter and it was going to set the tone for our new life together. I settled on an Erdem dress, a BLK DNM leather jacket, Tom Ford pumps, a blowout that said "I'm relaxed and free but could still be your wife," and a huge fucking scarf.

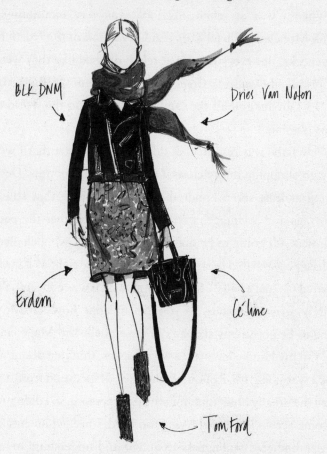

BLK DNM

Dries Van Noten

Erdem

Céline

Tom Ford

Robert and I were meeting at Café Gratitude, a restaurant that serves only vegan and raw food, juices, elixirs, etc. Instead of ordering things on the menu by their names, each item is listed as an affirmation, like "I am glowing" or "I am refreshed." I liked this because it made me feel like I wasn't really ordering food.

I arrived at Café Gratitude fifteen minutes early, which was a first for me. I was greeted by a female server who had the face of Blake Lively, the hair of Adam Duritz from Counting Crows, and the voice of John Leguizamo. She was the cutest ugly person on the planet. I'd seen her there before but never learned her name because I generally don't do names, and also because I'd always just referred to her as "Purple" on account of the two-foot-long purple rat-tail dreadlock that hung down her back. Purple immediately escorted me to my favorite table and within minutes served me my favorite juice, "I Am Energized," which is a perfect mixture of baby kale, lemon zest, and turmeric. So fucking yummy . . . oh my God. I sipped it very slowly and waited.

I was sitting alone, letting my mind be still and active at the same time, when something that Jackson said popped into my head. He'd been teaching a master class on Instinctive Well-Being, and I had fallen asleep during the seminar because it was boring as fuck. As I slept, Jackson knelt down right next to me and whispered, "It is very possible to be clear of your soul's beliefs that you are limited, and to be clear of your physical ailments and misalignments, if you can engage with your own sagacity. Unlimited awareness is within you. You are a beam of light that is part of God and a part of the universe." Those words of wisdom seeped into my subconscious and had gotten me through some tough times in rehab, because it made me realize that Jackson may be a fucking hippie crackpot, but he knew me a lot better than I thought he did.

The sight of Robert walking into the restaurant snapped me out of my meditative trance. I'd forgotten how tall 6'4" actually was. Plus, he was wearing a suede Bottega bomber jacket and perfectly tailored Prada pants. I stood up as Robert walked toward my table, and when he was right in front of me, he stopped and just stood there, staring at me, communicating with his eyes everything good and bad that stood between us. He didn't say anything. He didn't have to. Then he threw his arms around me and picked me right up off of the ground. I felt so small in his huge arms, which I obviously loved. He smelled like he'd just stepped out of the shower after spending two long hours on a treadmill. Our bodies were totally recognizing each other. We took our respective seats.

"You look amazing." Robert smiled.

"So do you," I blurted out a bit too loudly. I started sweating. Keep it together, Babe.

"Are you nervous? 'Cause I gotta admit I'm a little nervous, and I'd just feel better if we were both nervous." He was so cute when he said it.

"You weren't the one who lay on your boyfriend's stoop for a week in a puffy North Face jacket begging him to 'give our unborn baby a second chance.' You have no reason to be nervous . . . Or maybe you do."

Robert laughed. "True, but then again, I did dump my fake-pregnant girlfriend, so maybe we're both dickheads."

"Maybe."

"So, how is our baby?" he asked.

Is he flirting with me? Am I going to flirt back? "Oh, he's fine. I named him Bruce and sent him to a toddler boarding school, so hopefully we'll never have to see him again . . . Seriously, though, I'm great. Never been better."

"You look like you. Like the real you."

"Thanks. So what brings you to LA?"

"One of the Lakers needed knee surgery, so I flew out for that. He kind of needs someone to hold his hand through everything. I'm here for a few weeks while he recovers."

"Did it go well? Is he going to be able to play again?" Even I was impressed with my thoughtful line of questioning.

"That's sweet of you to ask. Yeah, Reggie's gonna be fine. I just came from Cedars. I actually introduced you to him a couple years ago in New York, and when I told him I'd be seeing you today, he told me that life is all about second chances."

"I happen to agree with Reginald."

"Yeah, and then he shit himself. He's on a lot of painkillers."

"Ew. Well, he's lucky to have such a good guy rooting for him." This made Robert smile, and feeling emboldened, I said, "Can I be honest with you? I've thought about you a lot. Like, a lot a lot. I'm sorry I turned into such a fucking psycho at the end—"

"Babe. You don't need to explain. I get what happened in New York. I totally understand."

"What do you mean?"

"I mean, I forgive you."

I wasn't expecting to hear those words come out of his

mouth. Obviously I'd hoped we could put the past behind us, but I never thought the day would come that Robert would forgive me for being such a nightmare. Was this some kind of pity thing? God, I hoped not. I'd rather be hated than pitied. My heart was sinking.

"I don't understand," I said, staring into my juice.

"Mabinty. She sent me your book. Or at least an advance copy or whatever it's called. I got it in the mail randomly one day about a couple months ago with a note that just said, 'Read dis, boy. Trust me. Love, Mabs.' "

I was shocked that Robert had read my book, then I was horrified, then I was angry, then I was embarrassed, then I made a mental note to fire Mabinty, then I deleted that mental note, because Mabinty's like my mom and what she'd done might have been a good thing, then I got anxious because I realized that meant Robert had read all about my labiaplasty, and I said: "What the fuck are you talking about? You read my book? You know about my old vagina?"

"Yes, and I was really impressed by your bravery. It's an excellent book. I'm serious. I had no idea that you were even a writer."

I must have looked like I was going to faint or puke, because Robert put his hand on my shoulder.

"Babe, chill. It's fine. I get it."

"But you know everything now. You know how deeply I felt for you. You know that you're the one person who made me realize I might want to say 'Happy tenth anniversary' to someone someday. I'm embarrassed."

"Don't be! You made me realize the same thing, but back

then, I had no sense of what had gone wrong. One moment things were amazing with us, and the next you were a different person. I told you I loved you, and you immediately changed. You're the first person I've really been vulnerable with and your reaction scared the shit out of me. It was really tough to lose you like that. I lost faith in love for a while . . . Don't get me wrong, I still think you're a little bit insane, but at least now I have a frame of reference."

Whoa. Hearing Robert's relationship monologue was slightly overwhelming, but he was still sitting next to me, so I was still happy.

"I thought I was going to come here today, make amends for everything that I put you through, drink some juice, and leave," I said. "My goal wasn't to convince you of anything or change your mind about me, Robert—I just wanted you to hear my side of the story. But I guess you already know it, so . . . "

There was a long, pregnant pause, during which Robert and I just moved our respective glasses of water around the table. It was really weird, but I could feel our hearts healing. After that little moment, it seemed like he was about to tell me something else, but then Purple came over and asked Robert what he wanted to order.

"You should get the 'I Am Opulent.' It's filtered water enlivened with essential oils of grapefruit, lemon, peppermint, ginger, and cinnamon to calm digestion and uplift your being. It's a bit on the heavy side, but I usually get it after traveling." I smiled.

"Sure. I'll have that." He smiled up at Purple, then looked back to me. "So, your childhood sounded ridiculous. Did Marilyn Manson really perform at your twelfth birthday party?"

"Totally. I thought he was going to bite the head off my kitten, Percy."

Robert let out a huge laugh. "That's insane. I love it. Listen, is it too soon for us to start hanging out again? Even just as friends? I don't want to mess anything up for you." He looked genuinely hopeful.

"It's not too soon. I wouldn't be here if it were," I explained.

We spent the next hour just catching up. I mostly asked him questions about his work and he asked me about my life in Utah. I only thought about him naked once. Robert was very impressed that I had stuck it out in rehab for so long. He told me that my skin looked radiant (which it did) and that he still eats at the same sushi place where we had our first date. Actually, I thought about him naked four times. Honesty.

After lunch, he walked me to my car, gave me a sweet kiss on the cheek, and we made plans to meet the following morning for a hike at Runyon Canyon. Anyone who knows anything about love knows that going on a hike with a guy is basically code for spending the rest of your lives together. Yes, somewhere in between sipping juice and making amends, I had fallen madly in love with Robert. Again.

Of course, the next morning when I woke up it was pouring, but Robert texted that he was still up for a hike if I was, and we arranged for him to pick me up at ten a.m. When we got to Runyon it was still raining pretty hard, so we just sat in Robert's rental car, which was a weird Ford midsize SUV scenario. I was unclear on the vehicle, but it was oddly romantic. We were just two normal people in a totally normal-people car having a real moment. I was wearing a really cute Stella McCartney for

Adidas top and pants that I'd purchased when we'd first started dating. Robert was the first person whom I'd ever allowed to see me sweat, besides my trainers and Mabinty.

He immediately recognized the Stella.

"I can't believe you still have those gym clothes. I remember buying those with you in SoHo."

"I know. It's part of my recovery. I'm not really shopping right now," I said proudly.

"Well, they look just as good on you now as they did back then. Maybe better."

I laughed so loud that I kind of snorted.

"Did I say something funny?" asked Robert.

"No, I'm just happy," I said. "I had forgotten what this was like. I feel like the end of us was so incredibly disappointing that I rarely think about how amazing things were in the beginning."

"I know what you mean," he agreed, exhaling harder than normal. "This just seems too good to be true."

It *was* too good to be true. We were re-clicking on all the right levels. Robert's sense of himself, his sense of humor, his belief that I had so much potential, left me feeling more confident than I had in years.

At this point we'd given up on the hike, and we just sat in the car chatting about books, ujjayi breathing, and the effect the Kardashian family has had on professional basketball and hip-hop culture. As Robert talked, he kept reaching across and putting his hand on my leg and my shoulder. At one point, while telling me a story about how tiny a certain NBA star's penis was, I laughed so hard that a piece of my hair came out of my chic little topknot. Robert reached out to my forehead and used his middle finger to tuck the rogue strand back behind my left ear before resting his soft, strong hand on my cheek. Then he looked right inside of me and said, "I'd forgotten just how beautiful you are when you let your guard down."

Full. Body. Chills.

I normally hate when people touch my face. I don't really even touch my own face, but that thought didn't cross my mind. I leaned in to him, and we had the most incredible (second) first kiss in the history of kissing. It was simple and perfect and everything I had hoped it would be.

That is, until Robert turned his beautiful face away from mine and said, "I really shouldn't have done that . . . I'm engaged."

four

BE THE PEACE YOU WISH TO CREATE AND GET THE FUCK OUT OF THIS CAR.

*H*ave you ever been at the doctor's office, waiting in the examination room in your socks and paper gown, silently surveying your cuticles, and had the doctor walk in and tell you that you have cancer . . . and HIV . . . and you're pregnant . . . with triplets? That's how it felt to hear the words "I'm engaged" come out of Robert's mouth.

My brain was on fire. I started to sweat, shake, and convulse all at once. But only on the inside. On the outside, I was cool, calm, and collected. Rehab taught me that trick.

"Oh. Um, okay. I'm so . . . I'm sorry. Congratulations?"

"No, Babe, I'm sorry," Robert said. He slammed the steering wheel with his fists. Then he reached across the car to grab my hand, but I pulled it away. "I should have said something. But

I also knew that I—that I— Fuck, Babe. Seeing you again has been really confusing . . ."

Silence.

I could feel all the rage and hate and love from Old Babe bubbling up in my chest.

"How goddamn dare you," I whispered.

Robert looked at me with a mixture of apprehension and fear. I needed to pull it back a bit before I totally hulked out. *Be the peace you wish to create and get the fuck out of this car.* I smoothed my leggings down with my hands, took a breath, and looked up into his eyes.

"So, this has been really fun catching up with you, Robert. And I wish you well on your path to matrimony. But I need to go home now."

"Okay," Robert said, starting the car. "I'll give you a ride."

"Noooooo, that's okay," I said, forcing a smile. "I'm just gonna walk! It's so nice out."

"Babe, it's pouring. Just let me give you a ride."

"Nope, gotta go."

Then I got out of the car and ran away. Like, really ran. "Sprint running" I think is what it's called. Once I knew I was out of his sight I downgraded to a slow walk, dashed into some bushes, and threw up that morning's smoothie. The engagement news and exercise were too much for me to handle. I tried to pretend that the rain was the universe sending me a message of renewal and purification, but this is LA and rain is filthy here.

Tears were pouring down my face. How could Robert do this to me? On one hand, his being engaged was horrible, but on the other hand, he definitely still had feelings for me. I knew this because I sensed the presence of a boner while we were kissing (a skill you obtain when you really start to pay attention to the world around you).

I was glad that I'd escaped the situation before I'd totally lost my shit. It took two hours, but I walked all the way to Bel Air in the pouring rain with my hoodie pulled over my face so no one would recognize me on my death march. Once I was back at the guest house, I showered for three hours, put on a super flowy white Chloé dress that looked like a nightgown, and wandered barefoot around the property, lightly trailing my fingers along the walls, sitting silently in corners, and floating face up in the pool for an hour. After that, I went to sleep early (at 7) in an attempt to distract myself from thinking about Robert and everything that could have been.

Chloé

I awoke fifteen hours later dying for sustenance, so I threw on a robe and made my way to the main house to satisfy my cravings. Mabinty, my dad, and Lizbeth were all in the kitchen drinking coffee and going over a new landscape design scenario that they were considering for the summer. I politely contributed that the concept was unpleasant and depressing, and that I hated it, but that I wasn't going to get involved in the reconstruction or maintenance of anything besides myself. I didn't need any more distractions at this point in my already shaky recovery. I made a hearty glass of celery, kale, and lemon juice infused with spirulina, parsley, and a hint of cayenne, and got the hell out of the kitchen.

As I walked back to the guest house I felt uneasy—you know that weird, creepy feeling you get when you think you're about to be murdered? I get that feeling every time I take a taxi and every time I take a shower, so every day. But I was especially overcome with this emotion as I entered the guest house. I walked into my bedroom cautiously. Everything seemed to be normal. I picked out my ensemble for the day and went into the bathroom to take a long steam shower. That's when I saw it. Written in black lipstick, scrawled across the length of my entire fucking bathroom mirror:

You'll never be with him because you're too fucking fat.

Maybe I should cut off your love handles, make a smoothie out of them, and force you to drink it.

TTYL

All I recall after that is the sound of glass shattering as my green juice dropped to the floor.

five

I'M NOT WEARING
A CUTE DEATH OUTFIT.

"*G*enevieve?!" I screamed. "I know you're in here somewhere. I can smell your Tory Burch flats. You have five seconds
to come out and apologize."

Silence.

I speed-dialed her cell.

"Babe, I'm not in the mood to fight. I'm in a much better
place today."

"Fuck. You."

"What?"

"Where are you?"

"Um, in Beverly Hills? Why, where are you?"

"At home, staring at my bathroom mirror."

"Okay . . . ?"

"Do you think I'm stupid, Genevieve? I know what you did."

"Well . . . don't tell anyone, but I've been getting a colonic every Saturday morning for the past two months. And I'm obsessed. It's like having anal sex but you lose weight instead of just feeling like a slut afterward. There, I said it. I love colonics. What are you doing later? Want to come over and lay out? I forgive you for the whole Jonathan thing. And for being such a raging cunt at the party."

"I'm not talking about your sick colonics habit, Gen. I'm talking about that shit you wrote on my mirror."

"Exsqueeze me?"

"How'd you do it? Did you break in while I was sleeping?"

"What the fuck are you talking—"

"The black lipstick was a nice touch, but it's so 'not you' that it totally gave you away. Congratulations, you're the rudest person I've ever met, and we are no longer friends."

And with that, I hung up. I didn't need to hear Gen's desperate protests. I was totally frazzled and I wasn't willing to accept that she might not be the creepy note-writer.

If the black lipstick note wasn't from Genevieve, then I didn't know what the fuck to think. I had to tell myself that she was feigning ignorance; otherwise the possibility remained that a murderous stalker had snuck into the guest house, written that horrible note, and was now watching me, waiting to kill. "Cut off my love handles"? Terrifying.

I called my dad and cried about the note. He told me to "get a bodyguard." While bodyguards are unarguably chic, hiring one is a two-to-three-month process that requires tons of interviews and background checks. I wasn't about to put myself through that. That being said, I also wasn't about to sleep alone in the same house where I'd been victimized. Looking around my bedroom, the entire space felt compromised, like everything had been moved two inches to the right. I had to go somewhere safe, somewhere I could be me, the new me, the simpler me: Chateau Marmont.

I needed privacy. I needed space. I needed to have one bedroom to cry in and another for sleeping. I needed two bathrooms. I needed a sundeck that let the light filter in ever-so-slightly, enough to keep the room warm but not hot. I needed plants. I needed big windows. I needed a huge fireplace. I needed my own carport. I needed to feel like I was my own housewife. So I had to stay in Bungalow 1.

I called Chateau and reserved the bungalow indefinitely. Then I called Roman.

I tried him on his house phone because I find calling house phones classic and graceful.

"Hey. Are you okay?" he said. Not the hello I was expecting.

"I'm fine, of course I'm fine. What do you mean?"

"I mean, you haven't answered any of my texts, you're calling me on my house phone, which no one does, and when you left the party the other night we weren't on very good terms." He actually sounded concerned.

"Oh, I'm over that," I half lied.

"Really? Because it's not like you to ignore my texts. I figured you needed space to, like, adjust, or whatever?"

"Yeah, dude. Really." I don't know why I said "dude," it must've slipped out as part of my charade.

"Dude?"

"I know, I heard it too. Let's just move on."

"Okay . . . what's . . . up?" He sounded like he was getting dressed or engaging in some other activity that involved long pauses for decision making. I was annoyed that he wasn't devoting all of his attention to me.

"So, Romie. This is going to sound nuts, but I'm in danger and my dad thinks you should be my bodyguard."

"Wait. What?"

"I know. Someone broke into my house and wrote a heinous note on my mirror and I think I might get serial killed if I don't get out of here so I'm moving to Bungalow 1 at Chateau. And you're really big and strong, so I want you to move in with me." As I said the words into the phone, the reality of the situation started to settle in.

"Holy fuck. Insane!" he said. "Do you want me to pick you up? Oh my God, this is so intense!"

"I know!"

"And actually kind of fun!"

The moment he said it I realized he was right. Having a stalker might actually be super dramatic and fun. Was this a sign that I'd made it as an artist?

"You really think I'm big?" Roman asked.

"You're huge, babe. Huger than ever," I said, finally starting to feel like myself again. "And don't come get me, I'm fine. Just gonna grab some stuff, throw it in a bag, and head to the hotel. I'm stopping to pick up a juice, you wantsies?"

"Duh. Thanks."

"See you in one to six hours."

"Love that. Text me."

That evening, once a moving truck was loaded with the twenty pieces of luggage (Vuitton this time) that I was bringing to Chateau, I got the fuck out of that plagued guest house. It felt like running from a fire, but not a scary fire. More like a giant, beautiful explosion, incinerating my dark past and igniting the spark of my next chapter.

*B*ungalow 1 was bigger than I remembered from the last time I'd been there, and also very, very, very, very chic. But not Babe chic, and not even gay chic. Imagine a sparsely decorated, art deco-y apartment, with a maroon-tiled kitchen, vintage appliances, and an empty refrigerator. Now imagine sliding doors in both the master bedroom and living room opening out to a quiet sitting area that looks out onto a lush green lawn enclosed by tons of gorgeous greenery. Now imagine two bedrooms, one with a queen-size bed and one with two twin beds. Obviously that wasn't going to work, so I relocated to Bungalow 2.

Bungalow 2 was a cottage situated right next to the pool and the valet area. It had three bedrooms, two bathrooms, and an enormous patio that reminded me of the solarium in the guest house. This scared me, so I re-relocated to the two-bedroom penthouse, where I finally started to feel safe. It had a dining room, a living room with a piano and another living room with no piano, two beautiful bedrooms with king-size beds, and a 1,500-square-foot terrace. Perfect. My room was all beige, which I actually loved for me, a blank slate. I knew I wasn't going to be living at Chateau long-term, but still, it was nice to feel at home. Basically, the penthouse would be chic enough to provide the perfect setting for my daily inverted meditation practice, a routine I needed to ramp up if I was going to unscramble my increasingly malnourished meridians and reestablish a balanced chi.

Roman wasn't happy that we'd had to change rooms twice, and that I'd brought so many trunks of clothes, boxes of shoes, boxes of hats, chests of Sanskrit literature, and Pilates equipment, but he understood that in order for me to feel secure in a new place, I needed certain objects around me. As far as the whole Genevieve issue was concerned, I'd made the hotel staff promise me that she wouldn't be making any cameos on the grounds while I was there seeking refuge. Gen and I were in a rocky place, and being in the same hotel together would make me sad, which would make me mad, which would annoy me, which might cause me to melt down again like I did at the party. I was still coming to terms with her ugly brown aura, and the fact that she might have written that note. Everyone needed to respect that.

The first few days at Chateau were whatever: waking up at noon, ordering some juice, going for a hike with myself, ordering more juice, not drinking it, late lunching in the courtyard with Roman, making fun of the celebrities' plastic surgery, wondering what Robert was doing, wondering if my stalker knew where I was, ordering a piece of salmon for dinner, showering for an hour before bed. Very typical Zen Babe. I was starting to realign myself. Roman seemed to be doing well too. He'd been writing a lot of new lyrics, and getting a great tan from lying out on the balcony.

A week into our Chateau experience, I was sunning by the pool and flipping through the pages of *Vogue Paris* when I came across a familiar face. There, in a dominatrix-themed editorial was Donna Valeo, my biological mom, growling up at me with a whip in her hand, draped in Balmain and Fendi. I didn't know she'd started modeling again. Her body looked insane and so did her face (but in a good way), which made me feel great about my own body and face. At that moment, I was really grateful to know Donna, simply for the fact that her face was proof I would age well. I felt compelled to email her, so I pulled out my iPad 3 and composed the following message:

FROM: Babe Walker <Babe@BabeWalker.com>
SUBJECT: Saw your editorial in Vogue Paris
DATE: April 2nd, 2012 3:22:56 PM PST
TO: Donna Valeo <valeo.donna@yahoo.com>
Chic.
How are you? How's Gina? Why do you still have a yahoo email?
BABE

She responded super quickly.

FROM: Donna Valeo <valeo.donna@yahoo.com>
SUBJECT: Re: Saw your editorial in Vogue Paris
DATE: April 2nd, 2012 3:27:45 PM PST
TO: Babe Walker <Babe@BabeWalker.com>
Babe,
Good to hear from you/glad that you liked the shoot. I'm trying to maneuver a bit of a comeback, as they say, so I've been doing a lot of Pilates and eating nothing but

organic salads from Gina's garden. She says hi, by the way. She misses you tons.

P.S.—We both read your book and loved it. Gina died laughing over what a cunt you made her sound like.

P.P.S.—I like yahoo. It's kind of early 2000s chic, no?

xDonna

FROM: Babe Walker <Babe@BabeWalker.com>
SUBJECT: Re: re: Saw your editorial in Vogue Paris
DATE: April 2nd, 2012 3:39:16 PM PST
TO: Donna Valeo <valeo.donna@yahoo.com>
Absolutely not.

Glad to hear you're both doing well. Gina's salad diet sounds major. Tell her I miss her. I guess I miss you too?

BABE

FROM: Donna Valeo <valeo.donna@yahoo.com>
SUBJECT: Re: re: re: Saw your editorial in Vogue Paris
DATE: April 2nd, 2012 3:58:10 PM PST
TO: Babe Walker <Babe@BabeWalker.com>
I miss you as well? Maybe we should get together soon.

xDonna

FROM: Babe Walker <Babe@BabeWalker.com>
SUBJECT: Re: re: re: re: Saw your editorial in Vogue Paris
DATE: April 2nd, 2012 4:10:38 PM PST
TO: Donna Valeo <valeo.donna@yahoo.com>
Totally.

BABE

This would've been a totally normal email chain if it wasn't for the fact that I hadn't seen Donna since meeting her for the first time ever while in rehab. Prior to that, the last time we were face-to-face was when I exited her womb twenty-five years ago. Long story short: my dad met Donna in New York when she was nineteen, she was a model, my dad knocked her up, she moved to LA for a nanosecond, had me, freaked out, left us, gave my dad full custody, and moved back to Ohio, where she was originally from (dark). After taking a few months off, Donna went back to modeling. Then she met Gina (a fellow model), they scissored, and fell in love. Things got a little too *Gia* for both of their liking, so they decided to take a leave of absence from the fashion industry and bought a farm in upstate New York to live happily ever after as farmer lesbians. After a few years, Gina went back to work (and heroin) and ended up at Cirque, where she and I were roommates, which is how I came to meet Donna. She showed up to visiting day, throwing me, my dad, Gina, and Mabinty for a total loop. I guess I know now who I inherited my knack for making an entrance from. The whole thing is really fucked up but kind of amazing.

Gina and I were close, but Donna and I hadn't really been in touch. We'd emailed a couple times and had a super awkward phone call where we both pretty much said, "Um . . . ?" back and forth to each other and talked about the weather until I pretended I'd lost my signal and hung up. Maybe it had to do with her guilt about being an absent parent? I don't know. At the end of the day it didn't really bother me that much. Even though we probably wouldn't be getting together any time in the near future, it felt nice to reconnect with Donna. My birth mother, the model. Chic.

I wish I could say that things didn't get weird between me and Romie, but I can't. In fact, the Chateau Marmont turned out to be the least suitable place for a best friends' staycation. Firstly, Roman's ex-boyfriend Uri was over all the time, which I felt was distracting Roman from his number one priority: keeping me safe. Also, Roman was in a CrossFit phase, which meant he never wanted to do hot yoga with me. And to top it all off, I could tell that he was starting to get annoyed with New Babe's lifestyle needs.

"Roman," I called from the kitchen one morning as he watched his DVR'd Anderson Cooper from the night before.

"Yesssss?" he called back, sounding annoyed.

"Where's the Vitamix?"

"What's a Vitamix?"

"Are you joking?"

"Babe, please. Anderson's talking about the election."

"Roman, please. I'm talking about my health!"

I heard the TV pause and then Roman was standing in the doorway to the kitchen.

"What? What do you need?" He didn't look mad but he didn't look happy, which usually meant he was mad.

"I'm just saying that, as someone who wants to contribute to the world with more focus and compassion than I was able to pre-Utah, I'm going to need the appropriate accoutrements to reach my goals."

"Okay . . . "

"So we need to get a Vitamix Professional Series 750. It's the only blender worth owning anymore, and it's perfect for making juices, nut butters, soups, and homemade organic cleaning solutions."

"Wow. Okay. Babe, look—there's a blender right there." Roman pointed to something behind me, but I kept my eyes locked on his gaze.

"Um, I've obviously sensed the presence of that machine behind me, but it's just not gonna cut it. I'm sorry."

"So just call the hotel staff and have them pick up a Vitamix for you."

"They can't be trusted."

"You're serious?"

"As butt cancer."

"This is next-level neurotic behavior," Roman said.

"Roman," I said as I turned away from him, looking down at the Mexican tile floor.

"What?"

"I'm scared and I don't want to die. Let me have a Vitamix."

"It's fine, it's fine. You're fine," Roman offered, walking toward me.

"Wait, am I being totally high maintenance?" I asked, tilting my head up and pouting for effect.

"No, you've been through a lot. But just go buy it yourself. I have a session with my voice coach in fifteen."

"Okay . . . well . . ."

"What?"

"See, I really shouldn't be getting in a car before one p.m. My shaman says the body hasn't located itself within the universe until around two p.m., and I believe him, so—"

"Babe."

"Fine. I'll do it myself, like everything else," I grumbled and walked off toward my beige room.

When I got back to Chateau with the Vitamix that afternoon, I went straight to Roman's room to apologize for being a cunt. I felt bad for giving him attitude, and he deserved an apology.

"Romie?" I said as I opened the door.

"KNOCK!" said someone very loudly. I don't respond to barked orders, so I walked right in and discovered Roman getting head from Uri.

"Fuck, Babe! Get out!" he shouted. Unfazed, Uri kept going.

"Actually," I said calmly, "would either of you mind if I hung out in here for a second?"

"Go for it," said Uri, who'd let up and turned to smile at me.

"Are you crazy??" Roman asked.

"The energy in here. It's amazing, so much power in the air," I said. It was true. The carnal energy in that room was beyond.

"Get out!" Roman screamed again.

"Gimme thirty more seconds, I haven't had good sex in forever, Roman. You know this. Let me enjoy these auras. Please," I pleaded back.

"Oh my God, this isn't happening."

"No, it's totally happening," I disagreed.

"Well, it's not, because I'm not even hard anymore. So, thanks." Roman rolled over and slipped on some track pants. Uri stood up to find his briefs, which were in a ball on the floor by the bed.

"Whoa, Uri. Roman was right. Your dick really is perfect."

"Okay, get out. Now," Roman said, crossing his arms. He was pissed, and I'd had my fill of the sexual vibes, so out I went, feeling refreshed. As I walked away from the room, I heard Uri thank Roman for telling me that he had a perfect dick. It was really cute. But that was the last straw for Roman. Later that night, we got into a big fight about him playing too much Mariah Carey in the penthouse and the Vitamix ordeal. I called him fat, he called me gay, we both cried, and everyone lost.

To make matters worse, there was construction going on outside the hotel the same day that Roman and I had our epic blowout. This meant there were deafening grinding noises constantly. The men in hard hats told me I should wear headphones or leave. I mean, how could they not have told me that my room would become uninhabitable? No warning, no nothing? No "Hey, Babe. You're not gonna be able to do yoga or meditate in the hotel because there will be a machine scream-crying in your face TWENTY-FOUR HOURS A DAY." Nope, they had no concern for my needs.

I tried to turn our kitchen into my bedroom, which basically meant I just started sleeping under a table because it was the only spot in the house that my spiritualist deemed "psychometrically balanced" enough for me.

One morning, I was jarred awake from my nap under the table.

"It's four in the afternoon. We're going to the gym. Get up."

"Why are you screaming? What's happening? I'm tired," I slurred.

"Muffin, I'm so not screaming. You just really need to get the fuck out of this zen kick from hell that you've thrown yourself into. We're over it." I could see that the blurry silhouette above me was wearing Jeremy Scott sneakers, so I knew it was Roman.

"Roman, please. Wait, who's 'we'?"

Then, as if the vibe in the room wasn't tense enough, Genevieve stepped in from around the corner holding a neon pink Céline Boston bag in one hand and a neon pink beet juice in the other.

"No!!" I screamed.

"Stop screaming!" Roman yelled.

"Okay!" I yelled back.

My behavior was out of control. I was watching myself turn into a monster.

"Okay," Roman said sternly, "you said you needed to feel safe, and I've been trying to make this a happy place for you. We're your two closest friends. You're losing yourself and it's not chic. You don't seem like Babe to us." So there we were. Three old friends. Three best friends. Three strangers.

"Hello, Babe," Gen said wryly, not smiling.

"Don't act weird. I'm still convinced you wrote that fucking note on my bathroom mirror," I replied.

"I'm not being weird and I obviously didn't write that shit on your mirror. Even if I was a stalker, I wouldn't be stalking *you*."

"Ew. That's like a really creepy thing to say."

"Ew. That's like a really creepy place to sleep."

"Ew. That's like a really funny joke, Gen."

"Fuck you, Babe. I was just stopping by to say hi and see if you were okay. Seemed like the adult thing to do. But clearly you're just going to be shitty and accuse me of being a murderer or whatever."

Silence.

"What?" I said.

"Babe," Roman dramatically whispered. Things were getting pretty elevated.

"What? I don't know what you two want from me. I don't trust either of you right now!" I was shouting at this point.

"I'm done!" Roman exploded. "I legit cannot believe you right now. I've put up with all your bullshit, Gen comes to check up on you, and then you tell us that we're not to be trusted? Oh, hell no. I'm done, hashtag shade, hashtag get a grip."

"You're a mess, bitch. Get it together and text me when you do," Gen added.

"GET THE FUCK OUT!" I screamed. "Both of you. Nobody gets that my life is in grave danger, and nobody's going to save me, so bye. Bye, bye, bye, bye, bye, bye."

With that they both left the suite without even turning back for a last look at me. Wow. This was actually happening. My friends had betrayed me, and once again I was a victim of this cruel and insensitive world. Had I completely lost track of who I was? I was so embarrassed/scared/angry/freaked out/confused/hungry. It started to settle in that Gen probably hadn't written that lipstick note in my bathroom. It just wasn't her style to take a sick joke this far. Was I in real danger? If Gen hadn't left the note, then maybe I was actually being stalked. Holy fuck. I'm going to die.

six

I CAN'T. I CAN'T. I CAN'T.
I CAN'T. I CAN'T. I CAN'T.

I spent most of the following morning and afternoon crying about being alone/not having any real friends. Luckily, rehab taught me that the only cure for disillusionment/doubt/depression is making a consciously positive and productive decision. Jackson called it Moving Energy Toward Happiness (METH). So I devised a plan to walk around the hotel looking like I was about to go for a hike until I ran into someone I knew. I needed to connect with someone in the world who wasn't in my inner circle. Someone who would ask me a bunch of vague questions to which I could respond with vague answers. Someone who would believe me when I told them that I was doing really well and that I was so happy and that things were really, really good.

I caught a glimpse of myself in the window's reflection as I walked toward the closet. I looked awful, but the kind of awful that actually makes you look amazing. Like when an actress is supposed to look strung out and disgusting in a movie but she just ends up looking strung out and chic. My eyes were massive and glassy from all of the cry-therapy I'd been doing, my hair was perfectly disheveled, and my skin was kabuki white. I had to be seen in this state. So, I quickly found some Pierre Hardy sneakers that said "Yes, I'm going for a hike, and yes, these are made out of snakeskin" and headed out the door.

I took the elevator to the lobby and walked out to the winding pathways that led to the garden and upper bunga-lows. I circled around them, and walked down to the pool, hung out there for a few minutes, and started back up the path toward the lobby. I almost tripped over my shoelaces, which would have been really embarrassing because I don't fall. Ever. As I bent down to re-tie my shoe, I heard a familiar voice.

"No way."

I slowly lifted my head to see Robert standing above me.

"You've got to be fucking kidding me," I said. I finished tying my shoe, got up, and started walking briskly toward the hotel lobby, pushing past him. I wanted to be seen, but not by fucking Robert.

"Wait, Babe—"

"I can't. I can't. I can't. I can't. I can't. I can't. I won't. I can't. I won't. Stop. Stop. Stop. Won't. Can't. Never. Never. Never. I am peace!"

He followed me through the winding garden pathways and finally grabbed my arm, spinning me around to face him.

"Get off me!" I shouted. "What are you doing here? Trying to ruin my life again? Because I'm trying to be healthy. I'm hiking."

"Can I just say one thing—"

"Can I just say one thing?!"

I might've been yelling. A maid carrying a stack of towels to one of the villas looked scared. I lowered my voice. "I've come to terms with the fact that we are never ever ever getting back together. I'm over us and us is over me. You're engaged, Robert. Those are the facts. When you keep popping back into my life, it fucks everything up. So just move on! Go back to New York."

Then he grabbed my face and kissed me. I let myself make out with him for 0.5 seconds before pulling away.

"No. Nope. No. I refuse to be the Glenn Close to your Michael Douglas. Good-bye forever." I turned and started walking away.

"Babe, I broke it off with Michelle. I've been staying in LA because things in New York are totally fucked. It's a mess, but I just couldn't do it."

"So, what you're saying is . . . you're not engaged?"

"No."

"So, you are engaged? Jesus, Robert. Fuck you and fuck this."

"No! I meant no as in I'm not engaged."

"Oh . . . well, good. I feel like it would be really hard to spend the rest of your life with someone named Michelle, anyway. Just saying."

He laughed. "Babe, I can't stop thinking about you. I was

trying to figure out how to get in touch, but I didn't know how—"

I didn't let Robert finish. I walked right up to him and kissed him hard on the mouth. When I pulled away, I looked into his eyes and I could see how much pain he was in. Our lives were miserable without each other, so there was only one thing we could do: fuck each other to death.

Smash-cut to Robert and me in his cottage tearing into each other. I pulled off his heather-gray suit jacket and ripped open his starched white Dior Homme button-down (this season), hungrily kissing his chest and neck. Then, without breaking eye contact, I pulled his pants down and gave him the most intense blow job I'd ever given anyone in my life. I'd forgotten what it felt like to be with someone whom I actually cared about. I wanted to please Robert and I also wanted him to know how much I loved him. His face was twisted in ecstasy. Suddenly he backed away; his gaze was smoldering, animalistic. I swear he growled as he threw me on the bed and began removing my clothes while kissing every inch of my body and teasing me with his hands. We knew each other's bodies so well that we were able to skip all of the bullshit guesswork that usually goes into these kinds of passionate encounters. He was so diligent about leaving no inch of me untouched. Even though I was writhing in anticipation of what was to follow, Robert was setting the pace and I was loving every second. This was definitely burning more calories than "hiking" around the Chateau.

The moment he finally pushed himself inside me, my eyes filled with tears of pure bliss. I was happy. I was peace. I was Babe Walker: the love of Robert's life.

For the next three hours we did nothing but laugh, drink huge, huge, huge glass bottles of Acqua Panna, and whisper "I've missed you" into each other's faces. So many nights in rehab were spent fantasizing about getting back together with Robert. How he would smell. How he would kiss. How it would feel to run my fingers over his chest. How his huge fucking hands made my arms feel tiny. But this, right now at Chateau, this exceeded all of my expectations, because it was real.

Afterward, as I nestled into Robert's chest, I saw our entire future flash before my eyes: the wedding, the house, the kid(s), eternity. We were in Hawaii, I was wearing a simple Calvin Klein wedding gown, Robert was wearing a puka-shell necklace, my hair was crimped, we were both barefoot, my French bulldog, Martin, was the ring bearer, and my miniature Italian greyhounds, Milan and Paris, were my maids of honor. There were hot-pink roses everywhere, my dad was crying, Mabinty was beaming with happiness and clearly stoned. Robert recited John Mayer's "Your Body Is a Wonderland" as part of his vows. I sang Seal's "Kissed by a Rose" as part of mine. Everyone was crying. It was beautiful.

Wait a second, I thought. *John Mayer? Roses? I hate singing. Who is this person? What is this wedding fantasy?* And then it hit me: I was crossing over to the dark side.

"What are you thinking about?" asked Robert, kissing the top of my head.

"You know . . . just, like, thinking about us."

"I know. I am too. I missed you so much."

"I missed you too, Daddy."

"Ha-ha, what?"

"Nothing. Hey?" I said, looking up into his trusting gaze.

"Hey," he said, smiling.

"Hey," I said, smiling back.

"Hey," he said back to me again.

Do something to show Robert how un-psycho you can be.

"Want me to toss your salad?"

Robert laughed, blissfully unaware that he was in the midst of a living demon.

"Babe, no. I want you. Come here," he said softly, trying to pull me toward him for a kiss.

"Nooooo, I don't think so, mister." I grinned, coyly walking my fingers down his happy trail. "I want to go down south."

Let me just clarify that I'm a total power bottom when it comes to anal play, and if the tables were turned and it was Robert wanting to toss my salad I totally would have let him, because it's the best thing ever. But I had zero interest in seeing Robert's asshole. Being the giver and not the receiver was clearly Babette's fantasy, not mine.

"You're joking, right?"

"Shhhh." I placed a finger over Robert's lips. "I would never joke about something as intimate as this. Now just lay back and try not to clench."

He grabbed my shoulders.

"Babe. No thank you."

"Ugh, FINE! Forget it. Forget everything!" I shouted, getting up from the bed and pulling on my underwear. I turned around to face him. "Are you even attracted to me?"

"What are you talking about?" Robert looked exasperated.

"Of course I'm attracted to you. We just made love for two hours."

"Then why won't you let me give you this gift?!" I demanded. "This is what future husbands and wives do for each other. Don't you want to marry me someday?"

As soon as I said that, I saw all the color leave Robert's face. This had spiraled completely out of control. All I was trying to do was tell him how much I loved him, but no matter how badly I wanted the right words to come out of my mouth, it was impossible to formulate a sentence that wasn't drenched in crazed desperation.

"I bet you let Michelle toss your salad," I muttered under my breath.

"What was that?"

"I said, I bet you let Michelle get all up in that ass of yours."

"Jesus! Babe, this isn't funny."

"Oh, I'm not joking. Maybe we should just call Michelle and she can come over here and give you a rim job because you're clearly still in love with her."

"I am not in love with Michelle."

"Well, then are you in love with me? Because I'm in love with you."

"Babe. I've always been in love with you."

We stared at each other in silence. This would have been the perfect moment to both start laughing and forget about this weird slip-up/fight. But Babette had something else in mind. "Dearly beloved, we are gathered here today to join Robert and Babe in holy matrimony—"

"What are you doing?"

"We're in love, so I'm marrying us. I'm an ordained minister."

"You are not."

"I am too. I got my ordination online when I was eighteen so I could officiate Roman's wedding someday. I married a dog couple at rehab. Now, I'd appreciate it if you'd let me continue without rudely interrupting me."

The light had disappeared from behind Robert's eyes, and he now looked as if he was physically in pain. He got up and started getting dressed.

"Babe," he said, "I know you've transitioned into Babette or whatever, but I hope you can hear what I'm saying to you right now. I've got to get out of here because I can't stand seeing you like this. My presence will only make it worse."

He started hastily packing his suitcase.

"I'll talk to you soon. Call your shrink. I'll check in with you tomorrow. I love you, but I can't stand seeing you this way. It's too dangerous for both of us. Bye for now, Babe." He kissed me quickly on the forehead, then was gone.

Side note: From this point on, I will refer to Babette in the third person, as none of the following actions are a true representation of who I am as a human being or who anyone should be.

Babette traipsed barefoot around Chateau in a robe for hours, asking staff and guests if they had seen "her husband." When she eventually gave up and returned to Robert's room, she called room service and proceeded to order what can only be referred to as Babette's Feast.

mac n' cheese

Chateau Marmont

pepperoni pizza

She ordered twelve liters of Diet Sprite, a bucket of ice, one bottle of Gran Maracame Tequila Platino, six liters of fresh-squeezed lime juice, the charcuterie board, a few of the heirloom tomato salads, and six side orders of mac and cheese, but requested that they be served in wineglasses.

And that was just breakfast. A few hours later, she rang room service again and ordered three of the bacon-wrapped bourbon apples, a half order of deviled eggs, and seven orders of the basil-soaked radishes, but instead of radishes she asked that they just do basil-soaked basil. She topped it off with two orders of roast chicken and a bin of deep-fried spinach. All of which she inhaled like a starving kidnapee. She was in such an animalistic fit that she barely cut the chicken, she just stabbed them with large steak knives and ate them like Popsicles. Sick, greasy, poultry Popsicles.

Then it was time for a text break.

Babette 4:30PM Hey Rob.

Babette 4:31PM Real dick move leaving me alone in a hotel room.

Babette 4:32PM What if someone tries to rape me? What if I've ALREADY been raped? Think about that for a sec.

Babette 4:33PM Are you thinking about it?

Babette 4:36PM Whatever.

Babette 4:40PM It doesn't even matter.

Babette 4:42PM I'm fine.

Babette 4:45PM Heartbroken but fine.

Babette 4:58PM Devastated but fine.

Babette 5:02PM Do you even care?

Babette 5:24PM What if I had been raped just now but I wasn't telling u?

Babette 5:30PM jk was def not raped LOL

Babette 5:36PM I have a perfect vagina so I'll be able to get another bf asap

Babette 5:37PM Go back to fugly Michelle

Babette 5:37PM I'll bet u call her meesh

Babette 5:38PM gross

Babette 5:45PM I'll just become a hooker

Babette 5:52PM At rehab, Jeremy Piven offered me 20k to fuck him

Babette 5:53PM I obvs said no

Babette 6:00PM But now I'm going to text him and see if he wants to cum over

Babette 6:08PM See ya

Babette's texting was interrupted by hotel security, who'd come to ask her to kindly go back to her own (my) room. Once she was back in the penthouse, she decided the only thing that would make her feel better was a movie marathon, so she made the concierge get her a DVD of every Nicholas Sparks movie. She kicked off her night with *A Walk to Remember*. All the crying made her hungry, so she called room service and placed a dinner order.

"Hi, let me get two orders of nachos with extra beef and extra jalapeños, two orders of your fish and chips with extra of that white sauce, I fucking love that sauce. Actually, can you put some of that sauce on the nachos too? Thanksies. And fifty fried oysters. Can you also go out and grab me a La Scala chopped salad, add cucumber, and include extra dressing and two seeded lemons on the side? You're the best."

Babette had finished *Message in a Bottle* and had made it

through *The Last Song* and most of *Nights in Rodanthe* when she decided she needed a midnight snack. So she had the concierge send someone to pick her up a double double In-N-Out Burger, and also stop by Bella Pita in Westwood and get her a black bean wowshi with cheese and extra onions, and bread. She also ordered a pepperoni pizza and hit on the seventeen-year-old delivery boy by telling him he looked "stupid and dangerous."

By the time I woke up the next morning, I felt like myself again, except for the fact that I was wearing a terrycloth robe and clutching a pizza crust, and the DVD menu of *Dear John* was playing on a never-ending loop. I was also the most bloated I'd ever been in my life, not to mention I'd driven away the only man I'd ever loved, and consumed more than ten thousand calories in twenty-four hours. I was devastated. But worse, Robert was horrified. Even though he said he'd call me, I knew deep down that he was scared out of his mind. And rightly so. We'd had a fucked-up relationship up until this point, but I was starting to believe that I could actually be the one for him. Robert and Babe forever. But Robert and Babe could never be, it would only ever be Robert and Babette. My heart shriveled to the size of a soybean and my life was basically over. What had I become?

seven

A DOBERMAN NAMED LARRY AND A GERMAN SHEPHERD NAMED TARZAN.

When I emerged from my hibernation I felt like I had the weight of the world on my shoulders. My life was destroyed. I had no one to love, no place to live, nowhere to be, no place to go, and no one to cry to. Once again I had lost the battle against my psychotic alter ego. Babette had ruined my chances at a happy ending, but I was Babette and Babette was me. Would there ever be a way to separate Jekyll from Hyde?

I grabbed my iPad to check the *Daily Mail* site and came face-to-face with this:

Nice binge, fatso. I'm gonna have to give you lipo with a knife and a vacuum cleaner.

TTYL

It was written in black lipstick across the screen.

"Noooooooooooo!" I screamed and threw the iPad away from me with such force that it shattered against the wall. A single sob escaped my lips, followed by a much larger one, and before I knew it I'd dissolved into the kind of crying that only comes from feeling completely violated or humiliated. I was alert enough to know that I had to get out of the Chateau as quickly as possible, but I couldn't catch my breath and my body was trembling out of control. Looking around the suite, I could feel the presence of an intruder. Few sensations are as frightening as realizing you're not alone when you thought you were. I got dressed, grabbed my purse, and got the fuck out of that hotel. The Chateau Marmont was not safe.

By sunset, all my belongings had been moved back into the guest house, a major security system had been installed, and I'd bought two guard dogs: a Doberman named Larry and a German shepherd named Tarzan. Even though the grounds were "secure," I was still so shaken by the experience that I spent the next few days moping around like a ghost stuck in purgatory, trying to cross over into the light of the living.

If there was an upside to all of this, it was that it gave me time to try to figure out Babette's reemergence. I guess I had a pretty serious personality disorder and needed professional help, but not, like, from an astrologer or facialist. There was only one person who'd be able to ease my woes, and that was my old therapist, Susan. The bad news is that Susan had terminated our doctor/patient relationship after a tiny incident (she fell asleep during one of our sessions and I drew a dick and balls on her forehead with a Sharpie in retaliation). One huge gift basket from Joan's on Third (her weakness) and an apology from me in person got me back where I needed to be: sitting across from Susan in her safari-chic, super Ralph Lauren-y, Santa Monica office.

"I'm a mess," I sobbed to Susan. "I have no one. Like, I woke up today and checked my phone and didn't have a single missed call or text."

"And how did that make you feel?"

"Um, lonely? Obviously."

"Mmm. Hmm."

"This isn't helping as much as I hoped it would."

"What do you mean?"

"Paying someone to talk about myself. It's kinda not as fun after so much rehab. Could I be over hearing my own voice? Oh my God, that's so dark."

Susan sighed. "I think it's time you take action, Babe."

"Action?"

"Create new relationships. Broaden your social circle. Los Angeles has so many different types of people to offer. Explore that."

Susan had never been more right in her life. It was obvious that I'd simply outgrown my friendships with Gen and Roman in the process of finding myself at rehab. Yes, I would always love (and mostly hate) them, but I was lost, friendless, and in need of a complete reinvention, again. Also the dark fact of the matter was that Robert and I hadn't spoken since our Babette/salad tossing/ Chateau Marmont rendezvous. It had only been a few days, but he hadn't gotten in touch with me, and I was far too embarrassed to reach out to him, so I figured he was probably over it. It was time to do exactly what Susan suggested and go outside of my comfort zone. As much as I hated trying to make friends, it was time to be open to new relationships. Ugh . . . fine.

I met my first new friend, Téo, one night when I was having dinner with my dad at the Sunset Tower Hotel. I was applying eyeliner in the bathroom when a super famous (but horrible) actress stormed in. I noticed her truly heinous Louboutins before I noticed who she actually was. When we made eye contact, she screamed "Leave!" in my general direction, covered her face, ran straight into a stall, and started snorting lines of blow. I did leave, but only because coked-out famous people scare the shit out of me. They're like the cheetahs you see while on safari—beautiful, but deadly if you pull out a camera.

As I walked out of the bathroom, I noticed a cherubic manboy leaning up against the wall, chewing gum and texting. His outfit (leather jacket, baggy-ish jeans, Jordans, baseball cap) said "straight," but his vibe said "gay." He shot me an intriguing smile. This was my chance to branch out.

"Isn't she so rude?" he asked. "She's like my best friend, but she gets so bossy when she's high, which is, like, all the time these days."

"Um, yeah, you might want to go check on her," I suggested as I walked past.

"Oh my God, you're Babe Walker."

"Yeah. I am. How do you know that?"

"What do you mean? You're huge. I've read your book, like, twice."

"Okay, I'm gonna pretend that you didn't just call me huge because if you did in fact just call me huge then I'd have to turn around, go back into the bathroom, and vom away my sadness."

"Oh please, you know what I mean."

"Kind of . . . Anyway, thanks for reading my book, I guess. Cute hat."

"You're funny," he replied. "We should hang out. Is that hot guy your dad?"

"Um . . . yeah?"

"Cool. I'm Téo." He nodded toward the bathroom. "I'm gonna check on homegirl and make sure she isn't choking on her own puke in there. We're staying in the townhouse suite. Come party with us after dinner?"

"I'll think about it," I said as I walked back to the table.

Normally I wouldn't deign to hang out with some weirdo celeb hanger-on, but I was in an especially vulnerable place, given my recent friend divorces, and in this case I was kind of the celeb who was being hung on to and that made me feel better about myself. So I finished dinner with my dad and up I went.

Téo answered the door with a full glass of whiskey in his hand. The suite reeked of Marc Jacobs Daisy and cigarettes. He dragged me into one of the bedrooms, past a few random crowds of random people smoking and not really talking to each other. No sign of the actress, but I had a feeling she was lurking in one of the bathrooms. Téo smoked a joint, I secondhand smoked a joint, and we had a totally deep conversation about how scary wealth can be. I confided in him about my stalker, he told me it was probably just an obsessed fan of my book, which I highly doubted. We even kissed for like five seconds, but he didn't get a boner.

Téo paraded me around the room, introducing me to all of his friends. "This is Babe Walker, creator of White Girl Problems. She basically changed the landscape of social media," he told everyone. Téo knew everyone so well, or at least he made it seem that way. If you know the first thing about me, you know that I have a strong distaste for small talk, especially when it's about myself and my career, but I was being open. So the night called for a lot of very quick mind-centering mantra reps and about six hundred Marlboro Lights.

Later, my new bestie told me that he and another guy also had a bonerless make-out encounter in the bathroom, so I accepted Téo as a chic asexual bisexual and proclaimed him my new Genevieve and Roman combined. I don't know what exactly Téo did for a living or where he came from, but everyone greeted him with a smile. I'd never seen anything like it.

By six a.m., everyone besides me was beyond fucked up. The actress had emerged from the bathroom (I was right) and was naked except for a thong, a fur coat, and a HUGE Rolex (which turned out to be stolen). She writhed around on the floor while Téo played a Lou Reed record and took pictures of her with his vintage Leica. He even got a shot of her throwing up into a Birkin filled with cash. It was kind of the most artistic thing she's ever done, besides *Machete*. I mean, I would totally buy that photo to put in my pool house or something. When the actress started going around the room pointing at all the guests one by one and calling them "fucking retarded," the party was officially over.

The next morning, I woke up to this text:

Téo 7:48AM Baby muffin, wake the fuck up and come to the pool.
We're relaxing. Wear something vintage. T

It was at this point that I realized Téo must not sleep, ever. I obviously had nothing to do all day, so I obliged.

When I got to the pool at Sunset Tower and located my new friends lying out next to a table of booze and untouched food, I texted Téo.

Babe 11:40AM I'm here. Where are you?

Sometimes, when you arrive somewhere, it's a good idea to pretend you can't find the person you're meeting, even if you're looking right at them. I can't really explain why, but it sets up a good power dynamic between you and your friends. Also, approaching large groups of people alone is not cute.

Téo 11:41AM I'll come get you.

He came and swooped me up, leading me to his group of friends, which included the actress and several other girls who were dressed eerily like the actress. Everyone was sporting vintage, but in an acceptable way, not a Coachella way. No one was talking. They all were sitting calmly flipping through crisp issues of *V* magazine, *Vogue,* and British *Vogue.* I wasn't entirely turned off by the vibe, which was a huge relief. Thoughts of my stalker occasionally popped into my head, especially when someone mentioned anything to do with lipstick (there were a lot of heavy lipstick scenarios going on with these girls), but I was able to keep my anxiety to a minimum.

"Everyone meet Babe Walker, creator of White Girl Problems. She basically changed the landscape of social media all from her phone. And she wrote a book," announced Téo.

"Hi," I said to the bevy of bikinied zombies.

"We have," said the actress, not looking up from her magazine.

"Excuse me?" I had no idea what she meant by that.

"We have met. In the bathroom . . . and in the room . . . and now. We know each other. I know about your book—it's funny. And if you're friends with Téo, then you're safe."

"Um . . . "

"Sit."

It was like she had this weird command over everyone—including me. I sat down at the foot of an empty chaise. The whole thing was very shameful for me. My power play had gone to shit.

Luckily, the actress and I didn't have to interact after that odd exchange where she totally queen-bee'd me. Téo and I just lounged while eating ice cubes and making fun of the B-list celebs who were also sunning out at the pool. Whenever someone remotely attractive walked by, Téo said hi to them and bragged about what a famous writer I was. He was basically acting like my publicist, which is tacky, I know, but I let it happen. If I was going to move onward and (more important) upward from my previous social strata, I could use the help from someone as connected and sharky as T.

Two of the girls in his posse were these very, very thin twins named Madalena and Helena. They spent the entire afternoon seeing who could stay underwater the longest. They may have been seventeen, not clear. Also in our group, making everyone uncomfortable, was an obese girl with a neck tattoo of a hummingbird. Téo claimed her mom owned Equinox, which I found astonishing and deeply sad. I was starting to doubt the integrity of my new friend circle. The usual questions swirled: Are they fun enough? Are they chic enough? Are they too LA? Am I the only person here who's been to rehab? Definitely not.

After a few hours of pooling I needed a nap, so I gracefully made my exit without saying bye to anyone. Everyone was asleep when I left anyway. When Téo invited me to come join in their group "relaxing," what he meant was group "Xanaxing."

Over the next few weeks, Téo and I hung out/went out a lot. He was never scarce with compliments and he always picked up the phone when I needed to talk about Robert. Plus, he was a male Gemini (my fave). We went to art openings, club openings, restaurant openings, and one weird party in Topanga Canyon that turned out to be an orgy. He even invited me to go to Sanya (google it) with him and this Japanese pop star he was friends with.

But I never made it to Sanya. Téo and I were supposed to have lunch a couple weeks before the trip to hash out the details and discuss our various Sanya looks, but he "got held up at a photo shoot" and told me I could fly private with him if I "just came to the Burbank airport on Friday," not specifying a date or time, and not responding to my texts inquiring as to when exactly the flight was leaving. Then the next Saturday morning he texted me that he'd landed at Fenghuang airport and that he would have called me but he "lost his phone." Whatever. I never heard from Téo again, but I did see a pic of him sitting at Nicole Kidman's Golden Globes table, so yay Téo.

Not long after Téo disappeared, I ran into his weird twin friends Mads and Hels at a macrobiotic cooking class at M Café. They were inappropriately excited to see me, so I let them have my number. I didn't want to like them, but I couldn't deny the fact that visually we made a lot of sense. Not only were they super tall, super naturally blond, and super bitchy, but my hair was in fact the perfect shade of chocolate brown to be hanging out with them. When they got into an epic screaming match (in the middle of our class) over a Balmain clutch that Helena had borrowed from Madelena without permission, and Madelena threatened to strangle Helena in her sleep with her own hair, I knew I'd found my new psycho besties.

We went out for drinks later that night and I was so right— we were the perfect trifecta of hair color and skin tone. I mean, yes, they were crazy and they drank too much and triple kissed with some guy, which was kind of gross, but they were also a lot of fun. They ended up spending the night in my guest house and we stayed up talking 'til sunrise. It was like I'd met two blonder, less pretty, less intelligent versions of myself as a teenager.

But after two weeks of hanging out nonstop, things got dark. Madelena and Helena were super competitive and they were always trying to put me in the middle of their drama. I mean, mostly they'd fight about clothes, so it was kind of a non-issue, but hanging out with twins in matching Isabel Marant Bekkets was really annoying. Especially when the truth was that I hated wedge sneakers and I wished they would go away forever. Also, they'd get really violent with each other if either of them happened to be on Provigil that day. I finally had to call it quits with them after seeing Helena pull out a chunk of Madelena's hair with her teeth because they both wanted to wear the same leather jacket to lunch. Not to mention the fact that Helena also bit me when I tried to play referee to their insanity. I thought fashion took me to a dark place, but I clearly had no idea.

My social life had been wreaking havoc on my skin, so I decided to take a night off from being out and reinvigorate with a HUGE bottle of alkalized negative ion water, hibiscus tea, and a tourmaline-charged radiance face mask. I had just washed the mask off and was slipping into bed when I heard the unmistakable sound of an American SUV approaching the back gate.

I checked the security camera via an app on my iPhone, and was shocked to see Robert's surly Ford rental parked just up the street. I knew it was his because I had taken a mental photograph of the license plate when I was with him last (just something I always do when getting into cars). My first thought was: *What the fuck?* My second thought was: *He's come here to ask me to marry him.* My third thought was: *Do something you'll regret.*

Suddenly the doorbell rang. I switched to the front door camera view and, sure enough, Robert was standing on the fucking porch of the guest house. I pressed the intercom button.

"I'd invite you in, but the stress of becoming a lovelorn psychopath every time I see you causes lasting damage to my pores."

"Ha-ha. Can we talk?"

"We're talking right now, aren't we?"

"Just let me in."

"Too dangerous. I wouldn't want to have another episode that causes you to leave and not talk to me for six weeks. So just say what you need to say."

"Fine. I forgive you for the whole Babette thing at Chateau."

"You forgive me?"

"Hear me out—"

"I forgive you for coming on to me even though you were engaged, telling me you loved me, and leaving when I got too emotional, then disappearing for a month and a half."

"I'm sorry. I fucked up. Can you please let me in so we can talk it out?"

"Please, Robert. There's nothing to say! You can't handle Babette. You left. You never called me. The end."

"You know, you could have called me when you got your shit sorted out, but you never did. So this is not entirely my fault."

"Oh, okay. What the hell was I going to say to you? 'Hey, Robert, it's me, the psycho who tried to force analingus and marriage on you. How's it going?'" Robert started laughing, which infuriated me. "It's not funny," I continued.

"Babe, come on. It's kind of funny."

"No, it's actually not. It's fucked up and sad. We're cursed."

"Let me in."

"No. Please leave."

"Is that what you really want?"

Of course it wasn't. What I really wanted was for Robert to bust down my front door, fight off the guard dogs, run up to my room, get down on one knee, and propose to me while slipping a four-carat Harry Winston emerald-cut diamond ring on my finger. I wanted him to tell me that I've always been The One, and then I would tell him that he's always been The One—that he would always be The One. Robert and Babe forever. But I couldn't say that to him.

"Yes, that's what I want. I can't be the girlfriend you're constantly forgiving for being a lunatic."

"Who said anything about you being my girlfriend?"

"What did you just say?"

"It was a joke, Babe."

"Okay. Clearly you're not taking this seriously. Leave now."

Robert stared into the security camera for what seemed like an hour but was really only two minutes and thirty-six seconds. I know this because I recorded the footage and saved it to my phone. He looked so sad.

"Fine, I'll leave." He turned around to go and then walked back up to the door. "No, you know what? You're acting like a child. Grow some balls."

"*You* grow some balls!"

"I have fucking balls, Babe. That's why I'm at your door trying to talk to you. God . . . fuck it. I'm sick of this shit."

"Me too. I hate this and I hate you."

"I hate you too."

"I don't actually hate you. That was a test. But since you clearly hate me, you can get the fuck out of here. Now."

And with that, Robert turned and walked back to his car, got in, slammed the door shut, and drove away. And I rolled over and cried myself to sleep.

I awoke two hours later to the sounds of someone frantically knocking on the front door. I thrashed about, looking for my phone, which had disappeared into my comforter, but my attention was quickly diverted from the bed to the wall next to my closet. A Terry Richardson portrait of me that I'd hung there upon moving into the guest house was smashed to bits. The frame was mangled and there were shards of glass scattered all over the floor beneath it. But the photo of me inside the frame was the scariest part. Whoever had smashed it up had scribbled out my eyes and drawn all over my hair with black lipstick.

I shot out of bed, screaming bloody murder, and ran down to the kitchen, where I grabbed the biggest butcher knife I could find. The knocking was intensifying.

"Go the fuck away!" I screamed at the top of my lungs. "I will cut you the fuck up!"

The knocking stopped. I crept over to the flat-screen security panel mounted on the kitchen wall and checked the front door cam to see who could possibly be trying to kill me at 2 a.m., praying that it would be Robert coming back to save my life.

But it wasn't Robert. It was Paul.

eight

REHAB IS FOR PUSSIES.

*P*aul was a fellow rehabber I'd been sleeping with during most of my time at Cirque. He had an enormous penis. If you took Josh Hartnett and added two inches to his dick and overall height, you'd have Paul. Unfortunately, in addition to being hot, he was also a total psycho, which made him great to fuck but hard to deal with when he wasn't inside me.

Our attraction started innocently enough—we'd make out in storage closets after our group therapy sessions while everyone was at dinner. But then once my roommate left, I started sneaking Paul into my bed at night. He developed feelings for me and things got messy. I was looking for someone to blow off steam with (and sometimes blow), and he was looking for someone to latch onto. He needed a real girlfriend who could handle listening to him read Bukowski aloud. Our "relationship" was doomed from the start. But here he was, at my house. My heart jumped into my throat. Was he the one who'd been after me this whole time?

I pressed the intercom button.

"Why aren't you at Cirque?"

"Baaaaaaaabe. I left. Rehab is for pussies. Lemme in."

"No. How did you know I live here?"

"You wrote me a letter a week after you were out and told me I was the most spesh person you've ever met, and that I should come visit you."

"Oh. Yeah."

Fuck. I had totally forgotten that, in a momentary fit of missing Paul, I'd written him a semi-love letter. Had I encouraged stalker-ish behavior?

"Did you break in earlier?"

"No way, dude."

"Liar."

"I just got here."

"When?"

"Just now! Landed at LAX an hour ago. This town is fucking boring as fuck, yo!"

"Hold on."

I rewound all the camera footage and sure enough Paul had gotten dropped off by a taxi and sauntered up to the door of the guest house five minutes earlier. Even though he was acting exactly like Skeet Ulrich in *Scream,* he wasn't the culprit. Truthfully I was kind of glad Paul showed up when he did, because he could provide protection from whoever was trying to eliminate me.

I ran back upstairs, swept up the broken glass, put the mangled picture frame in the closet, fluffed my hair, threw on a La Perla silk georgette chemise with a matching thong, and opened the front door, trying to look as bored as possible.

"Can I help you?"

"Molly for Pauly!" Paul screamed, scooping me up and running into the house with me in his arms. Oh great. Paul was high on molly. He carried me all over the house while I half-protested, and then ran up the stairs to my room, where he threw me on the bed. I wanted to hate him, but I was kind of loving this moment for myself.

According to our group therapy sessions, Paul Courtyard (Courtyard as in Courtyard by Marriott) had grown up with tons of money. His parents bought him his own mansion in Beverly Hills when he was fifteen. Then Paul got into a really intense relationship with some girl named Naomi. He also got into a really intense relationship with heroin, MDMA, and poppers. When Naomi dumped him because she couldn't deal with his other relationships, Paul lost his shit and beat up her dad (kind of hot) and almost killed him (kind of really hot, except not at all). Instead of going to jail, he was ordered to complete six months of rehab. He spent most of his time in treatment brooding, talking about Skrillex, and fucking me, so I guess it's not that surprising that he hadn't made much progress.

"Babe, you look hot!" he exclaimed, breathing heavily.

"Thanks, Paul."

"No, I mean your face is melting off."

"Ugh. Stay here, I'm gonna get you some water."

When I came back to the bedroom, Paul was wandering around naked.

"Paul, just because we used to fuck in rehab and you're naked in my bedroom doesn't mean I'm going to fuck you now." Of course I was going to fuck Paul. He was hot as shit, and somehow even more attractive in his altered mental state. Plus, the adrenaline rush from my near-death experience had left me kind of turned on.

"Babe, whyyyy?" he whined. "I came all the way here to find you. Jesus, it's like two hundred degrees in your house. Why do you have so many plants? Is this a jungle?"

"No."

"Oh." Paul stopped suddenly. "Do you hear that? The phone's ringing." He started crawling around on the ground, picked up one of his boots and held it to his ear. "Hello? Oh yeah, one sec." Paul handed the shoe to me. "It's for you."

I took off my chemise.

"She'll have to call you back," Paul said calmly into his shoe, smirking.

He jumped onto the bed and we started furiously making out.

"Babe."

"Paul."

"You are, like, the best kisser. My mouth is on fire."

"I'm glad you're out of rehab and having fun, but I'm kind of worried about you," I said, looking into his eyes.

"I think I love you."

"No you don't. What drugs are you on?"

"Babe, I'm not on drugs. I'm just chilling in my drug house right now."

"Excuse me? Your drug house?"

"Yeah. Like, the floors and walls are made of molly. There's also a whiskey garden, a weed chimney, and a cocaine skylight. It's my dream mansion, and I live in it most of the time, but sometimes I go outside."

"That is seriously fucked."

Paul licked my neck. "You taste like a marshmallow. I'm gonna take a piss. Be right back."

What is he doing here? I thought to myself. *Was he sent here to protect me? What is the universe telling me right now—that Paul is the new Robert?*

Five minutes went by.

Paul could totally kill someone if they broke in again.

Ten minutes went by.

Paul could be the love of my life if he were sober.

Then fifteen.

I'll bet I can get him to go back to Cirque.

Then twenty.

I'll bet I can get him to stop listening to dubstep.

Then thirty.

Paul is definitely the new Robert.

But where had he gone? Was he taking a shit? I really hoped not. That would be a terrible way to start the rest of our lives together. I got up, put on a robe, and walked by the bathroom door, but I didn't hear anything. I knocked.

"Paul?"

Nothing. I knocked again.

"Paul, are you okay?"

Still nothing.

"Paul, are you pooping?"

Still nothing. At this point I was irritated, so I just started repeating "Paul? Paul? Paul? Paul?" over and over, hoping he would answer me. Finally, I just opened the door.

The good news was that Paul wasn't pooping. The bad news was that he was dead. I'd never seen someone OD before, so I guess I went into a fugue state, repeating Paul's name over and over as I ran back into my bedroom and dialed 911. The whole thing was just too *Pulp Fiction* meets *Boogie Nights* meets that really scary movie with Liv Tyler and that guy from *Felicity*.

I was still awash in a chorus of "Pauls" when the ambulance arrived. The paramedics tried to zap Paul's chest or whatever, but it didn't work. He was too dead. Finally they gave up, and like a candle in the wind, he was gone.

Some people waltz into your life only to leave moments later. This was happening to me a lot, post-Cirque. Actually, it had been happening with pretty much everyone in my life, with the exception of my family. I'd been hemorrhaging friends since leaving rehab. Was this the universe telling me I was a bitch, or the universe telling me that everyone else was? Either way, I was starting to be over it.

I got a Facebook message from Paul's cousin saying that his family would prefer it if I didn't attend the funeral. So rude, but ultimately fine because the funeral was going to be too dark, and I didn't need that kind of negative energy in my life. Instead, I decided to have a light, uplifting memorial service for Paul in our backyard, which I felt would fully encapsulate his essence. There were no flowers, but there were lots of whiskey shots, and we all ended up pissing on the lawn. Trust me, it's what he would have wanted. I wore a McQueen frock that had been in my closet for ages, and I only invited Mabinty and Skrillex. I gave a short eulogy, praising Paul for being tragically misunderstood.

Alexander McQueen.

"We're gathered here today," I solemnly began, "for me to talk about Paul because his family wouldn't let me go to his real funeral. Basically, Paul, you were insane, but in the best way. The world will miss your unending rants about the evolution of dubstep music, and I know I'll miss how much you looked like Josh Hartnett. But most of all, I wanted to say thanks. Your death has taught me that sometimes people just need to leave. Like me. I'm at a point in my life where the only option is escape. Escape from old friends, escape from Los Angeles, and escape from my stalker. Good night, sweet Pauly."

My little speech was the least I could do. I dropped my head for a moment of silent remembrance, and as I lifted it up again to catch Mabinty shedding a tear I swear that over her shoulder I saw some sort of spirit float out of our pool. Paul? Maybe headed to heaven. Maybe hell. Who knows? I believe in neither.

All said and done, I was glad the McQueen dress got me through a funeral, even if it wasn't the real one. Paul's death made me realize that rehab doesn't work most of the time, and if I was ever going to be happy, then I'd have to move on with my life as the old me, the real me.

Moving on.

Growing up.

Losing weight.

Finding peace.

In Europe.

nine

MOVE, GROW, LOSE, FIND.

"I've always been the kind of girl who needs to run unfettered, like a Friesian horse. When I'm bridled by sobriety and caged in a guest house, everything around me turns to shit. Case in point: The past couple of months I haven't been myself— Hold on one second," I said into the phone, as I looked up into the eyes of a pudgy blond Air France flight attendant who was hovering over me. "Can I help you?"

"Madame, we're about to taxi out to the runway, so I'm going to need you to turn off all portable electronic devices, okay?"

I forced a single tear to roll down my cheek and attempted my best half-smile.

"Sorry, this is just really important because I'm on the phone with my rehab counselor and we, like, never talk. Plus, I know that electronics don't actually disrupt anything because my dad used to fly planes, but I will be sure to put my phone away once the plane starts actually taking off, I swear. That uniform is really flattering on you. Can I have another vodka soda?"

The flight attendant blinked and walked away. I gulped down the remainder of my first cocktail in six months and continued my conversation.

"The point is, Jackson, people don't change. They don't. I'm always going to be the same Babe Walker who crawled into Cirque Lodge Drug Rehabilitation Center last winter. And you are always going to be the same Jackson who loves telling people they need to 'search within their within' even though nobody knows what that actually means, including you. My Ambien's about to kick in, so I have to go, but I just called to say that Paul is dead and I'm going to Europe for a few months to shop my ass off. Hope you're having fun in Utah. Call me back if you get this. Or don't. Your choice."

I put my phone on airplane mode and threw it into my bag. Gazing out the window, I felt the kind of peace that can only be felt when you're about to take off on a direct flight from LAX to CDG. Or the kind of peace that can only be felt when you've mixed a double vodka soda and a 10mg sleeping pill. Either way it didn't matter, because in twelve hours I'd be in Europe putting the events of the past two months behind me. I reclined my seat to make a bed, sprayed some Evian mist on my face, and put on an eye mask. Good-bye, Los Angeles. Hello, Euro Babe.

Unless you've ever been the victim of a stalker at large, I wouldn't expect you to comprehend the levels of anxiety I'd been suffering. All the opiates in the world couldn't quell the nightmares I'd begun having after the notes first started appearing. I awoke the entire first-class cabin on my flight to France thanks to a nightmare involving zombie sorority girls covering me in black lipstick. There were hundreds of them. I was in a tube top and the lipstick they were smearing all over me felt like tar on my dream skin. I woke up screaming, which I guess was very disturbing to the other passengers. One very thin woman even told me to go fuck myself when she saw me at the baggage claim. The remarkable thing is that I was able to push through the fear, taking every day as a new challenge. Moving on, growing up, losing weight, finding peace. Move, grow, lose, find.

Running away to Paris was more than just a method of escaping the sick joke my life in Los Angeles had become; it was my way of truly rehabbing myself. Cirque had been a way for me to take a breather and examine my life choices, get some perspective, and lose some weight, but at the end of the day, did I really have a "shopping problem"? No. Was I a "drug addict"? Never. Did I like doing drugs? Absolutely. Did I have "anger issues"? Who doesn't? It was time to embrace my true self: The Babe who stole an Hermès cuff from Neiman's before she could walk. The Babe who would always be a little bit in love with Lance Bass. The Babe who sued Genevieve when she was sixteen for buying the same color prom dress as her. The real Babe is a woman who needs to shop and sleep late and roll her eyes at people who won't let her smoke cigarettes inside.

I was going to live my life the way I wanted to and listen to my gut (ew), which meant I would finally be free. And not like "zen bullshit meditation yoga namaste" free, more like "shoulder dancing, unbrushed hair, leather jackets, whispering in men's ears, salads, blowouts, the occasional blow moment, cigarettes, shopping, clear liquids, smoothies, and champagne" free.

Although I no longer subscribed to the universe and its ways, I suppose it was still kind of delivering, because my dad's partner's overweight daughter who'd been studying at the Sorbonne for a semester had suffered a nervous breakdown and was taking a few months off to detox at an Italian spa/retreat/fat camp. This meant her amazing apartment in the Eighth Arrondissement was up for grabs, and I was happy to take it over for her while she renovated her neglected midsection.

Even though it featured a little too much shabby chicness for my taste, the apartment itself didn't pose any problems that a quick feng shui session and a trip to *les marchés aux puces* couldn't fix. It had huge windows, molded ceilings, natural light, and super dark wood floors. Very inspiring once I'd gotten rid of most of her furniture. I was actually glad to have a project to keep me busy for my first week à Paris. Even though Cicily hadn't asked me to redecorate, I knew I was doing her a huge favor by creating a chicer, thinner space for her to live in once she'd lost all that weight. Upon arriving home to her freshly curated living quarters, she'd never want to eat frites again. That's the Babe Effect™.

I'd traveled light to Europe, only bringing a carry-on, three suitcases of vintage, a suitcase of basics, and two suitcases of shoes. The best way to revamp my wardrobe would be to start from scratch. I wasted no time in going to Colette and then traipsing up and down Boulevard Saint-Germain buying my spring/summer/fall/life staples. Being back in my element felt so empowering. After a couple days of very focused and selective acquisitions, I was ready to be a Parisian. My spirits were high. I was living in the now. Nothing could faze me.

I decided to send Genevieve and Roman apology presents (Louis Vuitton metallic cap-toe pumps and a Givenchy bird of paradise shirt, respectively) and invited them to come visit me via text. This was my attempt to make things right between us. Gen responded with "What? No!" which I knew meant, "Thanks and I love you too, but I can't leave my demanding job right now because I'm a total workaholic." Roman called to thank me. He was busy recording demos for an upcoming EP, but he offered to come out in a couple of months if I was still abroad. I was just glad they both still wanted to be my friend despite the fact that I'd acted like a wretched ogre. Well, Gen had really acted like an ogre too, but it was fine. All was forgiven.

One day I was in the middle of trying on the most incredible Creamsicle-orange Sonia Rykiel cocoon shearling coat when I got this email:

FROM: Donna Valeo <valeo.donna@yahoo.com>
SUBJECT: Hi
DATE: June 8th, 2012 8:22:56 AM EST
TO: Babe Walker <Babe@BabeWalker.com>
Hi Babe,
It's been a while. I'm sorry about Paul. Gina told me what happened, and says you're in Paris now. Are you enjoying your trip?
xDonna

Gina and I had been in touch via text ever since I'd left Cirque, and I assumed she told Donna some of the stuff I told her, but this kind of threw me. I took a seat on the dressing room floor, lit a smoke, fluffed my hair, and formulated a response:

FROM: Babe Walker <Babe@BabeWalker.com>
SUBJECT: Re: Hi
DATE: June 8th, 2012 8:30:24 AM EST
TO: Donna Valeo <valeo.donna@yahoo.com>
Hey?
Paris is Paris. You know.
Babe

FROM: Donna Valeo <valeo.donna@yahoo.com>
SUBJECT: Re: re: Hi
DATE: June 8th, 2012 8:41:59 AM EST
TO: Babe Walker <Babe@BabeWalker.com>
The reason I asked is I'm going to be there for a week at the end of the month to do another shoot for Vogue Paris. I'd like to catch up if you're free.

FROM: Babe Walker <Babe@BabeWalker.com>
SUBJECT: Re: re: re: Hi
DATE: June 8th, 2012 8:43:18 AM EST
TO: Donna Valeo <valeo.donna@yahoo.com>
Um, sure. Will Gina be here too?

FROM: Donna Valeo <valeo.donna@yahoo.com>
SUBJECT: Re: re: re: re: Hi

DATE: June 8th, 2012 8:49:37 AM EST

TO: Babe Walker <Babe@BabeWalker.com>

No, she's staying in New York. She just adopted two baby alpacas, so she's taking care of them. Couldn't make it out this time. Will be nice to see you.

FROM: Babe Walker <Babe@BabeWalker.com>

SUBJECT: Re: re: re: re: re: Hi

DATE: June 8th, 2012 8:57:26 AM EST

TO: Donna Valeo <valeo.donna@yahoo.com>

Totally. My # is (310) ###-####. Text me when you're here and we'll figure something out. Tell Gina alpacas make better sweaters than pets.

FROM: Donna Valeo <valeo.donna@yahoo.com>

SUBJECT: Re: re: re: re: re: re: Hi

DATE: June 8th, 2012 9:00:31 AM EST

TO: Babe Walker <Babe@BabeWalker.com>

Will do.

So that was that. Three weeks later Donna arrived in Paris. I'd been so busy shopping, drinking rosé, and making French friends (mostly fashion gays and one waify American girl from La Jolla) that I'd forgotten she was even coming until she texted me that she'd checked into her hotel, the Four Seasons Hotel George V. Her modeling thing was the next morning, so she was going to rest, shoot for a couple days, and we'd get dinner and have a night out when she'd wrapped. I was actually kind of nervous to see her. Yes, she was cool and modely for a forty-four-year-old, but we hadn't spent any time together since randomly meeting at rehab. What if she was crazy? I mean, I get that you have to be a little insane to still be modeling in your forties, but what if she was Sharon Stone crazy? I couldn't decide whether I'd love that or not.

When it came time for us to go to dinner, I was a little on edge, so I decided to formulate an outfit that accurately displayed my emotions. A T-shirt by The Row, underneath a crocodile Givenchy blazer with a huge shark-tooth pendant, Chanel hot pants, and Céline platform Mary Janes. Restrained, yet whimsical. Powerful, yet independent.

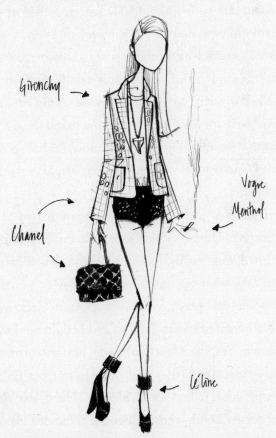

Givenchy →

Vogue
Menthol ←

Chanel →

← Céline

I met Donna at Café de Flore. She looked really fresh but kind of scared, which made me feel less scared. Neither of us ate much (obviously), but I guess it was nice to have a chance to catch her up on everything I'd been up to since leaving Cirque. Even though she'd never really be my mom, she was still my mom, so I figured I should try to get used to her. I mean, she'd missed every milestone of my most exciting years on Earth (everything after twenty-five is boring bullshit), so I figured we could, at the very least, be acquaintances who texted every now and then. Who knows? Maybe we would grow to have the kind of relationship where I could talk to her about STD scares. Either way, I was open to exploring our mother/daughter relationship.

We texted Gina a selfie of the two of us sipping rosé (no one drinks cocktails in Paris). Once we finished dinner, Donna mentioned she had to swing by Silencio, members only, to show face at the wrap party for her photo shoot and asked me if I wanted to come with. Um, duh. Little did she know I'd been a member since forever, and was already on the guest list. Like mother like daughter, I guess.

We arrived at Silencio and were promptly seated at a banquette, a bottle of Dom Pérignon Brut Rosé on ice placed before us. The crowd was mostly Parisian fashion people who were too chic to care what was going on. People were smoking cigarettes, Blondie was playing. I was stuck in a black mirrored room with a bunch of stylish demons and I could not have been more obsessed. Yes, the French are rude, but they secretly love Americans—especially if they find out you're from California. French people have it bad for California. There was this man seated in a corner booth whose silhouette reminded me of Robert's, but I was sure Robert wasn't in Paris and it was probably just my mind playing tricks on me. I wondered if I'd ever stop having visions of him.

I was shoulder dancing with a fashion gay I knew and congratulating him on his enormous Yohji Yamamoto coat, when I suddenly got this weird feeling that someone was staring at me. I turned around and saw this tall, tan Greek god looking right through my eyes and into my vagina. He had to be at least 6'7", with longish golden-y brown hair that was kind of slicked back, but not in a gross way. He was wearing Hermès everything and it was working. I rolled my eyes at him because I wasn't going to give him the satisfaction of knowing that I gave a shit, and poured myself another glass of champagne. As I took a sip, I felt someone come up behind me, move my hair off my neck, and say in a low, husky voice:

"You are without a doubt the sexiest person in this club."

It was the dumbest pickup line I'd ever heard, so dumb that it actually worked on me. He continued. "My name is Calisto, but everyone calls me Cal. Come have a drink with my friends."

"I have my own friends, but thanks."

"Then come have a drink with me."

"No."

Smash cut to Cal and me sitting in the banquette, so close to each other that our legs were touching and I could smell his cologne. Tom Ford Neroli Portofino. Chic. He was talking about his passion for Formula One racing when Donna walked brusquely over to me.

"We have to go."

"What do you mean?"

"See that woman over there?" she said, pointing to a really upset and drunk-looking model type.

"Yeah . . . ohmigod, is that Kate Moss?"

"Yes, it is. Come on." She motioned toward the exit.

"Wait, why?"

"Just get your purse. I'll tell you when we're outside."

I turned to Cal.

"Gotta go." I smiled. "Bye."

I leaned in to give him a kiss on the cheek, and he turned his head at the last second so our lips touched briefly, sending an unexpected wave of chills through my body. His gaze on me felt so intense that I had no choice but to write my phone number on the nearest matchbook, thrust it into his hand, and leave immediately without saying another word. It was a bold move, but well played.

I pushed my way out of le club and onto rue Montmartre to find Donna basically hyperventilating in the street, cigarette in hand. I hailed a cab and got us the fuck out of there. Once Donna had calmed down, I pressed her for more info.

"What the fuck was that?" I asked. "Last I checked, everyone was having fun. You were talking to Nicolas Ghesquière, and I was being seduced by a Greek Clive Owen. Remember?"

"I threw a glass of champagne at Kate Moss."

"Oh. Dark. You two know each other?"

"Not really. She and I had a thing years ago. It was nothing, but I just get so crazy when I see her. We came to blows at this gala in London. I 'accidentally' ripped the train of her dress."

"I remember that! That was you? All the papers said it was Courtney Love."

"No, that was me."

"Genius!"

"I don't know what it is, but she just makes me insane. I literally can't control myself around her."

"Whoa."

"I'm sorry," Donna said under her breath. She seemed genuinely embarrassed.

"It's okay. Does Gina know about your Kate Hulk-outs?" I asked.

"Yes, that's not the issue. Gina doesn't care. It's just—"

"Jesus, did you sleep with Kate Moss! Is she noisy?" Then I remembered that Donna was my mom, not a friend. "Oh God, is that totally inappropriate? I don't really know how to talk to moms, much less my own mom. You don't have to answer that."

Donna laughed. "No, no. It's fine. She's a very sweet girl, actually."

"Oh, well, that's boring," I said, disappointed. I'd always thought of Kate Moss as the girl who drinks all the booze, does all the drugs, and has all the fun.

"But . . . it's almost as if she elicited this crazy fucking alter ego in me," Donna said, shaking her head and looking out at the rainy Paris night. Although she said it in passing, it hit me like a Rick Owens boot to the skull. Alter ego? *Is Kate Moss my mom's Robert?* I thought. *Is Babette genetic?*

I grabbed Donna's hand.

"I know what you— Whoa, Jesus, your hands are freezing!"

"Yeah, bad circulation. Guess you didn't get that from me. Lucky."

"No, I guess I didn't inherit your weird, cold hands . . . but,

um, I think I may have gotten your split personality disorder."
And right as I said this, Donna turned her head to me and looked
right into my eyes.

"When you fall for someone?" she asked.

"Yes."

"Someone who actually fits into your life?"

"Yes," I said, catatonically staring back at Donna. It felt like
I was meeting myself for the first time.

"The second you fall in love, you become someone else. An
archangel."

"Babette."

"Donatella."

"Oh my God."

Then the weirdest thing happened. Donna and I scooted up
next to each other and hugged, almost involuntarily. After a split
second, we broke away awkwardly and I gave her an abridged
lecture in Babe Loves Robert 101, which was basically just me
weeping and Donna telling me it was okay. She confided in me
that when she first met Gina, she was exactly like that. Donatella
was her Babette. It took her years of therapy and self-explora-
tion to exorcise her inner beast, but she did it. Seeing Kate Moss
must've triggered Donatella's psycho habits. For the first time
since we met at Cirque, I felt actually related to my mother.

Luckily the snotting, nose-blowing, and retelling of embarrassing anecdotes had ended by the time the taxi pulled up to
the front of the Four Seasons.

"Hold on, you can keep the meter running," Donna said to
the driver, who didn't understand a word she said.

"Babe"—she grabbed me—"you have more spirit inside of

you than you know what to do with. You are a beautiful woman and you have to trust me when I say this: You are stronger than Babette and you will find a way to accept love. You will believe in yourself. You must believe that you can find love."

"Whoa," I said.

"I mean it."

"I believe you. This is just all so intense."

"I know."

As we held each other (for way too long) I wondered if Donna was right. Could I eventually exorcise Babette from my being? She seemed to have done it with Gina. But was it possible for me to do it with Robert? Maybe there was hope for me after all.

"Okay," said Donna, wiping her nose. "I have to head up to my room and call Gina. I'm sure she's waiting to hear from me. Thank you, Babe, thanks for talking. You know . . . I have some handbags that were gifted to me from the shoot today. Do you want one? You could come by in the morning and take a look at them. We could have coffee before I go." I was glad to move on from the topic of "impossible love" to bags.

"What kind of handbags?" I asked.

"A couple Célines, and I think there's a Proenza, and maybe a Jérôme Dreyfuss? Not sure though."

"Okay. See you at ten."

And that was that.

*B*reakfast was whatever. We made some small talk and drank coffee. I didn't take a purse from Donna. It felt weird for some reason. Getting on an emotional level with her in a taxi the night before was one thing, but letting her give me a bag would have been way too intimate. Plus, they were all kind of ugly, and I already had the Célines.

I walked Donna downstairs and waited while her driver loaded her bags into the car. I didn't know what to do, so I went in for a limp hug.

"Thanks for emailing me."

Donna squeezed me and held on really tight. Like, really hugged me before pulling away.

"I'm sorry I freaked out last night, but I'm glad it made us talk about our shit. I feel like I know you now, Babe."

"Yeah . . . "

"And I'm sorry you inherited my emotional bullshit."

"It's fine."

"You can always call me. I know how it feels."

"Okay."

"Okay. Then I guess I'll see you when I see you."

"It was good to see you, Donna. And I don't blame you for Babette. But I kind of do."

With that, Donna kissed me on both cheeks and turned toward the black Mercedes idling by the curb. Before shutting the door, she turned to me and yelled, "Just call him!" The words stung, but I pushed out a smile anyway. I obviously wanted to call Robert, but I couldn't let myself go down that path. Forward motion was the key to my growth, I knew that. Robert and Babette were my past. Forward motion. Forward motion. Forward motion. I kept repeating those words to myself as I made the trip up to my apartment and let myself in. Forward motion. Forward motion. All this talk about Robert had made me want to call or text him more than ever, so I decided to take a shower. It was the only way I could be alone without reaching for my phone. I disrobed and headed for the bathroom. Forward motion. Moving on. Growing up. Losing weight. Finding peace. Forward mo—

That's when I saw it. Written in black lipstick, on the mirrored bathroom door:

Wouldn't it be fun to get murdered in Paris? Enjoy your time on this earth while you still can.

TTYL

I must have passed out cold on the marble floor, because when I came to, the random maid who cleaned the apartment every week was standing over me looking extremely concerned. She helped me to my feet and I hugged her and started weeping.

"How is this possible? Did you see anyone in here? Who is doing this to me?!"

The maid looked completely freaked out. She tried to console me, but she couldn't speak a word of English, so I couldn't really understand what she was saying. She started wiping the note off the door.

"No! Don't touch that!" I screamed. "It's evidence. We need to get a forensics team in here, pronto. Somebody is trying to fucking murder me."

The maid stared at me blankly.

"Can you call the police?"

Silence.

"The police? POLICE? 911?"

Nothing. She was clearly going to be of no use to me.

"I'm fine. I'm fine. Just go ahead and clean the rest of the apartment," I said, wiping my tears away as I nudged her out of the bathroom. Confused, she hustled out into the bedroom.

I locked the bathroom door behind her and began to have the world's biggest panic attack. Whose handwriting was this? How had my stalker followed me across the world? How could they have known I was in Paris? How did they get into the apartment? All I had were questions and no answers. I sat on the floor, curled up next to the sink, shivering and hyperventilating for the next two hours while the maid cleaned the rest of the apartment. I waited until she left and then emerged. I obviously had to get out of there, but I had no idea where to go next. America and France were no longer safe. Fuck it. I'd just go to Charles de Gaulle and choose a destination once I got there. The point was, I needed to escape, and fast. I started shoving clothing into random suitcases.

Suddenly I heard my phone ringing. I fished it out of my purse, praying it was my dad or Mabinty or someone familiar, but it was a foreign number I didn't recognize. Maybe this was my stalker? I answered.

"Listen, you motherfucker. If this is the person who's been threatening to kill me, you're not gonna get away with it," I said in the most authoritative tone I could muster.

"It's Cal. Come with me to Greece."

"When?"

"Now."

"What?"

"Is this Babe?"

"Yes?"

"This is Calisto. We met last night at Silencio. You have been on my mind ever since. I am leaving for Mykonos this afternoon and would love for you to join me. My private jet departs from Paris–Le Bourget airport at sixteen hundred hours. If you tell me your address I can send a car for you."

This was exactly what I needed to hear at that moment. Cal's words made me feel protected from the vicious forces of evil in the world. Plus, I needed an out and a flight to Greece wasn't a bad option.

"Okay."

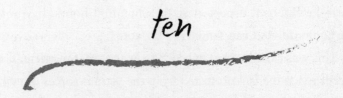

ten

FOOD IS NOT WHAT I'M HUNGRY FOR.

I left the Paris apartment with all my shit shoved haphazardly in suitcases. Nothing was organized, but it didn't matter. I would figure it all out once I was in Greece.

I met Cal on the tarmac of the private airport around 3:45 p.m. The car he'd sent for me pulled up right next to his plane. My mind was still racing, desperately trying to process the fact that someone had followed me to Paris with malicious intent, but despite my mental unclarity, it was a really chic moment overall. Getting on a private plane with a complete stranger felt like an organic decision for Euro Babe. Also, I had to get the fuck out of Paris before I got murdered, and Cal had provided a direction that at least solved that part of the equation.

Fortunately for me, there was something about Cal that was so captivating. He was brooding and sexy, and he had really honest eyes. The energy between us was palpable and exciting. Our spirit animals must have mated in their past spirit lives.

On the short flight from Paris to Mykonos, we made it through the usual "here's my background" talk. Cal was born in Greece and raised in Paris, his grandfather was the son of a shoemaker and then became a billionaire shipping magnate, and now Cal was running the "family business." He was thirty-two, divorced, no kids, and he drove Formula One race cars for fun (unclear). His plane was nice, but not as nice or as big as you would think it would be, for a billionaire. I expected more rooms and more white leather. Just more everything, really.

"That's a beautiful Hermès bag you've got. Whoever bought that for you must really care about you." Cal smiled.

"Oh, this old thing? It's my travel Birkin. I bought it for myself as a middle school graduation present."

"I noticed you had a different Hermès bag when we met at Silencio."

"Hermès is kind of my thing."

"My ex-wife asked for a Birkin every birthday, but I never obliged. Deep down I guess I knew it wasn't going to work out in the end."

"I get it. Birkins represent eternal devotion."

"Yes, they do. I would buy you a Birkin, Babe."

"That's so sweet."

Apparently Euro Babe had it all figured out.

Two huge men were on the plane with us. I could only assume they were Cal's security detail. They wore dark sunglasses, didn't say a word, and had matching Brioni suits (so chic). It was weird, because Cal never introduced them to me or even mentioned them. They just sat there in silence the whole flight (soooooo chic). Their stoic presence was not only calming, it also made me feel incredibly secure, which was a huge turn-on considering the fact that my stalker still very much wanted to assassinate me.

On the plane, as I was looking out the window at the Mediterranean below us, it occurred to me just how much I was looking forward to being in Greece. My dad and I had spent a couple of Augusts in Mykonos and I had loved it. My Parisian lifestyle encouraged far too much espresso drinking, cigarette smoking, and death threats. I was wanting a beachy, sunny, sandy scenario. Basically anything that would let me not think about the danger I was clearly in.

I wanted to be in Mykonos with my new super-rich boyfriend, under a giant fucking umbrella, where nobody could see me beneath my huge sunglasses and hat. As soon as we landed and I stepped off the plane I could smell the sea, imagine the tan bodies, and taste the vodka sodas that I was about to imbibe to keep my little body hydrated in the warm Mediterranean air. Heaven.

The two huge security randos helped me with my suitcases and we all loaded into SUVs that were waiting for us on the tarmac. Cal had booked the most amazing room for us at the super luxe Apanema Boutique Hotel: a suite with two bedrooms and bathrooms (thank fuck), both with Jacuzzis, a huge kitchen, and a private pool with amazing views of the sea. Of course, I'd also gone ahead and reserved a luggage room next to our suite. "The Luggage Room" is the extra room I always need at hotels. It's where I store my suitcases and travel gear once the clothes have been unpacked or dumped onto the floor. It's not a good idea to sleep near large, empty vessels like luggage—ask any shaman.

Everything in the hotel was white. The walls, the floors, the halls, the sheets, the furniture. You have to love any isle that features an all-white backdrop with pops of bright color.

Cal and I sat out on the terrace to look at the stars and have a few glasses of champagne. He'd arranged for the hotel's head chef to come up and cook us something fresh and low in sodium, per my request.

"I've never done this before," I admitted.

"And what is this?" asked Cal.

"Picking up and running away with a man I don't even know. In fact, I pride myself on being very untrusting."

"Well, if it makes you feel any better, I've already met your mother—who is extremely beautiful, I might add."

"Thanks, Cal. I'll let Donna know you're into her." I smiled.

"That's not what I meant."

"I know. I'm fucking with you. She's a lesbian anyway."

"I want to make love to you. And I don't want to wait any longer," Cal said as he looked deep into my eyes.

"We haven't eaten yet."

"Food is not what I'm hungry for."

It felt really great to be in the presence of a man who was strong, a little dangerous, and totally taking control of the situation.

"Okay then." I relented.

"Good, then go take a bath and meet me in the bedroom when you're ready. No more than twenty minutes, please."

I didn't respond. I just got up from the table, smiled, and headed to my bathroom. I'd never been bossed around like that, but I kind of loved it. I drew a hot bath, did a quick ten-minute meditation/Kegel ritual, got out, and stared into the mirror for thirty seconds while repeating my new mantra: "Fuck you, Babette."

I left my skin damp before putting on a robe. My body was warm from the bath, and my heart was pounding in anticipation. I hadn't been this nervous about something sexual since I was about to try anal for the first time when I was eighteen. When I entered the room, Cal was already sitting in a chair next to the bed. He was fully clothed but the top few buttons on his shirt were undone. He wasn't smiling, which was very unnerving. Cal gestured for me to come closer to him, which I did. Then, he beckoned me to come even closer. I slowly closed the gap between us until I was standing right in front of him. With his hands he indicated for me to lean down to him and when I put my face next to his, he whispered in my ear.

"*Chorépsoun gia ména.*"

I don't really speak Greek, but I knew enough to understand. He wanted me to dance for him. And the strangest part was that I wanted to dance for him.

Euro Babe was all about expressing her body through the power of naked movement and strategic hair flips, so I dropped my robe and started to sway back and forth in a Stevie Nicks/Eddie Vedder kind of way, which eventually led to more Eddie Van Halen–esque undulations, but I didn't feel weird about it. My heart was still pounding with nerves and excitement, but I wasn't embarrassed in any way. Plus, I could see that Cal was getting turned on, which made me feel even sexier. He smiled at me and almost immediately pulled me down onto his lap. He whispered into my ear again.

"Close your eyes."

"I don't want to," I replied.

"You are mistaken if you think that this is about what you want. What you want is what I want. So you want to close your eyes."

I gently closed my eyes and he picked me up, threw me on the bed, and lay down next to me, kissing my neck. I wanted to open my eyes to look at him, but I didn't know if I was allowed to. So I just lay still as he caressed my breasts with so much attention and grace that I almost said, "Fuck me." My body was pulsing with heat. Cal took off his shirt and I could feel his warm skin against mine as he slowly lay on top of me. His body was hard, smooth, and heavy. Although my eyes were closed, I could imagine what he looked like based on how he felt on top of me. This was his plan all along: by making me close my eyes, Cal had forced me to rely on the way he felt, smelled, and tasted. I could feel how focused he was on our lovemaking. He spent a lot of time making sure that I was good and ready for him.

When he finally pulled me close and pushed himself inside of me, I let out a sound that I've never heard anyone make. It wasn't an ugly sound, but it caught me off guard because it was coming from my own mouth. Cal was massive. Not like, "Oh yeah, I'm sleeping with this really hot guy who has a big dick," but more like, "I'm pretty sure that less than half of my boyfriend's monster cock can actually fit inside me." I was glad he made me close my eyes—if I'd seen that thing coming at me,

I would have never let this happen. The weirdest part was that it didn't hurt at all. Cal was clearly an artist who had thoroughly prepared his subject for what was about to happen. His diligent groundwork had ensured that the only thing I'd be experiencing was sheer pleasure and ecstasy.

Each thrust felt orgasmic. I could barely differentiate between when I was coming and when I wasn't. I didn't ever want it to stop. This was next-level fucking. I was more present in that moment than I'd been in any meditation, yoga class, or sweat lodge experience.

After at least an hour of unwavering intensity, as I was about to climax for the fifth time, I felt Cal's body rhythms begin to shift. It felt like we were syncing up to each other. Our breath was matched, our movements choreographed, our bodies communed.

"OPEN!" Cal shouted.

I opened my eyes and stared deep into Cal's soul as we came at the exact same time. He had saved the best for last. It was the orgasm to shame all other orgasms.

"Fuck. Fuuuuuuuuuuuuuuuck!"

"Well done," Cal said as he looked me in the eyes and cracked the slyest smile.

"Well done to you. I don't know what to say. You literally opened my eyes . . . to a lot of shit."

Cal laughed, kissed me gently on my neck, my collarbone, and my breast. Then he rolled off me and hopped off the bed.

"I'll be right back," he said as he walked out completely naked.

"Me too."

My legs were so weak as I stood. I wobbled back to my bathroom and it occurred to me that I had never had so many orgasms during one sexual encounter. Usually I don't even climax until the second or third time I've slept with someone. My body was in shock, I felt at least a pound lighter, and I was sure that I'd finally achieved sex hair perfection.

I walked into my bathroom and looked in the mirror. I was glowing. My cheeks were bright red, my hair was major, and I felt like I was on top of the world. I grabbed a towel and took a short thirty-minute shower. Once I was all cleaned up, I put on my robe and went into the living room, where Cal was sitting on a couch with an open bottle of white and two glasses.

"Babe. This is what we are going to do: You and I are going to get dressed, leave all of our luggage here, and walk out that door. We are going to spend the night on my yacht, which is moored just over there," Cal said, gesturing out the window. "Konstantinos and Dimitris will gather our belongings and meet us on the boat later in the morning. Does that sound good?"

"Yes, please." I really feature a yacht scenario, and I had brought a bunch of nautical looks from Paris that were going to be thrilled to make their debut on a shipping tycoon's yacht.

Before I knew it, Cal and I were alone in a tiny little dingy, speeding out to his yacht. It was midnight and I was freezing. As we approached the ship I realized that it was completely dark and not one crew member came to greet us. The whole thing was odd, but it was an unexpected visit so maybe the staff didn't know we were coming.

The yacht was spectacular, tasteful, spacious, and there was something very familiar about it. Almost as if I'd seen it before. Cal quickly showed me to our room.

"We are not staying in the master suite, because they are in the midst of refinishing the wood. I hope that's okay with you. Chemical fumes are disgusting and not good for the skin."

"Cal, it's fine. I can't thank you enough for everything tonight. This has been really special."

"To me as well. Let's have another adventure tomorrow."

I was exhausted. It had been an amazing day. I hadn't even thought about my stalker once. I curled into bed with Cal and fell asleep as soon as I put my head on his shoulder.

The next morning I was awakened by a maid who barged into our room. She looked right at me, her eyes widened, and then she quickly left. It was a very strange encounter, but I guess she assumed the room would be empty. Cal wasn't in bed, so I got myself together and headed to the deck to get a cup of coffee and see what he was up to.

As I passed a few more of the yacht staff on my way to the kitchen, they all seemed unreasonably icy. No one was acknowledging my presence or saying good morning. They actually seemed weirded out by my presence. Maybe Cal never brought girls onto his yacht? Then, rounding the corner, I recognized a distinct male voice that was very distinctly NOT Cal's. I'd heard this voice before. It was slightly nasal and boyish, but undoubtedly sexy, and it very distinctly belonged to Leonardo DiCaprio.

"Could it be?" I whispered softly to myself. I looked over the deck and confirmed what I had suspected. Sitting at a table, eating breakfast, was Leo. "NO!" I gasped to myself, turning away and pressing my body against the wall. It took me five whole seconds to register that this was not a dream, and when I looked back around the corner, he was still sitting there with four incredibly beautiful blond women, three of whom were topless, (and Jonah Hill) but whatever, not important.

So, this was happening. I was on a ship with Leo. I'd thought so much about this moment but never thought it would be like this. He was clearly Cal's friend. Why else would he be here? I had become the real-life Rose DeWitt Bukater, except not a redhead or fat. This was my *Titanic* moment. It was going to be messy telling Cal that I chose Leo over him, but the heart wants what the heart wants.

I grabbed the closest deckhand I could find.

"Where is Calisto?"

"I'm sorry, ma'am?"

"You know, Cal? Tall, handsome, Greek. The owner of the yacht?"

"Ma'am, this is Mr. DiCaprio's vessel."

I wasn't clear.

"Wait, I was with a man last night named Cal. Where is he?"

"There is no one named Cal on this boat. Who did you say you were again?"

Something was gravely wrong with the entire situation. Cal was missing, my bags had never arrived from the hotel, and I was somehow trespassing on Leonardo DiCaprio's ship. As I was putting all of this together, the deckhand radioed yacht security to make them aware of my presence. Everything was happening very quickly, but it dawned on me that Cal and I had illegally boarded Leo's yacht, and he'd left me there to deal with the aftermath. I refused to meet Leo for the first time as a dirty stowaway, so I had to get his security team off my ass. I grabbed the deckhand again and smiled warmly.

"I'm soooo sorry. I took a ton of ecstasy earlier and had no idea where I was for a sec!" I pulled my dress over my head and handed it to him. "I meant to ask where Leo was, not Cal. Who's Cal? I don't even know a Cal! Hahaha." I undid my bra so that I was topless and wearing just my black panties. "But I just saw Leo and Jonah and the rest of the girls having brunch, so it's all good." I handed the deckhand my bra. "That was scary! I should stop doing so many drugs. I'm gonna go for a swim. Will you put these in my room for me? Thanks a mil."

He seemed to have bought my "confused-druggie-model-girlfriend-of-Leo" act and walked away with my clothes. Then I ran as quickly as I could to the back of the ship, and jumped off of the deck and into the Med.

It took me about forty-five minutes to swim back to the beach, which was plenty of time for me to realize that this whole trip had been a setup. My suspicions were confirmed when I got back to the suite. Cal had robbed me. He was gone and had taken all of my possessions with him. My clothes, my Birkins, my phone, my iPad, my computer, my jewelry, my cash, my credit cards, and my dignity. Gone. Well, almost gone.

Whenever I'm out of town, there exists the possibility that I might leave my travel Birkin in a restaurant or on a yacht, or have it stolen by a creep like Cal. That's why I stay prepared by putting photocopies of my passport, British passport, and driver's license in a plastic bag, along with a travel-size Evian mist spray and a handful of raw, sprouted almonds. Then I ziplock it shut, fold it into a tight packet, and tape the bag and its contents to the bottom of the mattress in my luggage room. That Greek assface might have thought he'd gotten everything of mine, but he was wrong.

The police confirmed that Cal was a modern-day Thomas Crown. Apparently he'd done this to other unsuspecting women throughout Europe. The police were really nice about helping me get to the American embassy in Athens. Once everything had been sorted, I was fine to go on my merry way. My dad wired me some money, I had a massage, and I bought some new clothes.

As hard as I tried to be mad at Cal, my body remained in such a relaxed state from our incredible sex session that the whole thing kind of seemed like a fair trade. Sex with Cal was better than with Robert, it was better than that super expensive G spot stimulator I'd bought in 2009, and better than any fantasy sex I'd ever imagined having with Ryan Gosling. But Athens was kind of a dark place. It was not as island-y and definitely not as peaceful as Mykonos had been. Plus, my sex-tasy was wearing off and I was starting to be insanely shaken by not only being stalked in Paris, but also being Bling Ringed by Cal. The only thing that could possibly revive me after this elaborate debacle was a good, strong joint. So I booked a one-way flight to Amsterdam.

eleven

A SAFE SPACE TO GET STONED AND DRINK DIET COKE.

It was around ten a.m., and I was soaking in a huge tub in my hotel room watching some bad Nicki Minaj video (that probably only came out in Europe) on the little TV built into the mirror, when I realized I was actually relaxed. I'd let myself saturate in the bath for two whole hours (as opposed to my dermatologist's recommended thirty minutes), so it was time to get out. As I stood naked and wet in front of the mirror, Nicki in the background, I caught a glimpse of a strange sparkle in my eye. I have, like, really pretty eyes, but they don't sparkle. They're not sparkly eyes, never have been. Charlize Theron has sparkly eyes. Cameron Diaz has sparkly eyes. I guess Babe Walker had that same sparkle in her eyes now, and it was an amazing thing to see. I couldn't tell you why I suddenly had

A-list eyes, but I chose to believe that I was being rewarded for the immense strength I'd been exhibiting over the last few days.

The last time I was in Amsterdam was for a Kylie Minogue concert in 2002. I came with my dad (who has done work for Kylie) and Mabinty. We only stayed a night and I was fifteen, so I stayed off the heavy drugs. I mean, I obviously smoked several joints with one of the roadies at the after-party, but my aforementioned chaperones indulged in some of Amsterdam's finest offerings. Long story short, my dad puked on Mabinty's boobs, which caused her to puke on my face. We were in an elevator and they were on too many mushrooms. It's shocking I've ever touched that shit since.

Something I remember very clearly from that trip is my dad telling me not to "ever spend more than forty-eight hours in this fuckin' city, it'll bloody melt you." So I wasn't planning on sticking around for a long time. I simply needed a moment in a petite, urban European environment where no one would recognize me, including hopefully whoever had followed me to Paris and threatened to kill me. I needed to be somewhere where no one would judge me for sitting alone at a coffee shop with a lit joint in one hand while sketching pictures of my third eye in a Moleskine notebook with the other. It was time Euro Babe got a bit of much-needed relaxation. So I got a room at the Conservatorium Hotel, which was chic for the Netherlands, and had Mabinty ship me three suitcases of weather-appropriate garb.

• • • • •

I made my purpose in life to focus on Babe, get stoned, lose focus of my purpose, refocus, and forget about the fact that the world seemed to want me dead, or at least completely fucked over.

Once I was dried, dressed, and hydrated, I headed down to the lobby. When I asked the cute little Dutch lady at the hotel's concierge desk if she could recommend a "safe space for getting stoned and drinking Diet Coke," she suggested a coffee shop a few blocks away called Friends and Family. Sounded perfect.

The café was just what I was looking for. It reeked of pot, and there were chic little antiques everywhere, dim lighting, and zero dreadlocks in sight. I was safe. The guy at the counter was super hot in a Jack Nicholson kind of way, which is disgusting, but also kind of not if you think about it.

"Hi, can you help me find my spirit joint?" I asked.

"Hallo. What is it you like?" he said in a deep, husky tone. Dutch accents always make me laugh, so I laughed a little bit, but he didn't notice. I wondered how high he was.

"Well, it's been a trying few months. I'm just starting to get back on my feet," I said. "LA is weird right now, my mom told me that my whole crazy alter-ego thing is kind of her fault, then I was burglarized and basically soul-raped, but I'm okay. I'm getting through it. Forward motion, you know? So, I guess I'm looking for something inspiring and de-stressing."

Without a word, he turned around to the cabinet behind the counter and pulled out five perfectly rolled joints in plastic test tubes.

"These are good for girls. This one is the strongest and this one a little less, and so on," he said as he pointed to each tube.

"Perf, I'll take six of these super intense guys. And a Diet Coke. And a sparkling water. And a still water."

"Okay. I will bring to the table."

"Thanks. Oh, and are you married? Just wondering. I'm on vacation, so . . ."

"I am gay," he said in the straightest way ever. I was so into him.

"Oh, okay, cool. Yeah, I figured." Oh well, worth a shot.

I found a table in the corner, settled in with my pen and Moleskine, lit the first joint, and pressed play on a playlist I'd curated on the plane ride to the Netherlands. I make playlists when I need to get out of my head and/or when I feel bloated; it eases the racing thoughts and de-puffs my waistline. This particular list consisted of songs that I felt represented my state of mind at the time. So, that meant a lot of Kate Bush, a lot of old Whitney Houston, and a little bit of good No Doubt. I was a complex California girl with something to say.

I spent the next few hours sketching some of my lost belongings, in memoriam. I called it *Taken: The Soul Cries.*

I could tell that being in Amsterdam was helping me grow as an artist. I completely lost track of time, which is what happens when you do nothing but smoke medical-grade pot for hours, and when I emerged from Friends and Family it was night. Feeling happy, airy, and free, I embarked on an aimless journey along one of the canals on Keizersgracht. I was in an amazing mood. I had altogether forgotten about the Robert issue, the Cal issue,

SOUL CRIES

and my stalker issue. I was feeling social, so I told a few swans floating through the canal that they were chic. They didn't respond, but I sensed that they understood.

There were so many people on the street, and by people I mean scary tourists and drunk college kids. I get that I was also a tourist, but I didn't feel like one. Come to think of it, I never feel like a tourist, and yet, no matter where I am I always feel like everyone around me is. I was constantly becoming more aware of myself.

Anyway, I obviously wasn't interested in making friends with anyone I saw stumbling down the cobblestone streets. Lined up conveniently along the bank of the canals were glass doors, each lit only by one red light. Behind each door stood a girl in what looked like good lingerie but that had to be bad, cheap, and probably dirty. These women (girls? children? mothers?) looked super friendly, and some of them were even beckoning me to come closer. I perused my options, judging each of them by the way they stood and the way they presented themselves. They were totally hookers, but at the time I had no clue. I just thought they were friendly people behind glass doors, obvs.

I approached one girl because she kind of resembled Rihanna, with wide, optimistic eyes and a blond weave.

"Come in," she said to me, smiling and sliding open the glass door. "I'm Femke."

Once I was in the small room, which smelled like vanilla and bodies, Femke closed the door and pulled down a curtain, giving us some privacy. There was a bed, a chair, a sink, and a red lightbulb hanging from the ceiling. Very editorial. I sat on the chair and lit a cigarette.

"You're not gonna kill me, are you?" I asked politely.

"Ah, you are American? I loooove America." Her accent was thick as shit, so I laughed.

"So, you're not gonna kill me?"

"Whatever you want, darling," she purred.

"Cute. I'm Babe, I'm from LA. You know what LA is?"

"Yes, I know what LA is. You think I'm fucking moron?" she said coyly, leaning up against the pinkish wall, arching her back. Her body was actually kind of amazing. And she had gorgeous caramel skin.

"You're, like, way prettier than you need to be, right? Do you get that a lot?" I remarked.

"You are very pretty too, LA girl. Nice hair."

"Oh, no, my name's Babe. You can call me that. People in rehab used to call me 'LA Girl,' among other names." I continued to take long drags from my European Marlboro Light. I was totally getting into the weird scene and the buzz from the cigarette was sobering me up a bit, which in turn caused me to start realizing that Femke was a hooker and not a friend-for-rent, or whatever I thought she was.

"Nice to meet you, Babe." With that, she slipped the cigarette from my hand and took a few drags herself. She took off her bra and tossed it onto the bed. Great tits.

"Love that name, Femke. Very model-y."

"*Dank je.*"

"*Que?*"

"It means 'thanks.' "

"Oh, right."

"I used to want to be model. I follow all of the big ones. Christy, Kate, Karolina, Laetitia. I read all the big magazine."

"You like fashion?" I was actually shocked.

"I love fashion. You think I want to do this job forever?"

"I don't know, I've always thought being a hooker must be kind of terrifying. But then there are days when I think it's the chicest job there is."

"Chic?" she asked, handing me back my smoke.

"Chic," I repeated.

"What is this?"

"What is what?"

"Chic."

"What?"

"What is this, 'chic'? I see all of time in magazine. We don't have this word in Dutch."

"Oh . . . wow," I said. I was dumbfounded. I don't think I'd ever had to define the word *chic* before. Not in my entire life. Chic was just chic. I had no clue how to define it using only the mere English lexicon. How could a word so important, such a pillar of my being, be so hard to define?

I put my cigarette out in a little heart-shaped ashtray near the bed, found a hair thing in the bottom of my bag, and proceeded to tie Femke's blond weave up into a tight yet messy bun. Then I took the navy cashmere Miu Miu cardigan that I had been using as a scarf and gave it to her to pull over her bare chest.

"Fits perfect, I knew it would," I said.

Then I slipped out of my black crocodile Tom Ford pumps and kicked them to Femke's feet. She slid into the shoes, hunched a bit, and cocked her head to the left like a model (she knew her shit), and was magically a new girl. Tight bun, tight cardigan, black panties and pumps. It was kind of major, actually, and I was very impressed with my styling. I pulled out my phone to snap a photo.

"Look sad," I directed. She gave me a brilliant scowl.

Handing her the phone to look at the photo, I happily proclaimed, "That is chic."

Femke and I spent the next two hours talking—talking about bodies, talking about sex, and smoking Dutch cigarettes. I told her about rehab, my book, Robert, Cal, my stalker, and Leo. She told me about the different types of penises she's seen, and the time someone accidentally shat on her. We laughed a lot. There was a certain freedom in knowing nothing about each other. The newness of our bond was something I hadn't felt with someone in a while. My life had been so inundated with issues from my past, but Femke represented my future. She was my Pretty Woman, my Julia. I asked her to move to LA to be my assistant/bff, but she said she couldn't move because she had five kids to take care of. I totally understood. Kids first.

I settled up with Femke and decided I wasn't ready for my night to end. So I went to the Van Gogh museum, but being that it was 4 a.m., the doors were bolted. So I lay down on an open lawn near the museum and Google image searched "Van Gogh paintings" while smoking more cigarettes for about three hours until the sun rose. It was fucking major.

Turns out Van Gogh was, like, deeply troubled. He had every disease that anyone has ever had, and also sold only one painting before he died in 1890. He was completely unknown while he was alive. I think my life will be like that: underappreciated until I'm long gone.

I eventually found my way back to the hotel and took another long soak in the tub. I mean, Femke was cute and everything, but her little room was fucking disgusting, and I wasn't trying to catch another VD from a Dutch whore. Just kidding, I've never had a VD. Just kidding.

twelve

STRONGER THAN YESTERDAY.

So I ended up staying in Amsterdam for a little longer than two days. I was into this city. I even adopted its sense of style. Yes, I was royally fucked out of my head for most of my stay, which is why I firmly (albeit momentarily) believed that the Dutch had the best fashion sense in the world. Gone was my urge to present as a carefully disheveled ambassador of color. All I cared about was black. Outside of a particularly dark phase I went through during my freshman year of college, I had never fully realized the potential of dressing in all black. I could be a vision of drapeyness in Rick Owens, or structural meets slouchy in a combination of Céline and Ann Demeulemeester. The world was my dark oyster. I even went so far as to dye my hair obsidian, pierce my nipples, and experiment with different dramatic eyeliner shapes.

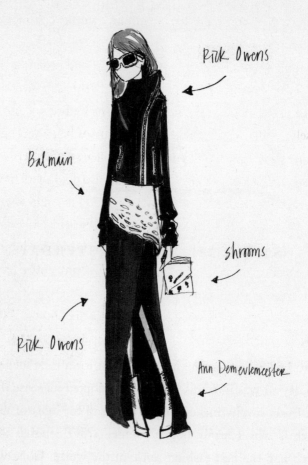

Rick Owens

Balmain

shrooms

Rick Owens

Ann Demeulemeester

I started doing special facial exercises to ensure my cheek-bones would be sharp as knives. I wanted to look impenetrable, dangerous. My inclination toward all things colorless probably had to do with where I was emotionally, combined with all the hallucinogens I was taking. When you've made a full-time job of doing drugs, drawing, and not really speaking to anyone, the last thing you want is to look in the mirror and have your sarto-rial choices ricochet your fragile mind into the throes of utter insanity. No. You must become your own beacon of stability. Therefore: blackness is key.

I took a vow of silence from my family and friends in LA and decided to communicate with them only through the power of imagery, meaning I group texted everyone I knew one portrait of myself per day. Conveying my daily state of being through photography instead of words was a fun challenge. Who needs words, anyway? Sentences are overrated. I was also doing a lot of sketching in parks around the city, and could feel my soul expanding. I was actually—dare I say it?—calm. I'd evaded whomever had been stalking me (thank God); I hadn't received a death threat the entire time I'd been in Amsterdam. I could drink coffee for hours, walk around the city, sketch, lie in grassy knolls, text photos to loved ones and ex-boyfriends, shop, text more photos, take a pill, put on eyeliner, go clubbing at night with Femke, and stare into space for hours. I was engaged in a truly fulfilling lifestyle. Much like the Britney Spears song, I was stronger than yesterday.

One morning, as I returned to my hotel from a wild night at this leather-daddy dance party called Filth Master, I noticed a sort of chic girl standing at the front desk having a quiet and controlled meltdown. She was wearing a Dolce & Gabbana crop top and miniskirt, which was kind of loud for 7 a.m., but caught my eye due to all the mushrooms I was on, so I sat down on a suitcase that I thought was a chair and watched her lose her shit. I live for confrontation when I'm tripping.

"You do not seem to understand that I have a standing annual reservation," she stated to the meek hotel attendant with a handlebar mustache standing behind the desk. "Please check the computer system again. The name is Thalia Alexandrov."

"Ma'am, we have nothing reserved under the surname Alexandrov."

Sighing, she reached into her Kelly and pulled out a wad of cash, placing it lightly on the counter. "There must be other suites available. This is the only place in the city that knows Magnus's walking and feeding schedules."

She was referring to the massive white Pyrenees mountain dog sleeping next to her on the floor.

"Unfortunately, Miss Alexandrov, we are full. May I recommend Hotel de l'Europe . . . ?"

"That will not do," she muttered darkly, putting the cash back in her purse.

"I offer my sincerest apologies for this misunderstanding," said the mustache man.

"What is your name?"

"Sergio, Miss Alexandrov."

"I once had a boyfriend named Sergio. He was very athletic, loved to ski."

"That's nice, Miss Alexandrov."

"Unfortunately he also loved to fuck whores."

"Oh."

"Shortly after I discovered Sergio's habits, he suffered a terrible skiing accident and broke both his legs and a rib, and his beautiful face was forever mangled. It was quite the tragedy. But very karmic, if you ask me. Now"—she reached back into her purse and pulled out another wad of cash—"how about that room?"

"I'm sorry, Miss Alexandrov, but as I said before, the entire hotel is booked."

Thalia kept telling Sergio about all the horrible things that had befallen those who had wronged her and kept asking Sergio for a room, and Sergio kept saying that the hotel was full. I was kind of zoned out until I locked eyes with Magnus. "Help us, Babe. Help us," he seemed to say. I love huge dogs. So much chicer than tiny dogs. Magnus's aura reminded me of my dearly deceased rehab dog, Soda Water, so I got up and walked over to Thalia, who was in the middle of describing to Sergio how a waiter had once served her a dairy-based soup and his balls had mysteriously been cut off the next day. I crouched down next to Magnus.

"It's okay now," I whispered with a reassuring smile. "Babe's here."

"Namaste, my queen," said Magnus with his eyes.

I rose to my feet.

"Sergio, please move the contents of my luggage room to the storage safe downstairs, and place Magnus's belongings and his owner in there for however long they wish to stay." I looked back down at Magnus. "I just can't have you shedding on any of my chunky knits."

"Certainly, Miss Walker," said Sergio with a smile.

"Thanks, Serg."

"I can't thank you enough," said Thalia, giving me a stiff hug. "I'm Thalia."

"I know. You've been screaming your name for the past twenty minutes. Anyway, I'm going up to my room."

"Is that dress Alaïa?"

"What does it look like?" I responded without turning back around.

And with that, I went up to my room and passed out.

I woke up to the doorbell ringing. It was about three o'clock the following afternoon. I pulled off my eye mask and stumbled over to see who was harassing me.

"What is it?" I muttered, opening the door.

"I am so sorry. I did not mean to wake you." It was Thalia and Magnus. "We will come back later."

"No, it's okay. Come in."

"I just wanted to bring you some champagne and marijuana to say thank you for letting us stay in your luggage room."

"Oh, no problem. You're welcome."

"Would you care to get high with me?"

"Um . . . sure, why not?"

We sat down on one of the sofas and Thalia lit the joint, taking a long drag.

"Fuck this fucking place," she said, exhaling. "I cannot believe they lost my reservation." She passed the joint to me.

"Yeah, that totally sucks." I took a hit. Notes of strawberry, mellow aftertaste.

"I usually stay in this suite."

"Oh. Sorry?"

"It's fine. I am over it."

"I was originally going to be here for a couple days, but I extended my trip and paid extra to rent it out for the rest of the month, so that's probably why your reservation got all fucked up."

"Ha, yes, probably. Well, whatever. This trip has been doomed from the start. I was supposed to meet a lover of mine here, but his flight got canceled and he's not coming anymore."

"Oh. Your boyfriend?"

"No. My boyfriend's back in Spain, attending a charity event. This man is an artist I see sometimes. We make love, and he paints me."

"Cute."

"What are you doing in Amsterdam?"

"Oh you know . . . just chilling out, drawing, doing a bunch of drugs, not eating, hiding out from a stalker. The usual."

"A stalker?"

"Yeah, like someone who is obsessed with me and follows me around leaving notes—"

"I am familiar with the term 'stalker.' "

"Okay. You seemed confused."

"No. Do you know who your stalker is?"

"No."

"Well, that is quite the accomplishment," she said, smiling.

"Are you kidding? It's terrifying."

"Nooooooo, no no no. It is chic."

"How is someone trying to murder me chic?"

"Because it means that there is someone out there who wants you, who cannot stop thinking about you," Thalia said, opening the bottle of champagne and walking over to the bar to grab a couple of flutes. "For all you know, this 'stalker' you speak of could be your soul mate who just doesn't know any other way of communicating his or her feelings." She carefully poured two glasses and held hers up. *"Za vas,"* she said, nodding to me. We clinked. I took a sip.

"I highly doubt my stalker is a hot guy who's dying to meet me," I said.

"You never know," she said. She finished off her drink and

poured herself another glass. "My father is, like, this kind of important person in Russia, so I had a stalker when I was seventeen. His name was Yosef, and he'd write me notes every day and wait for me outside of my school. One night my bodyguard caught Yosef in my room, watching me sleep, and he went to prison. But I'd seen a picture of Yosef in the papers, and he was a beautiful twenty-one-year-old man. Not so scary. I wrote him letters for a couple of years while he was incarcerated. Then we were lovers for three months when he got out. Best sex of my life."

"Why did you guys break up?"

"I got bored and slept with another man and Yosef tried to kill us both. He's back in prison now. Probably forever."

"You're insane," I said.

"I know." She giggled.

We both started laughing hysterically. It was really nice meeting someone who was crazier and slightly less pretty than me.

"I have a wonderful idea," declared Thalia. "Let's fly to my dad's chalet in Gstaad. The ski season just started and all my friends will be there. We need to get out of this awful hotel."

"I don't know. I really can't deal with flying commercial right now."

"You are in luck. I have my pilot's license and my plane is sitting in a hangar at AMS."

"You flew yourself here?"

"Some girls are into horses. I am into planes."

"Chic."

"Yes, I know. Will you join me?"

"Don't you want to get back to your boyfriend in Spain?"

"Absolutely not. Everyone thinks princes are the most glamorous boyfriends, but they smell and they're all racist."

"Right?! I've been saying that for years."

"Except for Prince Harry. He has a magnificent penis."

"Tell me about it. I'd fuck him."

"As would I. So what is your decision, Babe Walker? Stay here and hide out from this stalker person, or come away with me to Gstaad?"

Gstaad it was.

The flight to Switzerland was only mildly frightening (six-seat private planes are glorified death traps, in my opinion) and we made it to Gstaad in one piece. Thalia's dad's chalet was kind of everything. A quaint ten-bedroom, thirteen-bathroom A-frame home, with a beautiful pine exterior and intricately carved white wood balconies outside every room. What I loved about it most is that it was super rustic on the inside, with plush couches and sheepskin rugs and tons of pillows, but it also had some of the most modern amenities I'd ever experienced. I'm talking electronic toilets with facial recognition, an espresso machine built into the wall, and a water spigot near the sink that spouted ice-cold Pellegrino. Obsessed. I had my own suite (of course), but I mostly stayed in Thalia's room because we'd stay up all night talking and laughing.

Thalia was incredibly cool. I liked her because she was like me, but Russian. This meant that she drank vodka like it was water, and was always impeccably dressed. I'm kind of nymph-y and can pull off the whole chicly disheveled LA thing when I want to, but Thalia would never deign to step out in public without perfectly blown out hair, heels, and a dress. She never wore pants. It was kind of major. We also had the exact same sense of humor and could practically finish each other's sentences. I'd always been an only child, but I like to think that Thalia and I were like long-lost astral sisters. I also liked her friends, which is rare for me. She ran with a very international crowd who seemed to have nothing to do but travel and party. I don't know what they did for work, but then again, I didn't know what I did for work either, so it was all good.

One night when we were out I met a French guy named Guillaume. He was maybe 5 feet 11, kind of skinny, and had a big nose (sexy big, not gross big) and shaggy blond hair. He kept saying he wanted to marry me and I kept saying no. It was the best. I was about to head back to his hotel with him for a midnight romp when an extremely drunk Thalia stormed up to us, freaking out because she thought I'd left without her. She was yelling at me, which I thought was hilarious, but then her antics devolved into whimper-crying and it became clear that I'd have to abandon Guillaume and take her home. It was annoying. I mean, who hasn't been wasted off their face at a nightclub in the Swiss Alps? Why was it my problem? Call your driver. I was clearly busy with Guillaume.

The next morning things were back to normal, and I attributed her freak-out to a mild case of altitude sickness/too much coke. It could happen to anyone. But then a couple weeks later we were both enjoying a dry sauna in the nude and I noticed that she'd copied my nipple piercings.

"When did you get your nipples pierced?" I asked.

"Oh, these?" she said, looking down at her chest. "I've had them pierced since I was fourteen, but I don't wear jewelry. You are just now noticing?"

"I guess it's just strange because your nipple rings are literally the exact same as mine, which is weird because I had these custom made in Amsterdam." They were these super chic mini diamond hoops. I can't remember where Thalia said she'd gotten her nipple rings, but I didn't think twice about it. A couple nights later, when she Instagrammed a picture of me drinking beer out of a plastic cup, I had no choice but to get stern with her. I thought that would be the last of her weirdness, but I'd thought wrong.

We were trying on outfits one night, deciding what to wear to a dinner party she was throwing, when Thalia insisted that my white Helmut Lang dress (I'd switched from dressing in all black to dressing in all white) was "unflattering and a weird cut," so I opted for a different, less concept-driven dress. I was downstairs having a drink and chatting up Guillaume and the other guests when Thalia waltzed down the stairs wearing the exact frock she'd criticized thirty minutes earlier. I was obviously not okay with her borrowing a dress I'd never worn before, and even less enthused when everyone started complimenting her on it.

"Thalia, that dress is amazing," said some girl with weird man shoulders.

"Thank you! Babe gave it to me. Chic, no?" She winked at me.

"Um, no, I definitely didn't, but it does look pretty great," I said sarcastically.

"Babe, yes you did. You were going to wear it but took it off because you thought it was unflattering, and then you told me I could have it."

"What are you talking about?"

"What are you talking about?"

"I didn't give you that dress."

"This is making everyone uncomfortable. If you want it back, just say so and I'll give it back to you later. Now, please, calm down."

"Why would I want it back if I never lent it to you in the first place?"

"Babe, you are acting crazy. Do you want some champagne?"

"Thalia . . . forget it. I'm going outside to get some fresh air."

I stepped out onto the balcony and lit a cigarette. I didn't get the dress thing at all. Was Thalia mental? Had she had a mini break from reality? I guess it wasn't that big of a deal. It was just some Helmut Lang dress. It's not like she'd claimed some hard-to-find vintage item of mine. Plus, she was letting me stay at her dad's place, so I decided to let the dress thing go and talk to her about it later.

I didn't say much over dinner. I mostly stuck to drinking glass after glass of champagne while playing footsie with Guillaume's dick. I guess I ended up getting pretty drunk, because I woke up on a sofa in the living room around 3 a.m. I stumbled upstairs to Thalia's room and opened the door to find her and Guillaume sleeping together in her bed.

"What the fuck are you guys doing?" I said loudly.

"Oh . . . hi, Babe," Thalia said casually. "We were just sleeping. If you need an Ambien, they're in the pillbox on my vanity."

"Can I talk to you for a sec?" I asked coldly.

She sighed and got out of bed. We walked into the hall.

"What are you doing? You knew I was into Guillaume, why would you sleep with him?"

"Babe, I would have never thought of touching him if I knew you were interested. I am so, so sorry."

"Obviously I was interested, are you blind?"

Had I been too drunk to realize that Guillaume was flirting with both of us? I mean, he was French . . .

"Babe, it is too late to be fighting. What can I say? I'm sorry. Do you want me to make Guillaume leave?"

"No, it's fine. Have fun. He smells like shit, P.S., but you know that." I stormed off.

It wasn't fine. I needed a safe space to cry, so I went to the closet and crumpled into a ball. What was I even doing in Europe, anyway? I missed LA, I missed the sun, I missed the smog, I missed my dad, and most of all I missed my Range Rover. I was so sick of being driven around everywhere by faceless drivers whose names I could never remember. The next morning I would tell Thalia that I needed to get the fuck away from that chalet. I grabbed the nearest long piece of fabric hanging next to me and wiped away my tears. I almost felt bad, because I got my mascara all over an almost-chic vintage Pucci dress. A Pucci dress that I'd seen before . . . Was it on eBay? No that wasn't it. Wait a second. Wait two seconds. I suddenly knew exactly where I'd seen that Pucci dress before. I didn't meet Thalia in Amsterdam. I met her at Gen and Roman's horrid party that they threw in my honor when I got back from rehab. She was the random girl in Pucci who wouldn't stop trying to calm me down! Thalia had looked familiar to me, but I'd assumed it was because she was so average looking. But no. I knew this bitch.

Why wouldn't she have said anything? Where did she come from? Oh my God. She was the stalker. She had to be. Had she coerced me here to Gstaad to kill me and make a skin suit out of my flesh? There was only one way to find out. I went into the bathroom and started rifling through her makeup bag and that's when I found exactly what I was looking for: black lipstick.

"What are you doing?"

I whipped around. Thalia was standing in the entrance to the bathroom with a weird look on her face.

"You're the one who's been after me this entire time."

"What are you talking about?"

"You've been following me for months!"

"Babe, no. I'm not. I swear it."

"Liar. What's this?" I held up the lipstick. "Where did this come from? No one's worn this shade since ever."

"It's yours! I was just borrowing it."

"Oh, you were borrowing it? Just like you borrowed my dress?"

"Babe, please let the dress go. I told you, you can have it back if you want."

"You are literally insane! I've never seen this lipstick in my life. Where's Guillaume? Is he dead? Did you stab him in the head with a Louboutin?"

"You seemed upset, so I made him leave."

"Why didn't you tell me we'd met in LA?"

"We met in LA?"

"Don't play dumb, Thalia."

"I am not playing dumb. I do so much coke in LA I never know who I'm meeting." She laughed to herself like the psycho she was. "I love that we have met before. It's like our souls are cosmically connected."

"Can you call the driver? I don't feel safe here anymore."

"The driver is taking Guillaume home and then going home himself. It's almost four a.m."

"Fine. Then I'll call a car for myself."

She smiled creepily. "With what phone?"

Fuck! I had no phone. I'd dropped all three of my phones off a chairlift the week before and was waiting for my new phone to arrive in the mail. Thalia was a criminal mastermind. She'd planned this all out. Every detail. My heart was racing. I had no choice but to fight for my life. I pushed past Thalia and ran down the stairs toward the study, locking the door behind me and grabbing a fire poker to use as a weapon if need be. I couldn't call the police, because I didn't think 911 would work in Switzerland, so I called the only person on the planet who could get me out of this mess.

"Dad, it's me. I'm going to say this really fast because this is an emergency. Someone named Thalia Alexandrov is trying to kill me. She's the one who's been leaving the notes, she's stalked me all the way from LA, and now I'm trapped in her house in Gstaad, her huge dog is going to eat my face off, and I have no phone and no way out. Send the police. Send help!"

Thalia was banging on the door of the study.

"Babe, let me in! Let's just talk. I don't want to hurt you. You're my best friend!" she yelled. Magnus was barking like a wild animal. It was the most terrifying moment of my entire life.

"What in the bloody hell is going on?!" my dad yelled on the other end of the phone. I was so shaken up that I thought I'd been leaving a message. I guess not.

"DAD! I'm going to die if you don't get me out of here. I'm serious!" I cried.

"Where are you?"

"In Switzerland!"

"Jesus, alright. Hang tight, my darling. Send me an address and help will be on the way."

Instead of saying bye to him, I simply screamed as loud as I could into the receiver to ensure that my dad understood how dire the situation was. I rifled through the room, throwing anything into my bag that I thought I could use as a weapon. Thalia's fists still slamming on the locked door, Magnus's booming barks sending shivers throughout my body. Finally, I heard the sounds of a helicopter approaching the chalet. It got louder and louder until it was basically right on top of us. Then a voice with a heavy Swiss accent shouted over a loud-speaker.

"BABE WALKER. WE ARE HERE FOR BABE WALKER."

This was my emergency escape moment. I used the fire poker to smash through a massive stained-glass window and leaped out into the snowy night. I fell one story into a snowbank, but my adrenaline was pumping too quickly for me to feel any phys-ical pain. I ran into the trees behind Thalia's house, staying low to the ground, and zigzagging left and right, lest Thalia try to shoot me with the crossbow I'd seen hanging in the mudroom. It was beyond freezing. My limbs were practically numb, but I was powered by the animalistic need to live long enough to wear

Alexander Wang's first collection at Balenciaga. I would not die like this. Not in Gstaad, of all places.

There was nowhere for the helicopter to land, so they'd thrown down a ladder for me to grab on to while they pulled me on board. It was exhilarating. So nineties, so *True Lies*. Like, it would have been the most amazing photo op if I'd been wearing that fucking Helmut Lang dress, but whatever, Thalia.

I hoisted myself up into the helicopter and the crew rushed to wrap me in one of those emergency foil blankets. One of the chopper guys was hot. We flew straight to the closest airport, where I was instructed to wait for my dad (who was already en route from LA). Sitting in that little airport, I meticulously recounted every single word that had come out of Thalia's deceitful mouth. She'd obviously held a grudge against me for being rude to her at Gen's welcome-home party and stalked me all over LA and most of Europe because of it. I vowed to have Thalia arrested for bitchery, thievery, and stalkery. Some girls are such fucking psychos.

When my dad's plane arrived, we hugged for five minutes straight and immediately boarded another plane to London.

"Get me the fuck out of here," I said quietly to myself once we were wheels up.

I was finally safe.

thirteen

IT'S FINE, DAD.

"Welcome home, guys! You're just in time for warm roasted chestnuts!" shouted Lizbeth (my dad's girlfriend) as we walked through the door of my late grandmother's Chelsea duplex with all of my luggage. It was really nice to be in a familiar place after nearly being murdered. I feature a long, drawn-out, life-threatening travel moment, followed by a triumphant return to the familiar.

This was one of my favorite places to be, and other than our house in Bel Air, it was the place I'd spent the most time growing up. The home belonged to my father's mother, Rose. I'd always called her Tai Tai because she thought the word *grandmother* was an ageist slur, which I completely respected. Her Chelsea duplex sat on the top two floors of a beautiful, terraced pre-war. The view of the river from the top terrace has always been one of my favorites in the whole city. It was on this terrace that I had my first kiss (age eleven), had my first glass of champagne (age six), read my first *Paris Vogue* (age four), had my first period (age sixteen), and my first experience smoking dust (age seventeen, with Elizabeth Taylor).

As I walked through the entryway, an overwhelming sense of relief washed over me. I had been the victim of a deranged stalker for months. But now I was safe, or at least I felt safe. I could only hope that Thalia would give up on her obsession with me after seeing what lengths my father will go to in order to save my life. The Walkers are not to be fucked with.

Tai Tai's taste in interior design was the perfect blend of modern decor, mixed with a nod to old world chicness. Think antiques, Paul Smith rugs, mod furniture, Hermès china, and tons of taxidermy. It was weird to be back, considering the last time I'd been here was the last time I'd seen Tai Tai alive. After finding out she had rare bone cancer, she'd decided to take her future into her own hands and wore a zebra coat on safari in Africa. She was mauled and killed by a lion. It was dark. But ultimately light, because her lessons, such as "Never trust a man with a ponytail," will stay with me forever.

"Hello, love," my father said as he kissed Lizbeth's forehead.

"Hey, Liz. How are you? Merry Christmas?" I offered.

"Babe, I'm so happy you're okay," Lizbeth practically shouted, hugging me tightly. "I had a stalker in high school and then another one in college and then another one in grad school, so I know how you're feeling. That being said, for someone who's just been to hell and back, you look gorge. What supplements are you taking? You're glowing."

"Thanks. You look nice too," I replied on autopilot, checking out my hair in the hallway mirror.

Normally I loathe the women my dad sees, but I've come to be very conflicted over Lizbeth. The thing about her is that she's an overwhelmingly positive person, which makes her hard to hate. I know I'm supposed to be vehemently opposed to her perma-sunny disposition and everything it represents, but deep down I kind of respect her. Also, she would never blow smoke up anyone's ass, so I knew I must have actually looked good.

"Can I get either of you anything to eat or drink? I just went to the store and got some yummy stuff."

"Scotch neat, love," said my dad.

"Coming right up. Babe? Anything for you?"

"Nap time."

When I got to my room, I dropped my bag on the floor and collapsed on the bed. All I wanted was three days of solid, Valium-induced sleep, followed by a four-hour mani/pedi/massage, followed by a five-hour cleansing facial situation. But it just wasn't in the cards for me. After just three short hours my dad interrupted my restorative slumber and told me that I was needed in the kitchen and that he had great news. Rude.

I slowly got up, threw away all of the clothes I was wearing because they smelled like helicopter, showered, blow-dried my hair, put some makeup on, and walked out into the living room. The smell of roast chicken and potatoes was coming from the kitchen. My dad wasn't much of a cook—actually he never cooked, except for one dish: roast chicken, with whole-grain-mustard fingerling potatoes. He used to make it for Tai Tai and me. Of course, we only ever ate five ounces of breast, no skin, no potatoes, but it's always been one of those comfort foods that makes me feel at peace.

My dad popped his head out of the kitchen.

"Babe, darling. You're up. Come join. Can I fix you a drink? I think you'll be delighted to see who's stopped by to say hello," my father said.

Oh, great. What now? I took a quick self-survey: How was my skin? Fine. How was my hair? Seven out of ten. Was I wearing a bra? No.

The surprise guests were George and Maggie Dean, my dad's childhood bff and his wife. They still lived in London, but I hadn't seen them in years. They were also the parents of Charlie Dean, the first boy I'd ever kissed. The very same Charlie who'd turned up in my dad's kitchen in LA, looking incredibly handsome, the morning after I got home from rehab. George and Maggie were very nice, if a bit boring and pompous, but they certainly weren't the kind of snoozefests who'd make me want to leave my own home. I was safe. Or so I thought.

"Barbara, such a pleasure to see you, dear," said Maggie.

"I think she goes by Babe now," George chimed in.

"It's whatever. Hi, Deans. How are you both? It really has been forever."

"We're pretty much the same, love. Although George is retired, so we've been traveling quite a bit."

"Love that. I've been traveling myself, actually. I randomly hung out with my absentee lesbian mom in Paris before hooking up with this super sexy, albeit dishonest, Greek man who took me to Mykonos and stole all of my earthly possessions. Then I wandered around Amsterdam for a minute getting high and talking to prostitutes. It was really great for my soul, you know? Then I ran into this psycho at my hotel who basically forced me to go to Gstaad and then tricked me into being her slave, for like, months. Dad had to send Trump's helicopter to rescue me. And now I'm here!" I smiled.

"Well, doesn't that sound like fun!" exclaimed Maggie. "Regardless, you're even more beautiful than Charlie said you'd be."

"Charlie said I was beautiful?"

"Well, of course he did, Babe. He's always held a bit of a candle for you."

"That's so sweet of him. Please give him my best when you see him next."

"Well, you can tell him yourself, he's just in the loo, darling," said my father.

"Oh God. Please no," I whispered to myself.

"Babe?" I heard a voice say from behind me.

As I turned toward the voice, this thought raced through my head: *I look awful, I feel exhausted, and I can't compete with your "actress" girlfriend or whatever she is at this particular juncture.*

I turned around to find a tall-ish, handsome Charlie, looking better than ever. He was wearing a Barbour jacket over what looked like a navy Loro Piana cashmere sweater, khakis, and all-black Stan Smith Adidas.

"Hello," I replied awkwardly.

Charlie smiled. I froze.

I obviously wasn't thrilled with my father for not notifying me that this would be happening, but I decided to go with the flow, being that my dad had just rescued me from a hostage situation. Also, it was almost Christmas and I didn't want to come across like a totally ungrateful bitch.

"You look fantastic, Babe. What a special treat to see you again," Charlie said, kissing me lightly on the cheek.

"I didn't know that anyone was visiting today, but it's nice to see you all too."

"I invited them to stay for dinner!" Lizbeth said excitedly.

"How nice of you to have invited our longtime friends over to our house, Lizbeth," I said, slightly too rudely. I honestly don't know how to act around her.

"Barbara, congratulations on the publication of your first book! How wonderful," George interjected, clearly trying to change the direction of the conversation.

"Thanks, George. Not sure how much me being published says about the literary world as a whole, but I accept your affirmative positivity."

"I for one think the book is fabulous," my father added.

"You're my dad. You have to say that."

"Well, I'm not your dad," said Charlie, "and I thought it was really quite fantastic, Babe."

"That's really nice of you, but please don't feel the need to compliment my writing just because you're a guest in my home."

"I would never dream of it. I told you in LA, I read the whole thing in one sitting."

"By the way, how is your actress girlfriend doing? Did she like my book too?"

"Actually, my now ex-girlfriend did read it. She slept with David Duchovny on set. True colors, I guess. Don't worry about me, though; I'm fine."

"Her loss," I offered.

He continued. "And yes, she also loved your book. I think she even called it 'a brave exploration of the modern woman's psyche.'"

"She said that? You're kidding."

"Yes. I am," he said, grinning.

I love it when guys lie to me about their ex-girlfriends.

"Excuse me, Lizbeth," Charlie continued, "can I help you set the table?"

"How sweet of you to offer, but it's already been taken care of. Why don't you and Babe go into the living room to have a chat and relax. I'll let you know when everything's ready."

"Have a chat?" I asked sarcastically.

"Babe . . ." My dad sighed.

"What? She isn't British! Okay, okay. Give me a minute."

After a quick wardrobe change, a new hair choice, and a glass of champagne, Charlie and I were seated next to each other, catching up on the past fifteen years. Charlie (via his parents?) seemed like he had a pretty good handle on what I'd been doing with my life. It was sweet that, after all this time, he was still keeping tabs on me. I asked him what he'd been up to.

"Well, I went to the London School of Economics and hated it. Then I worked at Barclays as an executive for a few years. Hated that as well. But I just moved to New York City about eighteen months ago to run a hedge fund an old friend of mine started. To tell you the truth, I'm loving New York and I'm really enjoying my job, which is a nice change of pace for me."

"That all sounds amazing. I'm not used to being around people who are happy, or stable, or normal."

"Well, you seem like you're doing quite well for yourself. Writing books, traveling the world. Sounds exciting."

"It's definitely exciting, but not always in the ways you'd think."

Lizbeth came to tell us that dinner was ready, so we all piled into the dining room just off of the kitchen. My dad had really outdone himself. Two chickens, a mountain of mustard potatoes, and enough steamed spinach to feed the Paltrow-Martins for a week. I generally hate the holidays, as they involve being around an excess of food, but after my chaotic European travels it was nice to be with my family again. I'd missed seeing my dad and I think I'd even missed Lizbeth a little bit too.

"I hope everyone's enjoying the roast birds," my dad proclaimed. "I haven't made this in years."

"You haven't made anything in years!" Lizbeth shouted. She was always shouting.

Everyone laughed, including me, which was a first.

My dad stood, putting one hand on Lizbeth's shoulder and raising his wineglass with the other.

"I hope you'll all be available to join us in Los Angeles this June."

"Dad, I told you: no more birthday parties. I don't even care that I'm turning twenty-six."

"No, Babe, this is something else. Lizbeth has foolishly agreed to make me the happiest man in the world by being my wife."

Everyone at the table erupted with excitement and joy about this news. Conversely, I felt like I'd been hit by a bolt of lightning. My legs felt like they were melting, my head was spinning, and I could have easily thrown up. A wedding? A fucking WED-

DING? I'd accepted the fact that Lizbeth was going to be in our lives for a long time, but I never in a million years thought that she and my dad would get married. How could he not have asked me for permission first? I'm not sure if I was actually screaming, but I definitely heard the sound of my voice screaming, at least in my head. It was almost an out-of-body experience.

As I scanned the table, I noticed that the only other person who wasn't smiling ear to ear and staring at my dad and Lizbeth was Charlie. His eyes were on me. Maybe he had some preternatural sense that this news shook me to the core, but he gave me a look that let me know he was on my team. His eyes were blue. Very blue.

He stood up from the table.

"Lizbeth, Mr. Walker. My congratulations to you both. This is truly wonderful news and I look forward to June, but I've just looked at the time and unfortunately I'm running late for a work function that I must attend. It completely slipped my mind. A sincere apology to you all for jetting so abruptly. I must've lost track of the time." With that Charlie looked at me and raised an eyebrow. Then he continued. "Also, another apology for stealing Babe away from this celebratory occasion, but she's already agreed to accompany me this evening. I can't bear the thought of having to go to this dreadful event alone. We will make it up to you both. Right, Babe?"

"Yes. Soooo sorry to run out. Congrats, guys. Sooooo happy for you. Let's celebrate more tomorrow?"

With that, I reluctantly kissed my dad on the cheek, gave Lizbeth a hug that was more of a limp offering of my torso in her general direction, grabbed my coat . . . and was out the door with Charlie. We walked around the corner to a cute little pub that I'd passed by a million times but had never been in.

"I really can't thank you enough for rescuing me. How did you know?" I said to Charlie as we nestled into a booth in the back of the empty bar.

"You looked helpless."

"Was it that obvious?" I asked as we sat in a booth, sipping our respective G&Ts.

"I don't think anyone else in the room had a clue, but I knew I had to get you out of there before you exploded. I remembered how you can get."

"What do you mean?"

"You don't remember? When we were young—your dad and that woman Natalia?"

Hearing that name opened the floodgates. Natalia. The summer I turned twelve, my dad and I spent it here in London. Charlie had been around. My dad was dating this model named Natalia, who was a total bitch. She was a complete psycho when he wasn't there, but when he got home from work, she would turn on the charm. Toward the end of the summer my dad asked me how I'd feel about Natalia being my "mummy." I raged out, screamed at him, and told Tai Tai that if he married Natalia, I'd divorce him, emancipate myself, and become a gypsy.

"I forgot you were there that day."

"I know that we're all adults now and you don't need someone speaking for you, but I didn't want to see you go through all that again."

"Thanks. You were really helpful back then too."

"I'm not sure how helpful I could've been when I was thirteen," he laughed.

"No. You were. You totally calmed me down. You watched ten episodes of *Frasier* with me because you knew I loved that show. I think that was the day you kissed me."

"It was. I can't believe you remember that. It was my first kiss, if you can believe it."

"I can, because it was mine too."

Then Charlie put his arm around my shoulders for a few seconds. It wasn't awkward. It was just nice. We spent the rest of the night exchanging war stories about our failures at love. Charlie confided in me that all of his friends were either married or engaged and that he hated all of their wives and fiancées. I told him about Robert, and Cal, and Paul, and Thalia. I was even able to laugh about the entire Babette drama. Charlie didn't judge me for any of it.

It was weird, because I'd felt an instant connection with Charlie when I saw him in our kitchen back in LA all those months ago, but as soon as I learned he had a girlfriend I'd completely blocked him out of my mind. But now that we were here together, it felt like I was supposed to be in this pub with him. I'm normally so different when I'm around a guy, but with Charlie, I felt like myself. We had this incredible history and a similar upbringing and he just got who I was. Charlie was like a mood stabilizer. I didn't think about my dad and Lizbeth once after we'd left the dinner table.

Charlie walked me back home. I kissed him on the cheek, thanked him for everything, and told him I'd call him the next day. When I got into the apartment my dad was sitting alone in Tai Tai's favorite chair, looking out the window with a glass of single malt in his hand.

"I'm sorry, darling," he said quietly.

"It's fine, Dad."

I walked over and sat at his side. "I just wish that you could have filled me in about your decision to get married before you announced it to everyone at the table. I felt like an idiot."

"I'd planned on telling you about this when I first saw you in Switzerland, but you seemed so frazzled. Understandably, of course. I'd just had you rescued by the Swiss Secret Service in a helicopter owned by Donald Trump's son, Donald Trump. I didn't want to add any further stress to your life. I thought I would wait until we had a private moment to discuss."

"I just need time to process."

"I'm the same way. I hate being blindsided. I feel like a right twat for putting you in this situation."

"When did you propose?"

"Yesterday."

"Wait . . . why isn't she wearing a ring?"

"She didn't want one, can you believe it?"

"What?"

"She's an Ivory Coast activist—blood diamonds, you know the drill."

Maybe it was all the therapy that I'd been through in rehab, or maybe I finally understood what love was, or maybe it was that Charlie had calmed me down by being so cool and understanding, but I wasn't really mad at my dad. This engagement was inevitable. Lizbeth made my dad super happy, she obviously wasn't a gold digger, and her hair always looked stunning, even after the gym. It could have been a lot worse. My dad could have married Courtney Stodden.

"I'm really happy for you both, Dad. I know you guys really love each other and I'm glad you finally found your person."

"Babe, you don't know how wonderful it is to have your blessing. I do love Lizbeth, but I will never love anyone as much as I love you. You're my daughter, and nothing will ever change that."

"Unless I transition. Then I'd be your son."

We both laughed. My eyes started to well up with tears.

"Are those happy tears or sad ones?"

"Maybe a bit of both? I just want to be able to find my person."

"Babe, give yourself a fucking break. It took me years to find someone to love, who would love me in return. I thought that I was set when I met your mother. I was convinced that we would spend the rest of our lives together, but look how that turned out. Donna was a nightmare. She could've never been a wife, let alone a mother. She was batshit, dear. Crazy, jealous, out of control, and vindictive, and I fucking loved it. Nothing hotter than a gorgeous psycho-bitch model with a coke problem. But we both had a lot of growing up to bloody do. In order for two people to truly fall in love, they both need to love themselves first. It's taken me thirty-one years to figure that out."

"Please arrange for my assassination if I haven't found someone to marry in the next thirty-one years."

"It won't take that long, my dear. You're too special. But you need to be patient. I assume things didn't work out with that Robert fellow the way you'd planned?"

"Honestly, Dad, it's so complicated that I can't even get into it. I'm pretty sure we're never going to happen."

"That's too bad."

"Yes, it is."

"But there will be others, and probably better ones."

"You're probably wrong, but thanks."

"You need to be happy as you. Then you can be happy with someone else."

This was the most I'd spoken to my dad in months. I'd forgotten how nice it was. As we sat there in silence, I finally decided to give up on Robert once and for all. It wasn't in the cards for us, and I couldn't waste another minute trying to put those pieces back together. I needed to move on now or risk being stuck on him forever.

Charlie and I spent a lot of time together over the next couple of days. We saw a movie, had dinner, and then went Christmas shopping at Harvey Nichols. Maybe I'm a total slut, but this was the first time in a while that I'd really been into someone without having slept with him immediately. As the week went on I started developing feelings for Charlie. Not, like, head-over-heels/I-feel-like-I'm-on-heroin-whenever-I'm-around-you feelings, but definitely little cocaine-y heart palpitations here and there.

Christmas was uneventful. My dad got me a new Birkin to replace a stolen Birkin, Lizbeth bought me a new cold juice press, and I got them each a JAMBOX and a snowboard. Neither of them are snowboarders, so I thought it would be rude and funny. After everyone had opened their presents, Charlie and I went for a walk in Regent's Park. It was fucking freezing, and when Charlie rubbed my shoulders to warm me up, I got goose bumps. This was what I wanted to feel. Without hesitation I stopped walking, turned to him, and pulled his face toward mine.

When my lips touched his, there were way more sparks than I'd expected. His lips felt soft and full. Charlie didn't hold back at all. We finished the kiss, and he looked deep into my eyes.

"Wow. I don't think I want to wait another fifteen years before I can do that again," Charlie whispered.

"You don't have to," I said. "I could go back to New York with you."

"What do you mean, 'go back to New York' with me?" he asked, brushing a snowflake off my nose.

"Like, maybe we could be together in New York and be happy?"

"I love the sound of that."

Almost on cue, the sky started to dump snow on Charlie and me as we kissed again. It was like one of those bad Kate Hudson movies that make you think you actually like her and Matthew McConaughey together. But this was real life, and Charlie and I aren't annoying slores.

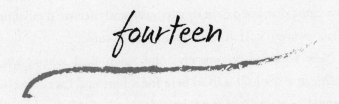

fourteen

HE SPOONED THE FUCK OUT OF ME.

I'd been in New York City for about four weeks when a truly bizarre and surprising thought popped into my head: *I think I'm happy.* I was lying in bed, staring out of Charlie's West Village bedroom window at the cobblestones on Jane Street, and it occurred to me that I had actually settled into a normal life for maybe the first time since rehab.

Charlie Dean had turned out to be so much more than I'd expected him to be. Never had a guy let me be myself so fully. I mean, I get it. I can be a lot to handle on occasion, but from Charlie's reactions to me, you'd never know it. He was actually a mega-workaholic, but I was fine with that. Most finance guys are. I really feature a boyfriend who is completely amazing, but only around in small increments. I've done the actor/DJ/artist thing and it gets old fast. Why the fuck would I want to be with any one person all day long? That sounds terrible. Charlie's busy work schedule allowed for me to be with me all day long, and then, if he wasn't out of town for a business trip, he'd come home at night for dinner. He would eat, we would laugh, I'd tell him about my day, and he'd tell me about hedge fund stuff and leveraging distressed debt or whatever, and then we'd talk about when we were kids. It was literally super cute.

New York had become my home again. Back when I was in college at Parsons, I'd lived here for a year and I was obsessed. I would've stayed had it not been for my horrible breakup with Robert. Regardless of how much I adore LA, there's something about the way Manhattan makes me feel that can't be replicated in California. Maybe I was finally ready to live here for good, or maybe it was that Charlie's apartment was so incredibly cozy that it made NYC feel like a safe place for me again.

It was classic West Village: sensible and vintage-y, all the while maintaining a good sense of humor. I'm talking high ceilings, original moldings, classic New York charm, chic. The whole apartment (including the bedroom) had original wide-planked wood floors, and huge windows that peered out onto the street just above the tree line. In addition to being an ode to antique tile, the master bathroom was also massive—two sinks, and a separate room for the toilet, thank God. The walk-in closet scenario in the master bedroom was equally as impressive, and the kitchen was light-filled and completely open. The living room, which overlooked the Hudson, was cool with dashes of warmth. A neutral color story that accented Charlie's great art collection, with some huge potted majesty palms hanging out in the corners. Charlie (or maybe his interior designer?) seemed to favor emerging New York artists' work (huge prints/bright colors) and really expensive cashmere throws. There was also a heated balcony off the living room that was perfect for smoking my biweekly Marlboro Light. His apartment was so comfortable that I felt like I was actually at home, even though I totally wasn't. It was almost like I wanted his apartment to adopt me.

Of course I'd purchased a few things to make "his" place more of "our" place. The usual suspects: a free-radical-neutralizing filtration system for the faucet, a proper spinach rinser, and all new silverware, dishes, pots, pans, etc. (for decoration only, of course). I was learning to accept that New York Babe was a little bit more "eclectic" than LA Babe. Upon first glance, I'd thought that Charlie's brownstone-lined street was going to be a little too Carrie Bradshaw for my tastes, but I was actually loving it.

On a chilly Monday morning, I woke up after Charlie left for work and made myself a cup of tea, spiked it with a touch of scotch, wrapped myself in a few throws, and sat on the windowsill and wrote for about an hour. I'd started a blog that I posted on a couple times a week in order to share my thoughts, feelings, and emotions with the world. I finished an article about how hair color directly correlates to confidence level and sent some very productive emails. Then I went back to sleep for about an hour, got up again, took a taxi to Aqua on Franklin in TriBeCa (underwater spin class . . . life-changing), grabbed a delicious turmeric juice and dandelion kale salad from Organic Avenue on Hudson, and then returned to Charlie's place on Jane, where I showered, stretched, moisturized, and meditated.

By 3:30 I was ready to shop. Shopping in LA is easy, but the shopping scenario in NYC is truly tough to beat. I think the city planned it that way to make up for the horrible fucking winters, which are not cute. I dropped in at Jeffrey, McQueen, Marni, Moschino, Theyskens' Theory, A.P.C., Margiela, and Helmut Lang. I'd been shopping regularly, but on this particular day I went a little overboard. Five pairs of Margiela sneakers (all for Charlie), ten gray Helmut Lang sweaters, an insane suede shearling Marni coat, and a Moschino blazer that reinvigorated my love for blazers, which is saying a lot. The fact that I was buying so much for the cold weather made me realize just how comfortable I was feeling. I was actually starting to picture myself having a life with Charlie here in New York.

I stopped to rest my tired legs and drink an americano at Soho House, where I sat in an obscenely huge leather chair and thought about my old friend, the universe. I wondered if someone (or something) up there knew all along that I was destined to end up with the same boy with whom I shared my first kiss. Then I noticed my waiter looked kind of like Robert, and I kindly asked him to stay away from me. I wondered what Robert was doing for about two seconds before re-exiling him from my thoughts. I was happy with Charlie and I was determined to keep it that way. He wasn't a fantasy lover like Robert. Yet.

We actually hadn't had a chance to do more than cuddle and make out, thanks to Charlie's hectic work schedule. In fact, he'd been going back to work for a few hours after dinner or out of town on business almost every night since we'd gotten to New York. But I was sure we'd get physical eventually and that it would be great. Charlie treated me well. He respected me, he thought I was funny, and he wore a lot of Paul Smith and owned more Moncler down jackets than anyone I'd ever met.

On the way home I stopped to pick up some pasta at Barbuto so that Charlie would have something to eat for dinner. He put in such crazy hours at the office, and my schedule was so loose, that I liked to have some food ready for him when he got home. I mean, there was no way in hell I was going to cook, because that would be a disaster, but he deserved to have a nice meal at the end of the day.

When Charlie walked in the door later that evening, there was an unusual fire behind his eyes. They were bluer than normal. He dropped his Valextra briefcase to the floor, took off his jacket, and began unbuttoning his shirt while staring right into my eyes.

"You look beautiful," Charlie said softly from across the room.

His chest was so smooth, his face was ruddy from the cold, and his hair was ruffled and windblown. It was hard to resist him. He closed the distance between us and kissed me so passionately and so fully that I melted inside. Then he picked me up like I was a fucking feather and carried me into the bedroom. I knew what this was. We were finally about to fuck, and I couldn't have been more excited.

Charlie threw me onto the bed and curled up alongside my body, spooning me. Actually, he spooned the fuck out of me. I wasn't exactly clear on his plan. Did he want me from behind? Were we just going to spoon really, really passionately for a few hours? Whatever, it felt good. He pushed my hair away and kissed the back of my neck. Then he took my sweater off and pressed up against me, cupping my breasts and kissing my earlobe. His skin felt cold against the warmth of my naked back. I wanted him inside of me. I arched my back, pressing my ass into his crotch. I turned around to face him. As we were making out, he slipped my underwear off in one slow motion.

"I want you so bad, Charlie."

And with that he began kissing my chest and stomach as he descended to my lady parts and began performing magical, ecstasy-inducing oral sex. Charlie knew what he was doing in the oral department. I've been with guys whom I'd consider gifted, but this was on a whole different level. I'm talking about multiple orgasms. Writhing, screaming, begging for mercy, and physical joy to the point of literal confusion.

My body was doing things that it had never done before. I undulated on the bed as his tongue took me to places unknown and unimagined. When it was finally over, I was exhausted.

"Charlie. You are so good at that it's disgusting."

"I love to do it, darling. You seem to be having fun."

"Oh, I am. But what about you?"

"What about me?"

Weird response, I thought.

"Charlie, it's not fair for me to have all the fun."

Charlie looked at me and smiled so sweetly.

"Babe, I appreciate your concern for me, but I'm fine. I love making you feel great."

This was very nice, but I needed to give Charlie the same amount of pleasure he'd given me. So I decided to take charge of the situation. I straddled him and started kissing down his neck and chest, prepping him for the blow job of a lifetime. Not to sound like a whore or anything, but I give amazing head. *We're going to fuck like the world is ending and probably fall in love and get married and have two children via surrogate and adopt a third one from Africa,* I thought as I kissed and licked my way down his chest and abs. Then I pulled down his briefs, revealing a two-inch, uncircumcised, erect midget penis surrounded by a mass of reddish-brown pubic hair. It had the width of a normal dick but was missing about six inches of length.

A shudder racked my entire body. *Abort! Abort!* my brain screamed.

"Oh . . . wow," I said, in an utter state of shock.

"I know. I'm so hard," Charlie moaned.

"Let's just make love!" I said a little too loudly, kissing my way back up Charlie's chest and lying next to him.

"Mmm. Okay," Charlie whispered huskily.

Before I knew it, he was on top of me, looking into my eyes and positioning his pelvis. He thrusted his hips forward and started moving them around rhythmically. It was weird, because he was acting like we were boning, but I felt nothing. Some humping was happening, some groaning was also happening, but I couldn't tell if his dick was inside of me or not. I didn't know what to do, so I tried to play along, thinking that with the right encouragement his dick could be a grower.

"Oh, Charlie. Yes, yes. Fuck me hard, Charlie," I cried out, silently begging God to let Charlie's dick be the Chia Pet of dicks.

"Yes, Babe. Yes! God, you're so sexy," Charlie carried on, his face buried in my hair, moaning in ecstasy as if all was right with the world. But nothing was right. After forty-five minutes of trying every position possible, mixed with a certain type of Kegel clenching to make my vagina more shallow, I still had yet to feel Charlie's dick inside of me. Finally, I gave him permission to come, which he did, screaming my name and collapsing next to me, kissing my shoulder.

"You, Babe Walker, are sex personified," he whispered. "Keep doing that to me and I'll have no choice but to fall in love with you."

Babe Walker on Male Anatomy
(with commentary)

I feel like it's important to note the types of penises I'm okay with and those on which I'm unclear:

Monster

Everyone loves a big dick, but a monster cock (over 10 inches) is terrifying in more ways than one. For example, The Greek. The fact that Cal and I only fucked once ended up being a blessing in disguise. Firstly, there's the issue of how a penis of that magnitude is even going to fit in a vagina/butt. Secondly, if said Monster does manage to get all the way in, there's the issue of stretching, and I'm not trying to have my lady parts look like I just birthed an eleven-pound baby after two years of fucking the same person. Unless you're content with doing at least 1,000 Kegels a day, the Godzilla penis is best suited for voyeuristic purposes, as opposed to regular sexual practices.

Husband Material

I consider dicks in the 7.5- to 10-inch range to be the kind of dicks you marry, have three kids with, grow to hate, divorce, and then become great friends with once the alimony's been paid and you're both a little older and wiser. Robert's was 8 inches. Obviously.

Boyfriend Dicks

Dicks 5 to 7 inches leave no lasting impression on me whatsoever, but can be great for a casual dating scenario. Packing a regular-size penis is fine, but I will probably cheat on a 5-incher within six months, and a 7-incher within two years. Sue me.

Makeout Dicks

Anything below 5 inches is what I like to call a "Makeout Dick," which means you go on a date with a guy, kiss at the end, feel his boner, gauge that it's not really your style, and never talk to him again. You can date a makeout dick for a few weeks, but it's best not to get up close and personal with the package, lest you come face-to-face with the unsavory realization that his wiener will never satisfy your needs.

Non-Dicks

This makes me sad, but there are some guys out there sporting 1 to 2 inches, or what I will now be referring to as a "Deen" (Dean + peen). The signs are there from the start, but you will want to ignore them because it's just too crazy to imagine that God would curse a grown man with a baby's penis. But it's real and it happens. Case in point: Monsieur Charlie.

The whole situation was torturous. Charlie was perfect in every way except for his lack of dick. I was so traumatized by the thought of facing his Deen again that I avoided having sex with him for a whole month. One week I said my vagina was sore from spin class. The next week I told him that my new spiritual guide, Courtney Love, told me not to have sex for fourteen days because resisting sexual urges gives you "a natural high." This was obviously a lie. The week after that, I had my period. Another lie. I haven't had my period since I was twenty-two.

To make matters worse, Charlie didn't seem to care that we weren't boning. He was happy as a clam. He was in and out of town due to work, and when he was home he was totally content to go down on me for hours and expect nothing in return. But I felt so bad about the state of his private parts that I eventually opted to fuck him. Once a week. With no blow jobs or hand jobs, because I couldn't bear the thought of touching the Deen with anything other than my vag.

As bleak as the whole "Charlie's penis" situation was, there was no getting around the fact he was actually an amazing lesbian/boyfriend. All the little things he did for me were adding up and making me realize how much he truly cared. One night I had a horrible nightmare that I was a piece of arugula and Thalia was trying to eat me with a giant fork. I woke up screaming her name. Charlie obviously knew about the Thalia situation and stayed up all night with me, rubbing my back and letting me cry it out. He told me that the stuff with my stalker had brought us together, in a way. He had a calming energy about him. I couldn't give that up at this point, no matter how tiny he was.

Another night, after being gone for a week on a business trip, Charlie presented me with four different Cartier Love bracelets so I could choose which one I liked best, and didn't even bat a lash when I decided to keep them all. He also didn't enable me to be the kind of Babe who was unmotivated and drank smoothies all day. Far from it. I admired how passionate Charlie was about his work, and it gave me drive to seek out the same kind of fulfillment. I started to realize that I kind of wanted a job.

On the other hand, I found myself reveling in the safety of domesticity. I even began cooking a few times a week. We had his parents over for dinner when they were in town. We'd stay in and watch movies. He loved to watch *Real Housewives* with me, calling them "crazy, inspiring bitches." So basically Charlie just got me. And I got him. I wanted to do nice things for him, like make him dinner sometimes, and go out to eat at non-sushi restaurants, and watch the boring History Channel shows that he was obsessed with.

My feelings for Charlie became clear to me during a conversation I had while on a shopping spree at Babeland, a serendipitously named sex shop on the Lower East Side.

"Can I live the rest of my life with someone who can't actually penetrate me?" I asked the salesgirl (who looked like Jennifer Aniston if Jennifer Aniston had a ton of facial piercings, jet-black hair, and had never gotten a nose job) as she rang up the price on several vibrators and a strap-on that I'd decided to purchase.

"Lots of ladies give up penetration for someone they love," she said nonchalantly.

"Is it love, though?" I asked, inspecting a massive black dildo. "I mean, I care deeply for Charlie, and I know Charlie's head over heels for me, but I don't know if I'm the kind of girl who can be in love with someone who can't really give it to me hard."

"I hear that. See this suction cup?" She pointed to the bottom of the dildo in my hands. "You can stick that thing anywhere with a smooth surface, like the wall in your shower or your coffee table, and just go to town."

"Really?"

"Yeah, dude. It's the best. My girlfriend and I use it all the time and we love it. Totally solves the whole penetration problem."

"You know what? Ring it up." I tossed the dildo over to her. "Charlie's the one for me. The Ellen to my Portia. We talk about our feelings all the time, and there's a lot of chic menswear involved. I can deal with never getting fucked by a real dick again." I slid my Amex across the counter.

"Charlie sounds pretty rad," she said, running my card and giving me the receipt to sign.

"Charlie is the best. I don't even know why I'm questioning this relationship anymore. Who needs dicks anyway? Blow jobs and hand jobs are so overrated."

"Exactly," she agreed, handing me my shopping bag full of goodies.

"Thank you for being my sex shaman."

"No problem. Good luck with your girl."

"My girl?"

"Charlie . . . ?"

"Oh. No, Charlie's my boyfriend. But I love him, and I respect his lifelong struggle of having a micro penis. God, this is great. I'm in love again!" And with that, I promptly returned to Charlie's apartment and fucked the shit out of myself with the dildo I'd just bought.

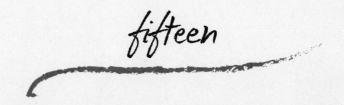

fifteen

SO . . . BABE IS YOUR ACTUAL NAME?

It was 6:30 a.m. and I was propped up in bed watching Charlie pack for a three-week business trip to China.

"Are you sure you don't want to meet me in Beijing? We can still get you a first-class ticket . . ." Charlie asked, folding a suit into his luggage.

"As much as I want to know what China smells like, the smog doesn't sound very pore-conscious."

I coughed to drive my point home.

"Plus, I have my second interview at *Vogue* tomorrow."

Charlie zipped up his suitcase and came to sit on the edge of the bed next to me.

"It's going to be very lonely at the Four Seasons without you," he said huskily, kissing my collarbone and up my neck.

"I know," I whispered, brushing back his hair. He kissed me on the lips.

"I have a surprise for you when I get back."

"What is it?" Somewhere in the back of my mind, I prayed that it would be state-of-the-art penis enlargement surgery, then felt horribly guilty, and then felt kind of turned on, then reminded myself to google penis enlargement surgeons.

"If I told you, it wouldn't be a surprise." He tugged the bedsheet down, exposing my breasts. A boyish smile spread across his face.

Suddenly his cell phone rang, interrupting our almost-sex moment.

"Damn. That must be the car service." He answered the phone. "Hello? Yep, will do. Be down in two shakes." He turned back to me. "Unfortunately, we're going to have to table this discussion until I return."

"Bummer." I smiled.

"Indeed. Total bummer. I'll miss you horribly."

"I'll miss you too."

"You know I love you."

"I know."

"So . . . Babe is your actual name?" asked a pencil-skirt-wearing woman named Kate, staring at me over a pair of tortoiseshell Oliver Peoples glasses, which were delicately perched atop her kind-of-cute nose job.

"Well, my name's technically Barbara, but as you can see by the way I present, that name doesn't really work." I smiled confidently. "People started calling me Babe the day I was born."

Thanks to my ex-model-mom's chic connections, I was in the final round of interviews for a position in *Vogue*'s new media department. Donna and I had been emailing for a while, and when I mentioned that I could see myself working in fashion, she decided to throw me a bone by setting up an interview for me with this "Kate" person. So far I felt like it was going well. I'd followed Donna's instructions: neutral lip, buffed nails (no polish), straight hair, a good boot, and at least one Hermès accessory. I stayed engaged. I hadn't yawned once, even when the HR woman in my first interview talked about "benefits" (unclear). I'd been maintaining strong eye contact and was selling myself to the best of my abilities. I still didn't really know why I was actually applying for a job job, but I guess being settled down with Charlie made me feel like I should stabilize other areas of my life. And working for the top fashion magazine in the world, around a bunch of Adderall-popping psychos thinking about shoes twenty-four-seven, is about as stable as I can get without wanting to kill myself. Plus, I was back into paying attention to the universe, and I think it really wanted me to be a writer. So *Vogue* it was.

"Hmm." Kate sighed passive-aggressively. "So . . ."

"So . . ."

"So . . ."

"So . . ."

"So, you wrote a book. That's great. Haven't read it, but I'm sure it's fun." Kate took an awkwardly long sip of her venti soy misto. "And you're obsessed with fashion. And your mother's Donna V., so that's chic . . . And you seem to have a good handle on all this social media bullshit. I don't really get it. But obviously our HR team sees you as a strong candidate, as this is your second interview. So good job."

"Thanks . . . ?"

"So why don't you go ahead and tell me about what changes you'd implement if you were to manage our social media outlets."

"Well, right now *Vogue*'s online voice is a little editorial and dry, so I would inject some much-needed personality into the brand. The *Vogue* reader wants to feel fabulous, rich, and expressive. Your online presence should reflect that. I mean, obviously I'd continue to link to your articles on Vogue.com, but I'd also tweet stuff that Anna says and capture general goings-on in the office. For instance, just this morning I rode the elevator with Olivier Theyskens and he was wearing his hoodie inside out. The world needs to know those details."

"Alright, Babe, I don't know the difference between a Twitter, an Instagram, and a Pinterest—"

"Oh, no one knows what Pinterest is."

"But you seem like you almost know what you're talking about, and you might very well be an acceptable fit for the job. We'll call you in the next few days and let you know what we've decided." Kate stood up and gave me a tight smile.

I popped up out of my chair. "Thanks, I'm confident you'll do the right thing."

*W*alking through the *Vogue* offices felt like a turning point in my life. Working here didn't sound like a terrible prospect, which represented a major shift for me. I mean, it was fucking

Vogue, for god's sakes. I got in the elevator after my interview and considered what life at *Vogue* would be like. Was it for me? Would I be happy coming to an office? Was I the next Grace Coddington: an angelic muse knocked from the sky, only to rise above the fashion industry like a phoenix? Could I deal with being around so many people, so much of the time?

I quickly exited the Condé Nast building and hailed a taxi. As I was getting into the cab, I swear to God I saw Thalia (or a Thalia look-alike) standing across the street, dressed in a full Haider Ackermann look, staring at me. It was creepy as shit, but I wasn't going to freak out, because today was my day. So, I slammed the cab door and hightailed it to a facialist/manicurist/seaweed wrap-ist/hot rocks masseuse in ChiBeCa (Chinatown/TriBeCa), silently thanking God for giving me the foresight to make the appointment. Prepping for the interview had been so stressful that I knew I'd have to spa it out for at least four hours afterward.

I finished my spa sesh around 8:30 that evening and was in another cab on my way home when I noticed I had two missed calls and two voicemails. Both from NYC numbers I didn't recognize. I pressed Play on the first one.

"Hi, um . . . Babe. It's Kate. I just wanted to let you know we've decided to offer you the position. Please give me a call back at the office when you get this. Thanks and congrats."

Holy fuck, I'd actually gotten a job. At *Vogue*! I mean, it wasn't *Vogue Paris* or even *Vogue Nippon,* but it was still *Vogue.* My dad was going to be so happy.

"Very chic," I said aloud, pressing Play on the next voicemail.

"Babe? It's Robert. Listen—I'm sorry to call you out of the

blue like this. I just . . . I heard you're living in New York now. Is that true? Please call me back. I'd really like to hear your voice."

"Stop the car," I said a little too loudly to the cabdriver. He pulled over.

"Ma'am, your stop is at the end of this block."

"I know. I'm sorry, I just need to walk the rest of the way."

And with that I handed the cabbie a twenty-dollar bill I found in the bottom of my bag, got out of the cab, and took a very cleansing, thirty-second walk to Charlie's building, during which I decided that I was absolutely not going to call Robert back and deleted both his voicemail and his number from my call list. I had a life now. I worked at *Vogue* and was dating an amazing guy who didn't drive me to absolute lunacy. Robert was my then, and Charlie was my now. After I washed my face and moisturized, I called Charlie in China to tell him the good news. We had phone sex, I came twice, and then I went to bed.

The next morning I called Kate and formally accepted her offer. My soul lost its wings for a moment when she told me to be in the office the following Monday morning at 8:30 a.m., but a trip to Marc Jacobs to invest in some staple work pieces helped me get over the loss of freedom known as "employment and resignation to a life of slavery." There's just something about buying twelve skirts that calms the spirit.

Monday morning rolled around faster than I'd expected. I'd spent most of Sunday night deciding on the perfect first-day-of-work look—which took hours—and ended up having to call over my hairstylist, Thorsten, for an emergency hair appointment to adjust my layers by half an inch. At first he was pissed because it was 3 a.m., but after taking one look at my face he realized the proportions were all off and was able to have me looking like a whole new Babe by 4. I slept for the few hours I had left propped up in bed with cucumber slices on my eyes and a pore-tightening masque on my T-zone, before my alarm chirped me awake at 7.

While I was getting ready for work (Work? Who am I?) a messenger delivered a package from Charlie. A beautiful bouquet of flowers and a red lizard-skin Smythson iPad mini case with the sweetest note.

> *To the chicest girl in New York. Knock 'em dead.*
> *Love, Charlie*

I don't take public transportation, and I wasn't going to take a taxi to my new job at *Vogue*. Placing my punctuality in the hands of a cabdriver who might ask me how to get somewhere was not going to happen. Ever. So I hired a car service to pick me up. That's how I met Felix the Dominican. He had the face of a twelve-year-old, the body of a thirty-six-year-old, and the hair of The Rock. Felix rolled up to my building in a huge Escalade. He had a vibe about him that said "I will get Babe Walker where she needs to be, even if it means killing a man or a child or a small dog."

I strolled into Kate's office at 8:25 a.m. She seemed surprised that I was on time, and I lied and told her that I've never been late to anything in my life. Then she showed me to my desk and walked me around the office, pointing out the "people you're allowed to talk to"—mostly assistants and junior editors. I kind of loved what a bitch Kate was. She was so cold and thin. Actually, everyone in that office was pretty cold and thin. There were lots of chic-to-death women, gays, and even a couple hot straight guys, all sucking fashion's dick. And I was Babe Walker: gainfully employed Voguette.

My first week went by smoothly. I had access to all the shoe closets, I went to all the New York photo shoots, and I even got to sit in on a creative meeting with Michelle Obama. It was a great position for me, because I didn't have to be anyone's assistant. Getting people's coffee and being passive-aggressively bitched at all day are two things that aren't in my skill set. There was one slip-up where I almost got caught sexting Charlie, and another where I almost overslept (I'd taken a Lunesta and forgotten to set my alarm). Thankfully, Felix had keys to the apartment and dragged me out of bed, dressed me, did a surprisingly decent job on my hair and makeup, tossed me in the car, and had me at work by 8:32 a.m. Also—I would never, ever brag about this if it weren't true (swear on my collection of PS1s), but one day I totally overheard Anna Wintour tell her second assistant that my blouse was "not heinous."

The thing I really loved about my job was that I didn't hate it. This was the beginning of the rest of my life. I was going to have a *Vogue* career. I was going to grow old wearing Charlotte Olympia slingbacks, mixing florals and prints, opting for a more sophisticated and polished look that included lots of couture from the nineties, and eventually (if things didn't work out with Charlie) marry an artist with a huge dick whose parents were filthy rich, retire early, and live out my golden years painting still-life portraits somewhere in Ibiza.

The following Monday I was picked up at 7:45 a.m., totally ready to take on week two of career-woman chicness at *Vogue*. Felix told me I looked "thinner and taller," which I attributed to the Giuseppe Zanotti boots I had just bought. They went up to my crotch, they were gray suede, and they were everything to me. We stopped by my favorite coffee shop, Ninth Street Espresso, before work so that I could get an oolong tea. Apparently they'd hired a new barista who was unclear on the art of steeping, so it took him fifteen minutes to prepare my tea. I grabbed the steaming-hot tea off the counter and was rushing out the door when I almost ran smack into the chest of a bedraggled man who was coming into the café.

" 'Scuse meeee!" I said, trying to edge around him without making eye contact. He smelled like a mixture of b.o. and Tom Ford Extreme.

"Babe?"

I turned around to confront this weird-smelling stranger who knew my name, hoping that it wasn't anyone from college, and was shocked to see Robert staring back at me. He looked . . . bad. He had a five o'clock shadow and dark circles under his eyes, and I swear his hair looked like it was thinning near his temples. Also, he was wearing drawstring pants that appeared to be medical scrubs, a white V-neck, and flip-flops?

"Robert?" I asked incredulously. I could tell he was embarrassed about his disheveled appearance. Especially since my outfit was insanely amazing (vintage Jean Paul Gaultier camel cashmere wrap coat, white Stella McCartney silk shirt dress, and, of course, my precious boots). Plus, my hair was incredibly shiny thanks to a five-hour conditioning mask I'd applied the night before. Normally I'm the one who's looking like a desperate mess. This was one of the greatest karmic shifts of all time.

Vintage Jean Paul Gaultier

Stella McCartney

Proenza Schouler

Work Birkin

Giuseppe Zanotti

I flashed Robert my friendliest smile. "How are you doing? You look very . . . relaxed."

"I'm . . . I'm good!" he said unconvincingly. If anyone wearing flip-flops tells you they're doing well, they're lying. "So, you live in the city now?"

"Yeah, I do. Been living here for a while now. I really love it. What about you?"

"I moved back a couple months ago. Right around the corner from this place," he said, motioning to the coffee shop.

"Oh, that's great."

"Yeah. Hey, did you ever get that voicemail I left you . . . ?"

"You know what? I might have, but I can't remember. I just got a job working at *Vogue,* so I've been really, really, really, really, really busy."

As if on cue, Felix appeared next to me.

"I'm sorry to interrupt, Miss Walker, but it's 8:05; we must be going."

"Thanks, Felix. Robert, this is my driver, Felix. Felix, Robert."

"Nice to meet you, sir," said Felix, giving Robert a firm handshake.

"You too," muttered Robert. God, this was the best moment of my life.

"Well, it's been so good seeing you, but I gotta jet. Take care," I said, placing my free hand on Robert's upper arm and giving him a reassuring, don't-kill-yourself-later squeeze. I smiled sweetly and turned to follow Felix to the car. As I slid into the backseat, I heard Robert calling after me.

"Wait, Babe!" He jogged up to the car, and I rolled down the window.

"What's up?"

"Can I take you to dinner tonight? I just . . . I really want to talk to you."

"I have plans tonight."

I wasn't meaning to be so curt, especially since he looked like Ted Bundy on vacation, but I needed to self-protect against the possibility of turning into you-know-who.

"What about tomorrow night?" he asked.

"What about tomorrow night?"

"Do you have plans?"

"Oh. Yes."

"Wednesday night?"

"Busy."

"Thursday?"

Looking into Robert's eyes, I suddenly felt a pang of sadness. Here he was, clearly in terrible shape, and begging me, his beautiful ex-lover, to go out with him. It was borderline humiliating. For both of us.

"Friday night might work for me."

"Great! Great. How about Koi? I can pick you up—"

"No, that's okay. Why don't we just meet there at seven?"

"Seven it is. See you then."

"Bye, Robert."

The workweek flew by, which I guess is what happens when all you do is look at clothes and talk about clothes. I got to Koi at 6:45 and took a seat at the bar. I was wearing a Burberry Prorsum metallic blue leather trench and chartreuse pumps with an ankle strap. Color = Power.

Robert showed up at 6:55 and seemed genuinely surprised to see that I'd beaten him to the restaurant. I stood up as he approached the bar and he greeted me with a kiss on the cheek.

"You look great. I made a reservation. Should we grab our table?"

"Let's just stay here," I suggested. I didn't want this to get too involved. Keeping things relegated to the bar meant we could grab a couple drinks, eat some sushi, catch up, and I'd be out of there in an hour. Even though Robert looked much better than he had on Monday morning—he'd shaved, he no longer looked like he was balding, and he was wearing a gray Calvin Klein Collection suit, no tie, crisp white shirt underneath—I wasn't here to get cozy.

"Bar works," he said, taking a seat on the stool next to mine. I ordered right away (vodka martini, seaweed salad, toro sashimi) so he wouldn't have the chance to linger.

"Thanks for meeting me, Babe," said Robert, leaning over his cocktail and taking a sip.

"You're welcome. You seemed a bit out of sorts on Monday."

"Oh, you noticed?"

"Yeah, unfortunately your drawstring pants and flip-flops combo gave you away."

He laughed. "It wasn't my finest hour, that's for sure."

"You also smelled like a hobo, so there's that."

"Ouch."

"But you clean up nice, I guess," I said with a forgiving smirk.

"To tell you the truth, I'm in a weird place."

"What's going on?"

"I miss you."

"Robert—"

"I just thought that if I could see you again, we could at least talk."

"About what? How I'm the worst version of myself when I'm around you?"

"You're not right now."

I sighed. "That's because I'm with someone else."

"I know, and it drives me crazy."

I loved that (a) Robert knew I had a boyfriend and (b) that he hated it. He kept going. "I called your phone on the off chance that it was still your number. I needed to hear your voice."

"Look, I appreciate the sentiment, but I have a boyfriend and we love each other and are very happy together."

"Do you go insane over him?"

"What do you mean?"

"You know what I mean."

"As a matter of fact, no."

"Then you're not in love with him. Do you still think about me?"

"Robert, what the fuck are you doing?"

"I don't know, Babe."

"Well, it's really poor form to ask me to dinner and then just—"

"I think I'm trying to tell you something."

"Tell me what?"

"I'm trying to tell you I'm still in love with you."

I inhaled sharply. What the hell was going on? I had expected to meet Robert for dinner and hear about how depressing his life was and feel even better about my own life. I never in a million years thought that all this time, all these months that I had tried to put him out of my head and move on, he had been trying to do the same thing with me. No. We couldn't go down this road. It was too late. I was with Charlie.

"Well, that's too bad," I said firmly. "We had our moment, it's over. Let's both move on."

"Babe, you disappeared. I was in LA, hiding out from everyone I knew back east, working like a dog, and you were off the radar in Europe or wherever. I wanted to contact you, but I thought you were done with me—or at least done with whatever it was we were doing. I stuck around, hoping you'd show up, but months went by and you didn't come back. And then I just let you go, decided to move back to New York and start fresh. I was doing okay for a while, and then I saw an interview with you pop up on Barneys.com, talking about how you live in the city with your new boyfriend, and I just kind of lost it. I realized I wanted you back and that I'd do whatever it took to get you back." He placed his hand on mine. Chills shot up my arm. I should have moved it away, but I didn't. I felt a lust trembling within me. A lust I hadn't felt in ages. I thought about Robert's touch. The way he kissed. The way he fucked. His massive hands and his perfect dick.

"You want me back?"

"I want you. Period."

"All of me?"

"All of you."

"Even Babette?"

"Yes. I feel like I am the male version of Babette right now. I'm not even kidding. You saw how I was on Monday."

"Are you attracted to me?" I asked.

"Very."

I knew I was playing with fire, but I couldn't help myself. "Do you want to fuck me?"

"Yes."

"Elaborate."

Robert leaned in close.

"I'd undo that trench coat you're wearing button by button until your naked body was in front of me, and I'd put my finger in your mouth and make you suck it. Then I'd trace it from your lips to your breasts. Then to your belly button and then slide it into your dripping wet pussy while sucking on your nipples."

I grinned at him.

"Do you have a boner right now, Robert?"

"Yes."

"Good. I'd take your finger out of my pussy and make you taste it. Then I'd kneel down in front of you, unbuckle your pants, pull your dick out, and start licking it from shaft to tip." God, it was refreshing to imagine being with a man whose dick I actually wanted to see/touch. Our food had arrived, but I'd suddenly lost my appetite. "Then, when you're rock hard—"

"I'd lay you down and fuck you slowly until you begged me to fuck you fast and hard. And then I would fuck you and fuck you more until we both came, screaming each other's names."

Robert and I just stared at each other, both of us basically panting. I had to get out of Koi before I actually fucked him.

"I'm sorry, I have to go. I have a boyfriend and I have to go. I'll talk to you later."

I ran out of the restaurant and into the street, hailing the first cab I saw. I couldn't stop picturing Robert's perfect penis. I was trying to wrap my head around what had just happened.

I'd mentally cheated on Charlie by having verbal unprotected sex with Robert.

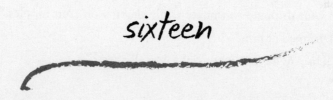

sixteen

NAMASTE, UNIVERSE. NAMASTE.

Charlie 7:15AM Good morning, love. Have the best day ever. Thinking of you.

This was the text I woke up to. It made me smile, but smiling turned to sadness when I remembered the events of the night before.

Babe 7:16AM Hi C.

Babe 7:16AM I hope you have a nice day too.

Charlie 7:17AM Miss you my darling.

Babe 7:18AM You too.

I needed to take some time to reset my aura, so I booked a full day of spa appointments and turned my phone off. Disconnect, exfoliate, reconnect. When I turned my phone back on the following day, I was shocked by the sheer volume of text messages I'd received, and made a mental note to drop off the face of the earth more often. Upon further inspection, I was especially shocked to see that most of them were from Robert.

Robert 11:11AM When can I see you again?

Robert 11:12AM I miss you, Babe.

Robert 11:13AM If we could just talk for five minutes . . .

Robert 11:16AM We could go get a Jamba?

Robert 11:17AM They have one on the secret menu that tastes exactly like a clear gummi bear. It's delicious.

Robert 11:56AM I'm so stressed out. I think I'm having a shingles outbreak.

Robert 1:48PM Just went to my doctor, it's definitely stress-related shingles.

Robert 2:20PM Babe?

Robert 4:00PM Babe?

Robert 4:02PM Babe, are you okay?

Robert 5:39PM Babe, are you dead?

Robert 6:17PM If you're not dead, just text me and let me know you're okay.

Robert 7:07PM Remember when we went to that Italian restaurant and you ate whole wheat pasta? Then we made love and told each other I love you?

Robert 7:10PM I miss that.

Robert 7:11PM I miss us.

Robert 10:45PM I feel fucking crazy.

What in the mother of fuck? Was I in a parallel universe all of a sudden? Robert was totally Babette-ing out on me. He had a dark side? He had a dark side. A Roberto! I was momentarily overjoyed that I had made him feel this way because I knew it was out of love and infatuation, but then I got really sad because I might've given him shingles by not responding to any of his texts.

I stared at my phone for fifteen minutes with no idea how to handle the situation. I couldn't engage with Roberto because encouraging someone's dark side only makes it worse, and also because he was never good at coping with Babette, so I figured I could let him suffer. Plus, all the desperation was kind of a turnoff. What was the answer? My head felt fuzzy; everywhere I looked, I was surrounded by boyfriends. I needed to get out of Charlie's apartment and walk out into the universe and let it tell me what the fuck I was going to do.

Please, universe, deliver yourself to me and help me find my way.

Once I was out of Charlie's building, I walked a few blocks and found myself descending into a subway station. It was brighter and smelled more like old, dry piss than I would've liked, but I was just following my instincts and letting the universe relay its messages. I got on something called the F train and took it to the Lexington Avenue station. Once I emerged from underground, I vowed to never take the subway again, said a short prayer for the unfortunate souls who have to take it every day, and started walking. It was as if I was being propelled by a force stronger than myself. Each step felt supported by the winds of fate. I was surrendering to a magnetic pull, not choosing my destiny. And then my legs stopped moving. I knew in that moment that the universe wanted me to stop, think, and look. I lifted my head slowly and realized that I'd been brought to the one place where I'd truly be able to clear my head: Barneys.

Namaste, universe. Namaste.

I took the elevator up to the second floor. I heard the faint murmur of sales associates greeting me as I floated through the racks. I addressed no one and I certainly didn't make eye contact. This phenomenon has happened to me a few times before, usually in times of extreme confoundment. Complete out-of-body shopping. I wandered over to a rack of perfectly sheer plaid shirts and pants hanging near one of the walls. Dries Van Noten S/S '13. I started sifting through the blouses. My fingers traced the seam of a feather-light maroon-and-black top, and I felt the cloth's soul connect with my own soul through my skin. It was as if the two of us had met in a past life. "Hello, old friend," I whispered to the blouse.

A saleslady with a chic afro walked over to me and before she could open her mouth, I preemptively addressed her presence.

"I'm in the middle of a crisis, and I would really appreciate it if you didn't speak to me at all. It's not you. You didn't do anything. Your hair looks really amazing and I love that dress. Is it by Suno? Blink once for yes."

She blinked.

"From last season, yes?"

She blinked again.

"So cute. So fun. Anyway, I just need to focus on me right now, and my mental processes cannot be interrupted by your or any other salesperson's agenda. So if you're okay with relaying that info to the other workers and can agree to being my silent sherpa, blink once again."

She blinked again.

"Okay, let's fucking do this, then. If you can just take this"— I handed her a silk floral caftan—"and this guy"—a silk floral skirt—"and these"—a light gray cashmere sweater; a sheer silk, high-waisted trouser; and another plaid shirt and dress combo— "and start a fitting room for me, that would be good."

She blinked again, grabbed all my stuff, and was gone just as quickly as she'd appeared.

I knew my Dries selections were going to be amazing, but I needed to counteract all that nouveau grunge with something a bit more sophisticated. The Balenciaga color story that season was basically a reinterpretation of my current state of mind, and the Givenchy ruffles were really speaking to all the changes I'd been through over the past six months. Up, down, right, left. You get it.

I found Safro (Suno + afro) and asked her to put both collections in the fitting room for me. Then I continued walking around the second floor, letting the universe guide me to a rack of romantic yet simple eleganza by The Row, and a denim pencil skirt/cape combo by Miu Miu, both of which were promptly delivered to the fitting room.

Instead of grabbing clothes in a frenzy like a starving rat, I was letting the clothes choose me. All the stalker/emotional roller-coaster relationship drama had left me feeling exposed, so the entire Alexander Wang spring collection focused around strategic cutouts was calling my name, obviously. I thumbed through the racks and settled on a white cutout skirt and tank set, as well as a blue paneled lace dress that I handed to Safro, who was following me around the store silently, which made me feel very safe. I was so lucky to have Safro. I explored the "Babe: Exposed" theme some more and added a black mesh Giambattista Valli tank top and a white floral crop top and skirt combo to my selections.

I headed upstairs to the seventh-floor co-op. As I held a 3.1 Phillip Lim shirt in my arms that read "I Heart Nueva York," I asked myself, *Is this where I belong? Do I love New York? Maybe I just need to go back to LA.* That's when, coincidentally, I locked eyes with a pair of Ksubi cutoff shorts that made me miss LA so much I almost cried, but I didn't because that would've been retarded. I hadn't cried in a Barneys since before rehab and I was not falling down that rabbit hole again.

I sifted through some Missoni bikinis, asking myself whom I'd rather go to the Hamptons with: Charlie or Robert. Did Charlie even have a Hamptons place? Surely he did. Maybe he rented. Next Safro and I journeyed down to the fifth floor and tried on a pair of Salvatore Ferragamo flats. They were perfectly sensible and sensibly chic. A must-have. Very Charlie. Then I spent fifteen minutes trying to decide between a pair of black Céline furkenstocks and a pair of bejeweled Céline furkenstocks and ultimately decided to get both. Very spontaneous. Very Robert. I also ordered a pair of canary-yellow fur pumps that I used to think were hideous but now needed in a way that I couldn't even verbally express, and contemplated the idea that I might be in love with both Charlie and Robert. Can a woman be in love with two men?

After my jaunt through the mecca of white marble that is the Barneys shoe floor, I felt like I needed to do something to protect myself, so I did a quick lap of the accessories department to try on some sunnies and maybe peep a few bags. *You need to learn how to be more of a bitch,* I thought to myself while trying on a pair of Tom Ford Anastasia shades. *No you don't,* I then thought, placing a pair of reflective Jil Sanders on my face. I handed both pairs to Saffro and informed her I'd be taking them. A Saint Laurent Paris hat called to me so I handed that to her as well. Then I headed back to the second floor to try on all my clothing selections.

I knew that going to Barneys was a dangerous move on my part, and I was definitely going to buy a lot of shit, but instead of feeling frantic and crazed, I felt completely in control. I kept hearing Jackson's voice saying, "It's not a breakdown, it's a breakthrough!" and I knew I was in the throes of a major power moment with myself. I was Babe Fucking Walker. I wasn't going to lose my shit at Barneys (again), or freak out about Robert or Charlie or any of the stuff going on in my life. I was going to decide what I really wanted and I was going to get it.

As I tried on all the garments I'd selected, I asked myself, "Is this what I want?" And carefully curated a yes pile and a no pile. Did I want to be with Charlie? He was perfect in every way except for his penis, and Robert was also perfect in every way except for the fact that he makes me act like a complete psycho whenever he's in my life. But apparently I have the same effect on him. Did this mean we were destined to be together? Or were we both just two psychos with overcommitment issues?

Even though I couldn't come to a conclusion about Charlie vs. Robert, I did come to a conclusion about everything I wanted to buy. After a couple hours of putting looks together in my dressing room, Safro hung my yes pile on a rack, rolled it to the counter, rang everything up, and wrote the total damage on a piece of Barneys stationery (she was really good at her job). I slid my Amex to her, closed my tired eyes for a few moments, and she processed the payment. As I handed her back the slip, I grabbed her tiny hand, pulled her close to my face, and said, "I appreciate you."

I grabbed my eight large bags and out I went.

I hailed a cab outside of Barneys and directed the driver to take me back to Charlie's. Despite all my amazing purchases, I was frustrated that I hadn't managed to come to a decision about the love triangle in which I was currently embroiled. Traffic was barely moving, weirdly mirroring my stagnant romantic dilemma. My phone rang. It was Charlie.

"Hi, honey," I answered. "How are you?"

"Well, hello there, Miss Walker. I'm well. You sound tired."

"I just did a power shop at Barneys. I'm exhausted."

"Ahh, that will take the air out of your tires. I'm sorry to say this, but I'm afraid I have some bad news."

"Oh, no. What's that?"

"The deal we're working on is taking forever to go through, so I have to extend my trip another week. I won't be back until next Monday."

"Oh."

"I'm sorry."

"It's okay. I just miss you, that's all."

But did I really?

"I miss you too, love. I can't wait to get back."

"I can't either."

But could I?

"I have a surprise for you that I think you're going to like." I could hear him smiling.

"Exciting!" I said, trying to match his enthusiasm.

"You have no idea. I have to run to a meeting. What's your plan tonight?"

"Nothing, just headed home to relax."

"Lovely. Maybe we can Skype."

"Yeah, maybe. I'll text you."

"Okay. Love you."

"You too."

With that, he hung up. The cab was at a standstill some-where in Midtown. I looked out the window and shuddered at the sight of the enormous Macy's. It reminded me of the time I'd eaten pot brownies and gotten lost in the Macy's at the Beverly Center during high school. It was one of the hardest days of my life. No matter how much I tried, or where I went in the store, I literally couldn't find my way out. I spent seven hours in there and was about to resign myself to a life of living among midpriced, American designer diffusion lines, when a security guard found me and escorted me out of the store. It was a waking nightmare.

Finally the cab turned a corner and we were flying toward home. It was on the West Side Highway that I had a realization: Charlie is like Macy's. He's accessible to the masses, he's sensible, and he has everything I need, but nothing I really want. Like kitchenware and comforters. I don't want any of that shit. Robert, on the other hand, is like Barneys. He has everything I want and need, like Missoni towels and The Row backpacks. And because of that, he makes me feel a little crazy at times. But now Robert was the one losing control of himself too. Maybe he and I were more in sync than I'd realized and maybe that's why we loved each other so much. Our connection was animalistic. It was full of fire. It was ancient.

Everything became crystal clear to me. I had to break things off with Charlie before things got completely out of hand. Robert was The One. He always had been. It was settled. I would go home, put my purchases away, get on Skype, break up with my boyfriend and his very small penis, and find Robert/Roberto and tell him that I'm in love with him.

seventeen

TOTALLY YUMSTER.

When I got back to Charlie's, I was flustered and starving, so I ordered a pepperoni pizza from Domino's and started doing my nails to try to center my chi. I'd executed a perfect French manicure and was celebrating this victory with a slice of pizza when I realized Babette had clearly taken over my body/mind. Domino's? French mani? I spat out the bite of pizza and threw the rest down the garbage chute. This could not happen. Not while *Vogue* was on the line. I tried every trick up my sleeve to get ahold of myself, but nothing seemed to work. I slapped myself, took two Xanax, took a bath, nearly Whitney Houston–ed, got out of the bath, and then lay in bed shaking for most of the night.

I woke up in the morning wearing silk leopard-print pajamas. I had no idea where they'd come from. I checked my bedside clock. It was 8:35. I could hear Felix pounding on my front door, and I could feel Babette pulsing through my veins. FUCK. There was no way I could enter the halls of *Vogue* like this. I couldn't let my alter ego sabotage me again, but I was powerless against her. So, under Babette's spell, I called the office and left a quick message that I'd gotten a really "big bad period" and would be late to work, then let Felix in. I was trying to get dressed, but I couldn't find anything to wear, it was all too chic.

"I'm gonna need you to take me to a few stores really quick," Babette said to Felix.

Three hours later, once her brief yet dreadful shopping spree was done, she slathered herself in Thierry Mugler Angel and changed into an Herve Leger bandage skirt, a Bebe leather crop top, a denim jacket, giant, sparkly platform Louboutins, and a rhinestone necktie, all in the backseat of Felix's SUV. Once dressed, Babette realized that her hair was not cooperating with her outfit.

"Feeeeeeelix?"

"Yes, Miss Walker?"

"You know that feeling where you just need bangs?"

"I'm bald, Miss Walker."

"Exactly. Stop here for a sec."

They stopped in front of the first salon Babette saw so that she could get chunky bangs. She also had one of the salon's manicurists apply pointy, leopard-print gel tips to her nails.

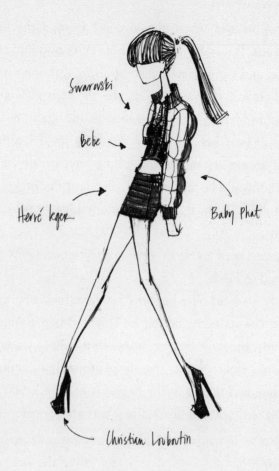

Swarovski

Bebe

Herré leger

Baby Phat

Christian Louboutin

Then she was ready to go to work. Babette strolled into the office at 1:27 p.m.

"Hey, bitches!" she said loudly to the people who worked in her area. "I hope you're hungry because I brought McDonald's breakfast for everyone! It's kinda cold because it's been sitting in the car, but I had a hash brown and a McMuffin on my way over here—okay, I'll be honest, I had two—and they were still totally yumster," she squealed, passing out an assortment of McMuffins and hotcakes to my stunned coworkers. "Notice anything different about me?" she hinted, pointing to her face. "I got baaaaaannngggssss—"

"Babe, what the fuck are you doing?" hissed Kate, grabbing Babette's arm and pulling me into the *Vogue* closet.

"Oh, hey. Nothing, just here to work. Should I tweet a pic of my new bangs?"

"No. Here, put this on for the love of God," Kate said, thrusting an ivory Oscar de la Renta cashmere shirt at Babette. "Lose the necktie and that horrible crop top thing. If Anna sees you wearing those, she'll fire both of us. And here—" She shoved a pair of black Manolo Blahnik pumps at her. "You need to burn those Loubs."

"I—"

"No. Don't say anything. Just do it. I don't know what's gotten into you today, but I don't have time to discuss it because you're late for the swimwear shoot, so please get over there and try not to act like a freak." Then she left in a huff.

The rest of the day was disastrous in ways that are hard to talk about because it ended with me losing the only job I've ever semi-liked. The following tweets that Babette tweeted from *Vogue*'s account should give you an idea of what was going on and why it was so dark.

@voguemagazine 1:40pm: Crying on the floor of the accessories closet. Why is everyone so mean here?

@voguemagazine 1:45pm: It's like you try to do something nice for your coworkers by bringing them McDonald's and they don't even care. #overworked #underappreciated

@voguemagazine 1:50pm: I miss Robert.

@voguemagazine 2:11pm: Swimwear shoot, starring Karlie Kloss and a bunch of beefy male models. Snooze.

@voguemagazine 2:15pm: I'm over Karlie Kloss.

@voguemagazine 2:22pm: She's so tall it's scary. Almost too tall. #KarlieKloss

@voguemagazine 2:24pm: These male models smell weird but I'm still totes DTF.

@voguemagazine 2:30pm: brb, gonna go take care of some business (aka touch myself).

@voguemagazine 2:45pm: Dear assistant who just found me in Anna's office, I was only smoking a cigarette under the desk because I'm addicted to them. NOT doing anything else. Swearsies.

@voguemagazine 2:57pm: I'm literally starving.

@voguemagazine 3:34pm: Holla! Ordered a delish lunch from @cheesecakefactory. Just one slice of cheesecake lol maybe three.

@voguemagazine 4:00pm: FASHION.

@voguemagazine 4:05pm: BCBG clutches are so cute but everyone here hates them. #why

@voguemagazine 4:10pm: I think Anna's hair is actually a wig.

@voguemagazine 4:29pm: Grace Coddington's hair is SO FRIZZY girl. You'd think Anna would have made her get a Brazilian blowout by now!

@voguemagazine 4:41pm: "Karl Lagerfeld is the chicest Nazi in the industry."—André Leon Talley

@voguemagazine 4:52pm: ROBERT.

*A*round 5:00 p.m., I was escorted out of the building and told to never come back. Felix drove me home. Somewhere along the way back to the West Village I transitioned back into myself. Babette was gone, but the damage had been done. Before I got out of the car I fired Felix, for obvious reasons. What kind of driver are you if you can't tell when your client is having a nervous breakdown and needs to be quarantined instead of taken into her place of business?

I was in complete denial about what had just happened to me. Robert? Babette? *Vogue?* I had landed myself on Anna Wintour's blacklist, right next to Kim Kardashian, and I had bangs that would take at least six months to grow out. I couldn't even deal. Not one part of me was able to process the shit show that was this day. I drew a hot bath and just as I was about to get in, my doorbell rang. Standing at the door was Charlie's doorman, Donald, who handed me an unmarked box that he claimed had been dropped off by a messenger. Fuck. It was probably a gift from Charlie. My eyes filled with tears, thinking about how far away he was, how much he trusted me, how much I was fucking everything up.

I took the package into the kitchen and opened it, hoping it would be Google Glass, or a Rolex, or at the very least a set of jade bangles, but it was none of those things.

The box was filled to the brim with unopened black lipsticks.

I shoved the box off the counter, and black lipsticks flew everywhere. Fucking Thalia! I thought confronting her in Gstaad had put an end to her reign of terror, but I was wrong. Apparently she was in New York and wasn't going to stop until I was dead.

But you know what? I was happy Thalia had followed me to New York. If Babette was going to destroy everything that mattered anyway, I wanted Thalia to kill me. This was my perfect out. I went into the kitchen, took out several knives, some duct tape, and some heavy-duty trash bags, and brought them into the bathroom. I arranged them neatly on the bathroom counter, took a roofie, and got in the bath fully clothed. It was my time. *Come and get me, Thalia,* I thought to myself. *End me. I'm ready to die.*

But I didn't die.

I woke up ten hours later, completely disoriented. The water was freezing and I felt like Leo in that scene from *What's Eating Gilbert Grape.* My dark reality was coming into focus. Thalia hadn't killed me, and now bits and pieces of my day were floating through my head like the trash that floats through the East River. I got in the shower and just stood there crying. Why hadn't she come for me? I'd made it so easy for her. All she had to do was put me out of my misery.

Leaving the shower meant facing the shitstorm my life had become. I had no job, no prospect of happiness, soon I'd have no boyfriend, and now my untimely demise was imminent. I was safe in the shower. Warm. Isolated. Denial. But I couldn't stay in there forever. I was at least clearheaded enough to know that. So I got out, grabbed a towel, quickly dried myself off, and cocooned under the covers on Charlie's bed.

"Please let it be over soon," I said to God, or myself, or whoever the fuck cared to listen. "Please."

eighteen

YOU LOOK HOMELESS,
BUT NOT IN A GOOD WAY.

If you've ever heard the ringtone for Skype, then you'd know that it's perhaps the most horrible way to be woken up from a deep sleep. I accepted Charlie's call despite the fact that I looked unpresentable on every level.

"There's my girl."

"Hi."

"What's wrong, Babe? You look truly worn out."

"I'm fine."

"You don't look that fine. You look sad."

"No. Really, I'm fine. I just . . . miss you. That's all."

"I miss you terribly, but I have some bad news. I have to push my return date."

"How long?"

"Another week? Maybe two?"

"Charlie . . ."

"I know, darling. It won't always be this bad. Once this deal is done, I will have far more free time. I promise."

"Well, good."

"What have you been up to, love? Anything new going on?"

I paused and contemplated telling him everything that had happened in the past forty-eight hours.

"Nope."

"I find that a bit hard to believe. We haven't spoken in a few days. You must've gotten up to something."

"Honestly, Charlie. I've just been here or at work. The usual. Hanging out, I guess? You know."

Now would have been the time to rip off the Band-Aid, tell him about Robert, my job, Thalia's return, Babette. But I just couldn't do it. Even though I knew Charlie wasn't The One, part of me wished he was in New York, comforting me. He was so good at that. I hated lying to him.

"Do you have a busy day at the office today?"

"I'm actually not going in today. It's like a Jewish holiday or something, so I decided to observe."

"But you're not Jewish."

"I know. But still."

"Are you sure you're okay, my dear? Something's off with you."

"Well, maybe it's Skype. I look a lot prettier on FaceTime. FYI."

"I'll remember that for next time. Listen, I have to run to this dinner for work. But I can cancel it if you just want to talk."

"You're so sweet. But no thanks. I have a super busy day planned. You go ahead."

"Okay, but I'll try you again before I go to bed. Love you, Babe."

"You too."

And with that, we clicked our respective hang-up buttons.

It was time for me to stop taking three-hour showers and lying in bed, waiting to die. I was sick of being a victim of circumstance. I might have felt forlorn in regards to my love life, but I needed to make a serious change if I wanted to live. Which I did. I wanted to live for a long time. Long enough to get married someday, have a daughter, raise her to be a supermodel, age gracefully, get a second face-lift, and die in my sleep. Rolling over and allowing Thalia to murder me was not an option.

I rehired Felix as my driver and my bodyguard, and enrolled myself in a week's worth of kickboxing and Krav Maga classes. I bought Mace and a Taser. I watched *Home Alone*. I was starting to feel physically stronger, but my heart still hurt. I was slipping deeper and deeper into despair about the Robert and Charlie situation, which I dealt with by turning to poetry. I Instagrammed pictures of my writing:

The Undead
An Invisible Poem by Babe Walker

My Soul Is A Rat King
my voice my hope my time my love my life my heart my tears
lost
my death my dust my depths my dear my dull my
darkness
cost
my happiness

*T*his must have been what tipped Gen and Roman off to just how fucked my life actually was. We'd been checking in periodically over the past few months, but within an hour of posting the poems (which each got like 2,000 likes, btw) I received a stupid number of texts from them:

Genevieve 3:45PM Babe. Are you dead?

Roman 3:45PM Babe?

Roman 3:50PM Hon? Gen said you died. True?

Genevieve 3:56PM Babe? If you're dead I want my pashminas back.

Roman 4:43PM Seriously, are you okay? Just text me one letter to let me know you're okay. Gen said to tell you she wants a pashmina or something?

Genevieve 5:01PM Ran into Mabinty at the Grove today. She got extensions. She looks like a young Lauryn Hill. You should call her.

I didn't respond. When my depression-fueled hunger strike entered a second day, I tweeted the following haiku:

Macaulay Culkin
is my spirit's reflection
Home Alone for life

. . . and mustered enough energy to look up the number of Organic Avenue and order a few cold-pressed celery juices to be delivered to Charlie's apartment. Twenty minutes later, the doorman buzzed up to the apartment. Donald will try to engage in conversation if you let him, so I just pressed the intercom and immediately said "Send it up," to avoid having to hear about the New York Knicks or some other stupid football team.

As I stood up to answer the door, I caught a glimpse of myself in the huge mirror hanging in the hallway. I looked dead. But not in a good, skinny, pale way. Like, actually deceased. I didn't really care, because it wasn't as if I was trying to impress the juice delivery guy, but I wrapped myself in a bright yellow Pratesi throw that was on the couch, grabbed my wallet, and opened the door.

I must have been staring into Genevieve's eyes for at least a full minute before I realized I was actually screaming out loud.

"What the fuck are you doing here?" I said, shutting the door in her face.

"Babe, we came to rescue you from yourself."

"What do you mean, 'we'?"

"Romie and I. He's downstairs flirting with your doorman."

"I'm not really in the mood to talk to anyone this month, so can you come back never?"

"Babe. Open the door. We flew Southwest. It was fucking sick and I need to shower, like, pronto."

I'd heard the elevator door open so I knew Roman was probably standing with Gen by now.

"Roman? Are you there too?"

"Yeah, Babe. We're both here. I gotta pee. Can you please let us in?"

"You can come in, but she can't."

"If you don't let us both in, I'm going to pee on the carpet right in front of your door. PS: This building is very *Factory Girl*."

As I opened the door, it occurred to me how terrible I looked. Gen hadn't seen me this stripped down since before high school, and I don't think Roman ever had.

"Oh, hey," I said quietly.

"You okay?" asked Roman.

"What do you mean?" I was being so rude.

"You look homeless, but not in a good way," said Gen. "We know you got fired from *Vogue,* and you haven't been responding to any of our texts."

"Why is there a handgun on your coffee table?" asked Roman.

"And who is that?" asked Genevieve, nodding to Felix, who was standing across the living room silently observing what was going on, doing his job.

"The gun is ceramic, the bodyguard is Felix. Thalia is still fucking stalking me, you guys. And I have a switchblade in my purse. Just kidding, it's a Taser."

"WHAT?" they both asked in unison. I was kind of loving the attention, so I continued.

"It's true."

"Didn't she drive a Range Rover into her ex-boyfriend's house after he cheated on her with Paris Hilton?" asked Roman.

"That was her?!" I asked, shocked. "I knew she was a psycho from the moment I laid eyes on her freaky face. She's the one who's been stalking me."

"Ew, sick," said Gen.

"I know. It's all been her. The notes, the creepiness. The lipsticks. But she doesn't deserve one more second of attention. I'm fine. I'm actually like so super great. I was just about to drink some celery juice, write another couple poems, smoke some cigarettes, maybe go lie down in Central Park for a while . . ."

"No, Babe," said Roman. "Take a shower and put on something Jil Sander-y—we're taking you to lunch at the Carlyle."

*W*hen we arrived, I told Felix to wait outside in the car until I texted him. Gen and Roman checked in while I laid on a couch in the lobby and fake-read emails I'd been avoiding. After what seemed like forever, Roman tapped my shoulder and the three of us went up to the room. I was in one of the shittiest moods I'd ever been in. I didn't want to be there, I didn't want to be with anyone (especially Gen and Roman), and I certainly didn't want to have to talk about any personal shit that had been going on with me. Which is why I almost passed out when we got up to the suite and I realized that I had been ambushed.

Sitting on a couch cross-legged, wearing a flowy, flower-print dress, was Susan, my fucking therapist from LA. I looked at Gen and Roman with all the disdain I could muster. They had tricked me into thinking that I was going to have lunch with them, but in reality they were plotting to intervention the fuck out of me, and they'd flown my goddamn therapist across the country to help in their efforts.

"And, uh, what the fuck is this?" I asked, infuriated.

"Gen and Roman thought, wisely, that it would be helpful to have someone here to help mediate," said Susan, looking serious/concerned.

"Okay, first of all, don't talk to me right now, Susan. You unloyal backstabbing bitch!" I turned back toward the door. "I'm leaving."

"Babe! Stop. We are seriously worried about what's been going on with you," Roman chimed in.

"Well, why the fuck do you care all of a sudden? You didn't seem to give a shit about me or my stalker when you left me at Chateau," I screamed.

"You are a mental patient. You are literally Angelina in *Girl, Interrupted*," said Genevieve. "No one 'left' you, you kicked us out!"

"Oh, fuck you, Gen. I was in a really good place when I came back from rehab, and you just couldn't deal with me being happy, so you sabotaged my life by throwing that disgusting party. You are literally Vanessa Hudgens in *Spring Breakers*."

"Whatever. You are literally Tilda Swinton in *The Beach*. Psycho."

"Honestly, you are literally Charlize in *Monster*. But fatter and greasier. You're scaring me."

"Oh, that's rich. When you opened the door to your apartment, I literally thought I was looking at Catherine Deneuve in that Roman Polanski movie where she kills like three guys and eats a rabbit."

"Nice try. That movie happens to be one of Catherine Deneuve's chicest moments, so thanks. You are literally Eva Mendes in life."

"That's literally so rude."

"I was fucking sober, Gen. I wanted a peaceful, zen dinner party with tropical wildlife in the backyard and around the pool. Not some kegger with a bunch of losers who didn't even know who I was and what I had overcome."

"There were Lakers there, Babe. For you."

"Exactly."

Gen and I stared at each other for thirty seconds. The tension in the room was palpable.

I finally broke the stare-off. "Why would I want to have frat guys and starfuckers who don't even know me at a party celebrating my triumphant, substance-free return to Los Angeles?"

"Babe," interrupted Roman, "you know I don't like to use this word, but sometimes it's the only way to get through to someone in need, so here goes . . . You're acting like a cunt. I've known you since we were four years old and never in my life have I seen you be so aggressive toward your friends. It doesn't look good on you, trust. I honestly questioned whether or not we could be friends anymore after Chateau."

"I wasn't that bad, Romie." I turned to look at him.

"You were absolutely that bad. You were the worst! You were cuntsville dot com slash Babe Walker."

"Roman—"

"The. Fucking. Worst," he deadpanned.

"Can we all just sit down and talk this through?" Susan gently interjected. "Emotions are running high, and I want to make sure that everyone is heard."

"I can't believe you guys lied to me about coming here for lunch," I said, tearing up. "No one should ever lie to anyone about going to lunch. That's just cruel."

"Babe. Please sit down. Genevieve and Roman flew a long way to—"

"Ambush me?"

"No."

"Fuck with me?"

"Babe."

"Make fun of me?"

"I think that's enough, Babe. I'm in New York because I want to help the three of you clear the air. You're lucky to have friends who care this much about you. In my practice, it's rare that I see this level of loyalty between people your age."

That statement shut me up. Susan isn't an idiot, and although I have a love/hate relationship with her, she was kind of making sense. I sat down on the couch opposite Susan, and Gen and Roman each sat in chairs so we could all see one another.

"Let the healing begin," I said smugly.

"That's exactly why I hate talking to you about anything real, Babe. You make a fucking joke every five seconds," Gen blurted out.

"Jesus, Gen. Chill out. This isn't about you."

"The thing is, Babe, it's never about me. It's always about

you. I feel like I'm always there for you, but when my life is falling apart, you barely notice."

"Um, exsqueeze me? When was your life falling apart? You are like Miss Perfect Pants. With the job and the tits and the job and the promotions and stuff. When have I not been there for you?"

"Always! When you came back from rehab, I was dealing with an AIDS scare."

"What?"

"Yeah. My ex-boyfriend Josh traveled to Africa with his family."

"So you thought you had AIDS?"

"Yes."

"Gen, he was on safari with his family," said Roman. "They drove around and looked at lions and shit. They stayed in a five-star resort. I've told you over and over, you can't get AIDS just because you fucked someone who went to Africa."

"Yeah, I know," said Gen. "I didn't end up having AIDS, but I was terrified for, like, three days. But I couldn't even tell you because you'd just gotten home and you seemed so fragile. There's always something with you, Babe. One-way street."

"She's right," Roman whispered under his breath.

"Oh, please, Roman. Throw me under the bus much? My life has been way too fucked up over the past few months for me to be emotionally raped by my two former best friends while my ex-therapist films it and posts it on YouTube."

"You're doing it right now, Babe," said Susan, making a note on her notepad.

"I'm doing *what* right now, Susan?"

"You're doing exactly what Genevieve is accusing you of. You're making everything about you. We've dealt with this stuff in our therapy for years: Narcissistic Personality Disorder. This shouldn't really come as a surprise."

"I'm not sure it's so ethical for you to be bringing my personal stuff from therapy into a group session with my friends."

"I'm not sure it's that ethical of you to call your therapist, who's just trying to help you, a disloyal backstabbing bitch, but who's really keeping track of ethics at this point?" Susan quipped.

"Susan's right. You aren't hearing what we're saying to you. I was feeling super abandoned by you at a time of need when I thought I had AIDS and needed to break up with Josh."

"Gen, you never had AIDS. Stop talking about AIDS."

"Well, I really felt like I did, and feelings are real. I was so distraught from all of it that I had to break up with him. But when you first got home from Utah you were so consumed with your own shit that I felt like I couldn't talk to you about it."

"But I remember you telling me about Josh. You said he was nineteen. See? I was listening."

"Me casually mentioning that I was dating this guy but I didn't think it was going to work is completely different than me telling you that my heart had been ripped out and I didn't know if I'd ever recover. I just downplayed it because you are always super judgmental about me dating young guys—for the record, he was twenty—and I just didn't want to get into it with you. But I was torn apart when I broke up with Josh. I ate a pizza."

"She really did. It was dark," added Roman.

Both Gen and Roman looked super serious as they were recalling the Josh situation. I felt bad for Gen.

"When Robert and I hooked up at Chateau after you guys left, I went crazy and ate, like, forty thousand calories' worth of food in one night," I admitted. "I didn't realize how hurt you were over this guy."

"Can you remember Gen ever being hurt over a guy?" asked Susan.

"Um . . ."

"No. She definitely can't." Gen was actually almost in tears, but she continued. "I really needed my friends at that time and you weren't there for me. Roman, you were pretty nice to me, but you totally forgot to thank me during your acceptance speech at the Gay Grammys."

"You won a Gay Grammy?" I interjected.

"Yeah, I did. Three of them. Best Single, Best New Artist, and Best Pop Vocal—Male."

"Congrats, that's really incredible."

"Thanks, Babe. It was a big night for me. And yes, I thanked you, but I just forgot to thank Gen and she's clearly still mad about it."

"It was just rude."

"Well, maybe I didn't feel like thanking you?"

"Why didn't you want to thank Gen?" Susan asked.

"Yeah, Roman," I prodded, "why didn't you want to thank Genevieve?"

"Because Gen tried to fuck my boyfriend the night she dumped Josh."

"I did not."

"But, like, you did."

"Genevieve, Uri? Really? What the fuck?"

"Whatever," muttered Gen. "I was drunk as shit, lonely, and who doesn't want to fuck Uri? I don't remember this at all, so why are we even talking about it?"

"Well, trust me. It happened."

"I'm sorry, Roman. I'm really fucking sorry, okay? You've seen me try to fuck lots of people's boyfriends in the past, and you never seemed to care that much."

"Other people's boyfriends are different from my boyfriend!" Roman shouted.

"I get that you guys have had some personal issues, and I hate to keep bringing it back to me, but I'm the one who has a stalker and a minor multiple personality disorder. Also, you flew my therapist here to help me. So can we deal with me or what?" I asked.

I could tell from Susan's expression that she was starting to get a bit annoyed by our bickering.

"This is like an endless tennis match—it could go back and forth forever and there won't be any resolution. From what I can gather, you're all mad at each other, and you have a right to be. But you're never going to get anything resolved in this way. I think we need to take a step back. So I want to do an exercise with the three of you."

Roman and Gen looked terrified. Neither of them had ever really been in therapy, so they had no idea what to expect.

"You're all having a hard time being sympathetic toward one another. I want you to each write down one negative belief that you have about yourself on a piece of paper."

Susan pulled a few small sheets of printer paper and some pens out of her bag and handed them to us.

"Do we have to do this?" asked Roman.

"Yeah. I don't want to fucking do anything like this. That sounds retarded," said Gen.

"You don't have to do anything you don't want to do. This is your time," Susan calmly explained.

Gen, Roman, and I looked at one another and smiled. I started to giggle because I knew they were as over this whole therapy session as I was.

"Late lunch?" Gen said quietly.

"Thank God. I'm fucking starving," added Roman.

"So you guys don't want me to continue with the exercise?"

"No, Susan. We're fine now. You fixed us. You're brilliant. Go back to LA."

"I'm over it," said Roman.

"Obviously," Gen agreed.

"Love you. Love you."

"Love you. Love you."

"Love you. Love you."

And with that, we finally went to lunch. I wasn't totally over my shit, but I would be with some time. My two besties had put in the time and effort to come to my emotional rescue and for that I was grateful. It was already 5:30 and none of us had eaten all day, so we went downstairs to the Gallery, which was the only restaurant that was serving food at that time. I ordered an Assam tea and the chilled poached salmon, Gen ordered a Cobb with no bacon, no blue cheese crumbles, and no dressing, and Roman got the steak tartar.

I was missing Robert. We'd gone to lunch at the Gallery years earlier when we were first dating. I looked across the empty restaurant and saw the table where we'd eaten. It was all a bit overwhelming for me, so I excused myself to go to the bathroom.

As soon as I was in a stall, I burst into tears. Maybe it was the hunger, maybe it was the therapy, but I was pretty sure it was the fact that I was going to end up alone. I cried for a while. Then I pulled my shit together, reached in my purse to grab my powder, and noticed the following words written in lipstick on the little mirror of my compact:

Soon.

TTYL

nineteen

GET OFF MY DICK.

I threw my compact against the floor and proceeded to stomp on it, smashing it into a million shards of plastic and glass. Not only was Thalia still at large, but she had gotten close enough to me to get inside my bag.

I felt violated. I felt scared. I felt like I'd been molested.

I stood there for a minute, just staring at the broken compact strewn across the tiled floor, and then I let out a sound that no human being has ever produced. The noise that came out of my mouth in that bathroom was like the battle cry of a prehistoric animal with hairy wings and a forty-foot penis. I went primal. Full on modus brute.

A cocktail waitress with wide eyes came barging in.

"Are you okay?! What's going on?" She was frantically searching the room for any sign of a fight, I guess.

I didn't exactly respond to her so much as stand there, rocking and breathing heavily.

"Excuse me? Miss? Are you okay?"

I tilted my head up, revealing my maniac eyes and trembling lip.

"Miss?"

"Thhhaaallliiiaaaa," I groaned.

"Are you . . . okay?"

"NO! I'm not okay. Where the fuck is that fucking bitch?"

Her gaze found the mess on the floor. She looked at me like she thought I might attack her, which was a strong possibility.

"You know something, don't you?"

"What? I just work here."

"I don't give a shit. I'm gonna end this motherfucker once and for all."

"Excuse me?"

"Excuse you is right," I spat at her. "Excuse ME!" I pushed past the bewildered girl and toward the door. Before leaving the bathroom, I grabbed one of those self-standing toilet paper holders to use as a weapon if things got out of hand.

Thalia was in New York. I knew she had to be close. I could feel her watching me, laughing at me.

I stormed directly over to Gen and Roman, who were sitting across from each other in silence, scrolling on their phones and sipping their vodka sodas.

"She's fucking here!" I told them, waving the toilet paper holder around and letting the room know that I was not to be dealt with lightly.

"What le fuck, Babe?" Gen said without looking up from her phone.

"You guys. Thalia is back."

"Wait, what?" asked Roman.

Gen looked up at me. "Prove it."

"Jesus, Genevieve, I'm not kidding! And I can't prove it because I broke the evidence. But it's her. She's fucking here, she has to be!"

"Thalia?"

"Yes, I fucking told you guys."

"How do I know you're not just being annoying?"

I slammed the table with my free hand. "Being annoying?!" I scream-whispered right in her face; she didn't even flinch. "There was another death threat. It was on my compact, which was in my bag, which means she must've gotten close enough to me to get in there."

"When was the last time you opened that compact?" Roman asked.

"I don't know, yesterday? This morning? I don't KNOW."

"Babe, sit down, people are leaving," he pleaded.

I pounded the table again. "Roman, don't."

"Okay, okay. Fine. So, the person who wrote that note could've gotten into your bag yesterday potentially?"

"But I can feel her presence!"

"Wait," said Gen dryly. "Show me the note."

"I destroyed it when I smashed the compact on the fucking floor, which I just told you."

"Babe, I can't."

"No, I can't."

Roman stood up and looked past me toward the bathroom, from which the terrified waitress had just emerged and begun to alert the rest of the waitstaff that a crazy customer was walking around the restaurant with a TP holder, threatening people's lives.

"So you're sure Thalia is the same person from Chateau?"

"Yes, Roman, Thalia! My stalkerrrrr. Why is this so hard for you to understand?!"

"I'm just saying it looks like Thalia is in jail," said Gen, looking down at her phone.

"What?" I was truly dumbfounded. "Gimme." I grabbed Gen's iPhone from her hand. It was open to the *Daily Mail*, to an article with the headline RUSSIAN SOCIALITE ARRESTED FOR THEFT, ARMS DEALER FATHER REFUSES TO COMMENT. And there under the bold type was a photo of Thalia and her family at the front of a yacht. I'd recognize that face anywhere now.

"Wait . . ." I speed-read through the post, searching for anything that would mean something to me. A clue, anything.

About three paragraphs in I saw it. "New York City . . ."

"Oh my God, you guys."

". . . in a MAC Cosmetics . . ."

I looked up from the screen. "She was arrested at a MAC store."

"Not chic," Gen said, shaking her head in disapproval.

"No, not fucking chic. And I told you it was her! New York?! The lipstick?!"

Gen took her phone back. "She probably got bailed out immediately and came to finish what she started with you."

"Genevieve, please," Roman said.

That hadn't even occurred to me.

"Are you serious?" I demanded. "What the fuck? Is that possible?" My body temperature in that moment was embarrassingly warm. "Roman? Is she still out there?" I was losing it all over again.

"Okay, okay, calm down," he said, putting an arm out to grab my weapon.

"No!" I ran across the room swinging the metal stand, creating a streamer of toilet paper behind me. The whole thing was very Olympics opening ceremonies, and everyone in the restaurant was staring at me.

The room's blue and gold wallpaper was swirling and I forgot where I was. I had one simple thought in my head: *Find this loser pervert psycho bitch who's been following me and kill her . . . to death.*

I began screaming with my arms open wide to the sky. "Come and get me! I'm right where you want me!"

End this now, I kept telling myself. I'd come too far on my life's journey and the stakes were too high to let this psycho fuck with my progress. I was a warrior. It was Thalia's blood or mine. I hadn't felt a surge of anger like this since they rebranded Yves Saint Laurent as Saint Laurent Paris.

So there I was, standing on a banquette with my toilet paper sword in my right hand, scanning the room. And then BOOM!

My body slammed against the carpet and my weapon went flying from my hand. I hadn't seen him coming, but Roman had tackled me.

"Babe!" he shouted, pulling me up from the ground. "We're leaving. NOW."

"What are you doing?!" I screamed back. My body

writhed and flailed as Roman dragged me across the floor like a hooked fish fighting for its life. Genevieve was giving random, scared patrons twenty-dollar bills and apologizing for my behavior. I let out one more extremely drawn-out pterodactyl screech as I was pulled through the door and out into the street.

The light glaring down Seventy-sixth Street that day was blinding. Pure whiteness. I actually thought I'd perished as I passed through the hotel's threshold to the street, which wouldn't have been so surprising. Death by psychotic insanity.

Roman let go of my arm, I made some sort of half-growling, half-grunting noise, and the next thing I remember is Genevieve's voice: "Okay, Babe. You're wearing a trench coat over pajamas, you have really unfortunate bangs, and you just behaved like a wild animal in a classy restaurant."

"Gen, get off my dick. I'm fine! And you know I hate the word *classy,* so please!" I shouted.

"You are out. Of. Control," she said loudly and slowly.

"You can really go blow yourself," I said as I prepared to walk away. But before I had the chance to, Genevieve dropped her bag on the street (which I don't think she's ever done), wound her arm back, and open-palm slapped me across the face. Everything went white again. I stumbled a couple feet backward and put my hands on my knees. It had been a long time since I'd been slapped like that. I was physically shocked, but it was exactly what I needed.

When we were in seventh grade, Gen and I began a tradition of slapping each other, based on our own private Fujita scale of cuntiness. If either of us was ever being what we used to call an F-5 Bitch Storm, the other would slap her as hard as humanly possible. It's like stabbing someone who's having an allergy attack with an EpiPen, without anyone's skin breaking. I mean, slapping is really the only way to snap someone out of a proper bitch fit. I would know, Genevieve is the queen of F-5s.

On occasion a single slap can birth a series of slaps. A slap war, if you will. I found my balance, assumed a steady position facing Gen—who stood there ready to take what was coming her way—and slapped back. She stumbled backward, allowing a highly unattractive tennis-groan to come out of her mouth. She quickly recovered, and before I knew it, we were throwing one slap after the next. It was on and I was committed to slapping Genevieve and getting slapped until I felt better. The blows got harder and harder as we took turns back and forth.

Roman obviously knew exactly how important this moment was, so he stood guard, making sure that no Good Samaritan tried to intervene and fuck everything up. It all went on for another minute or so, until I was drawing my hand back, ready to clap another one on a completely red-faced Genevieve, when I realized I'd forgotten about the note on my compact. My tunnel vision had cleared and I'd broken free.

"I'm done," I said, and lowered my hand to my side.

Roman turned around to face us, lit a Marlboro, and shot me a look of relief.

"It worked. I'm okay. It's gonna be okay."

"Are you sure?" Gen asked, taking Roman's cigarette from

his hand and taking a drag. "Because you were not okay inside. It wasn't cute and it wasn't safe, for anyone."

"Yeah, I know. Not cool." I took the cigarette out of Gen's hand and helped myself to a long inhale. "But you shouldn't have said anything about Thalia possibly being out on bail."

"I know," Gen said. "That was rude. I was just fucking with you. She's already been deported back to Russia."

Roman took the cigarette from me as soon as I finished my pull. "So we can be normal now?" he said.

"Yes. But why did she target me? I don't understand."

"I think it's kind of fun." Gen smiled, pulling out her own pack of Marlboros and lighting one.

"Ew, you would think it's fun. Try having a stalker."

"Don't ew me right now, Babe. Honestly."

"Ew to you telling me not to ew you, though."

"Ew to you having a stalker in the first place. It's so nineties."

"Your tits are so nineties."

"Whatever."

"Whatever."

Silence.

Before one more surprise slap could be added to the war, Roman put his arms around us and drew us both in for a limp, three-person hug. It was actually more like Roman was hugging us and Gen and I were just smushing our bodies together with our heads down and our hands at our sides. Inside the hug, I stole Gen's cigarette out of her hand and took a drag. I did feel better. Still shaken up, but better.

It was a relief to know that my best friends would always care about me even when I was acting like a righteous cuntface.

I was also happy that, unlike Thalia (may her poor soul rot in Russia forever), they'd never ask to borrow my clothes because they had their own. That's true friendship. That's genuine love. So I guess we'd come a long way, and I was sad that Gen and Romie had to go back to LA that night. Roman was performing live on *Access Hollywood* the next day.

twenty

I PROMISE I'LL NEVER FART.

I arrived at Charlie's apartment building with one objective: smoke a joint, weigh myself, take a bath, eat something small, weigh myself again, and fall asleep watching a black-and-white movie. So needless to say I was less than pleased to see Robert, or rather Roberto, sitting on a chair in the corner of the lobby. He was wearing a suede beret, a mock turtleneck with those weird scrub pants, and Crocs. It was so hard to see him dressed like that, which just goes to show you that even the hottest guy can be repulsive in the wrong outfit.

"Are you crazy? You can't just show up here and wait for me in the lobby of my boyfriend's building. You look like Art Garfunkel."

"I know, Babe. I'm sorry."

"Where did you even get that turtleneck? It's scaring me."

"Banana Republic," he said softly, eyes downcast.

"I knew it." I was devastated. "You need to leave. This is too
hard."

"Wait. Babe, at least take these."

Roberto reached behind him and handed me a bouquet of
rainbow roses. They were not chic.

"You can't be here, Robert. Please go home. We'll talk later,
but right now I have something I need to do."

I swear to God a single tear rolled down his cheek. He was
definitely on the verge of having a nervous breakdown. Donald
the doorman eyed him suspiciously.

"Miss Walker, is this man bothering you?" he asked.

I sighed. "No, he's fine."

"Babe . . ." Robert pleaded.

"WHAT?" I blurted out far too loudly.

"I love you."

"I know. But I have a lot of shit to take care of. Let's talk
later."

I turned and walked away, and my mind began to race. Was
I being an idiot/bitch? Robert may have been in the middle of a
psychotic break, but he was basically telling me exactly what I'd
always wanted to hear. I turned to look back at Robert only to
discover that he was standing right behind me.

"Hey."

"Holy fuck, you scared the shit out of me!"

The elevator doors opened and Robert followed me inside.
As soon as the doors closed in front of us, he reached into his
scrubs pocket and pulled out a napkin covered in black scribble.

"I want to read you this poem I wrote."

"Oh my God."

"Babe. My queen. My soul."

"Stop, Robert."

"'My body is a cage and you are my heart. My mind is a museum and you are my art. I promise I'll never fart. Let me love you.'"

"You're kidding me."

Robert dropped the napkin to the ground dramatically and looked right into my eyes. Either the color was coming back to his face or the elevator's lighting favored his bone structure, because he looked less sickening. And then he started kissing me. Roberto was just as good of a kisser as Robert was, but this couldn't go any further. I certainly wasn't going to hook up with him in Charlie's bed. I'm not some kind of she-devil. I just couldn't actually cheat on Charlie. He was too sweet and too caring for me to hurt him like that, so I removed my lips from Robert's and pulled the beret down over his face.

"I can't do this with you right now. We need to stop."

He said nothing. And just stood there with his face really close to mine, one thin layer of brown suede between us, until the elevator doors opened. I pulled the beret off his face and put it on playfully.

"I thought I was a freak, but you are next level."

We walked down the hall to Charlie's door.

"Are you sure that you want me to come in?" Robert said.

"No. But don't try to kiss me again or read any more of your weird poetry. Some of us are natural-born writers, while others aren't blessed with the gift of words."

I unlocked the door. As we walked into the foyer, I noticed that the lights were on in the kitchen, which was weird because I was 99 percent sure I had turned them off before I'd left. I walked farther into the apartment, with Robert trailing me by just a few feet.

"You wait here. I'll get you some water, but then you really need to go."

"All right, my sweet."

I went into the kitchen and walked to the shelf to grab a glass for water. When I turned around, Charlie was standing right before my eyes.

"Surprise!" he said, lifting me off my feet and hugging me.

"Hiiiiiiiiiiiiiiiiiiiii . . ." The word trailed off into oblivion as I realized how totally fucked I was. Charlie lowered me to the ground, and before I could give fair warning, Roberto came walking through the door, hideous bouquet in hand.

"Babe, who is this?" asked Charlie.

"This is Robert."

"Robert? As in ex-boyfriend Robert?"

"More like 'Soul Mate Robert.'" Roberto chuckled to himself, as if he'd said a joke that no one understood but him.

"I, uh . . . I thought you weren't coming back until next week?" I said to Charlie.

"Well, I was hoping to surprise you with a nice meal and an early return, but apparently you had other plans this evening." I could tell by how quietly he was talking that Charlie was fucking pissed.

"It's not as bad as it looks, I swear."

"Oh, really? Not as bad as it looks, love? Well, that's a bloody relief, because it looks pretty fucking bad."

"I'm going to bid you two farewell," Roberto said very quietly as he backed out of the kitchen.

"Brilliant idea," Charlie replied condescendingly.

I shot Robert my best "please stop acting like a freak on a leash" look, and he mouthed "I'll have you" to me before he left the kitchen. And with that, Robert was gone. I felt so bad for Charlie. I'd made a complete fool out of him. I was a monster, a ghoul, a goblin.

"Babe Walker. That was truly one of the most uncomfortable and humiliating moments of my life." He seemed to have calmed himself a bit. Angry, but calm. "How long has this been going on?"

"Nothing is going on, Charlie. But I do think that we are in different places emotionally right now."

"You think? I was planning on proposing to you tonight. Jesus! And you're out and about with Robert? I would say we're on different planets."

"Excuse me, what? You were going to propose what tonight? Marriage?"

Without saying a word, Charlie reached into his pocket and pulled out a small green ring box and set it on the kitchen counter.

"Oh my God, no. This is not happening right now."

"You're right. It's not happening."

I opened the box to reveal the engagement ring of my dreams. It was a four-carat, emerald-cut perfect diamond resting on the most tasteful yet over-le-top vintage platinum setting I'd ever seen. Tiny pavé diamonds sat inside the filigree design. It was as if Charlie had incepted this ring inside my head before I saw it.

It was stunning. It was the ring of my soul. It was the ring I'd never have. I started bawling.

"Why are you crying? Clearly this was never going to work."

"Charlie, I'm crying because I wanted this to work so badly. I'm crying because it's pretty clear that I'll never be in a normal relationship. I didn't cheat on you. Well, I kind of cheated on you, but also kind of not."

"What happened? Was it something I did? Have I been away too much? Were you lonely?"

"You did nothing wrong. This was completely out of your hands. Honestly, I just wasn't ever sure that this was the right fit because of how tiny your penis is, and I think I put off dealing with my concerns because I really hoped it would just work itself out."

After a long and very awkward staring contest, Charlie took a deep breath and continued. "Okay. I'm going to go out and get a drink. I'll be back in two hours. It would be great if you and your stuff were gone by then."

"I can do that," I said through my tears. "You won't ever have to see me again. I'm sorry."

Charlie grabbed his keys, wallet, and phone off the kitchen counter. On his way out the door, he looked down at the gross bouquet of roses sitting in the entryway and then back at me with a steely-eyed glare.

"Take care of yourself, Babe."

Then he walked out.

Charlie was gone. I had no time to wallow because gathering, sorting, and boxing all of my clothes and beauty products was going to take way longer than two hours. I called Felix to see if he could come up to Charlie's place to help me, but he was "at his daughter's quinceañera." No one is reliable anymore. No one.

The next couple of hours were a frantic blur of packing, crying, packing some more, whimpering a little, etc. Once I had all my must-haves packed (the rest were basics that I could replace), I decided it was time to get the fuck out of there.

I did a quick scan of the bedroom, bathroom, and office (where I retrieved my white iPad mini and my black iPad regular). Then I circled back into the kitchen to grab a trash bag, which is where I noticed that Charlie had left the ring box sitting on the kitchen counter. I couldn't help myself from trying it on. It fit perfectly. Was this my journey, to walk away from a life with Charlie? I stared at the ring, contemplating my decision, and realized that my ring finger was twice the size of Charlie's penis. There was nothing more to do but take off the engagement ring, put it back in its box, thank the universe for giving me a solid sign that Charlie wasn't right for me, and step boldly toward my future without him.

I went to throw away those disgusting roses, but discovered that the head of each flower had been chopped off, and a mess of rainbow petals covered the entryway floor. A small envelope now sat next to the bunch of headless stems. I was frozen. Someone had been in the apartment with me. They probably still were. I opened the envelope to reveal the note within.

This is all it said:

Tonight.

twenty-one

STALKER POTENTIAL.

"Heyyyyyyyy, Cassie, it's me, Babe Walker. I heard you're getting lipo in LA this weekend. Love that for you. Um, I'm actually kind of homeless and was wondering if I could crash at your place for a few days while you're out of town? What thread count are the sheets in your guest room? Call me back when you get this."

This was my third futile phone call for help. The realization that my stalker (maybe Thalia, maybe not, I had no fucking clue at this point) was still at large, and had clearly broken into Charlie's apartment and slashed Robert's roses while I'd been packing, caused me to run screaming into the hallway, letting the door shut and lock behind me. When I went down to the lobby to beg for help getting back in, I was informed that Charlie had already removed me from his "approved entry" list. This information caused me to brownout and utter some choice words to the doorman, and I quickly found myself being escorted out of Charlie's building and told not to come back or else the police would be called. I'd tried Charlie's cell, but of course he didn't answer, and now, in a matter of minutes, one of my worst fears had come true: I was on the cruel streets of New York City with a white iPhone as my only possession. To make matters worse, I was still in my packing outfit: vintage overalls, a T by Alexander Wang wifebeater, and Chanel flats. A look that was never intended for the public. And no wallet, credit cards, or ID meant no hotel. I was officially a homeless person.

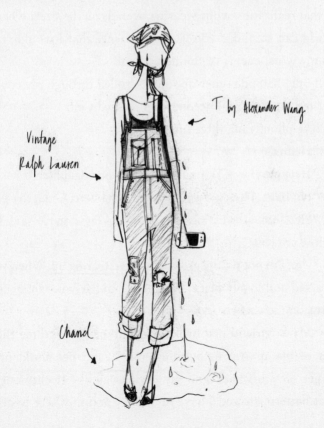

Vintage
Ralph Lauren

T by Alexander Wang

Chanel

I had to figure something out, and fast. I was starting to get cold and hungry, which was an altogether new sensation for me. I mean, I'm always cold but never hungry. There must be something about homelessness that causes hunger. My dad was on a yacht with Lizbeth somewhere with no Wi-Fi, and thus was unreachable, so asking him to save me was out, and having no hotel option was forcing me to rely on the kindness of others, which made me physically ill. Everyone I'd called was either at dinner, or in Miami, or simply refusing my attempts to seek shelter by not answering their phones. The realization that you are all alone in the world and have no one is tough, but coming to that realization while wearing overalls on the street where the world can see/judge you is an experience that I wouldn't wish on my worst enemy or thinnest friend.

I only had one other option. I scrolled through my contacts, located the number I needed, and pressed Call.

The phone rang three times.

"Hello?"

"Heyyyyyyyyyy, Donna. It's Babe, your daughter."

"Hi, Babe. How are you? I have Gina here. Gina, say hi."

"Hey, honey. Missing you like fucking crazy," said Gina. "How are you?"

"Um, I'm not totally great." I started tearing up. When you're in a sad and lonely place, hearing a familiar voice immediately turns on the waterworks.

"My boyfriend just broke up with me and had me thrown out of his apartment building and I can't get ahold of him to get my stuff back and my phone has like twenty-one percent battery left and I have no money and nowhere to go. I'm homeless. Also, someone has been stalking me for almost a year now and leaving me these death-threat-note thingies, I thought it was this crazy Russian bitch I knew, but whoever it is will probably murder me while I'm sleeping in a subway station tonight. And I'm wearing a really sad outfit. Like, I've never hated an outfit more in my life. That's how I am. How are you?"

"Oh, Babe," Gina said. "Come here. Come upstate for the weekend and stay with us."

"We'll have one of the guest rooms upstairs made up for you," Donna chimed in, taking back the phone.

"Oh noooooooooooo. I couldn't impose on you guys like that. I'll be fine."

"Babe, seriously, it's not an imposition."

"Oh my fuck, thank you sooooo much. I'm dying out here. This city is so harsh."

"Babe, stop it. You're family. There's a train that leaves from Grand Central at 8 p.m. We'll get you a ticket and email you the details ASAP."

"That isn't gonna work, because I don't have an ID."

"You shouldn't need an ID to get on a train, just a ticket."

"Are you sure?" I asked.

"Have you ever taken a train?" asked Donna flatly.

"Um. In Europe, yes. In the continental U.S., no."

"Okay, well, today's your lucky day. Babe's first train ride."

"Is it safe?" I was scared.

"We're sending you a ticket and you're coming here. No questions."

"Seriously, Donna, you don't have to invite me to stay with

you. I mean, I'll probably die tonight if you don't, but that wouldn't be your fault."

"Babe. Shut the fuck up. You're coming here!" shouted Gina. "Get to Grand Central before your phone dies. We're gonna text you our address, so take a cab when you get off the train and we will pay for it when you get to the house. See you soon!"

I made it to Grand Central in one piece. The train car smelled like farts, but luckily it was empty so I didn't have to sit next to any shims or mers. I'd been saved! I was momentarily ecstatic that I wouldn't have to sleep at a bus stop, but then completely terrified because my stalker situation was coming to a head. "Tonight"? What did that even mean? Who was this person? I had to get to the bottom of this mystery. I started making lists in my head. Lists of everyone who had been around me each time I'd gotten notes:

> My guest house (on the mirror)
> Chateau Marmont (on the iPad)
> Guest house again (destroyed Terry Richardson portrait)
> Hotel room in Paris (bathroom door)
> New York in Charlie's apartment (box of lipsticks)
> New York at The Carlyle (on my compact)
> New York in Charlie's apartment again (the roses)

Obviously the stalker was someone who had money/a relaxed work schedule, because they'd been able to follow me all over the world.

I jotted down a list of potential murderers on the back of a *Wall Street Journal* that I found on the train.

Potential Murderers

Thalia

Tara Reid

A Psycho Fan

Cal

Charlie

Paul

1. *Thalia*

The idea that Thalia was my stalker had been put to bed after I terrorized that restaurant at The Carlyle and we'd found out that she'd been arrested and deported back to Russia. But she still made the most sense, although her motives were unclear. Why would Thalia even want to kill me in the first place? Because I was rude to her at Genevieve's party? I mean, she's totally *Single White Female* obsessed with me, but I honestly don't think she's crazy enough to actually hurt me, much less kill me. She's the type of girl who'd hire someone to kill me, but this wasn't the work of a hired hitman. I've seen *A Perfect Murder* enough times to know that hitmen don't leave notes, they just fucking kill you. Plus, according to her sick habit of geotagging all her posts on Instagram, Thalia was still in Russia, so she couldn't have broken into Charlie's place. Thalia was officially no longer a suspect.

2. *Tara Reid*

Probably not.

3. A Psycho Fan

Psychos are legit so insane these days. An obsessed fan of my first book (or anyone who's seen how amazing my hair has looked over the past year) could have decided that they wanted to eat me in order to become me. I offered too much of myself in that book. Damnit. I should've never written about my labiaplasty.

But I never forget a face, and I'm constantly aware of my surroundings, so I'm sure I would have recognized a random stranger lurking about. Also, these notes and attacks weren't the musings of just any old stalker. No, my stalker knew me. Knew me well. It had to be someone I'd fucked.

4. Cal

He may have granted me the gift of Life's Best Sex, but Cal obviously had it out for me the entire time I was with him. In addition to his general malicious nature, Cal had to be at least semi-good at planning and plotting horrible things. His intrusion into my life was an assault on everything I hold dear: my body, my mind, and my Birkins. He was for sure capable of following a young, beautiful girl around the world if he wanted to. Stalker potential.

5. Charlie

He was in LA when I was there, he was in New York, still not sure what a hedge fund is, and he definitely has the dick of a stalker, but there was just no way. He's too sweet. And he really loved me. Fuck, I'm such a bitch.

6. *Paul*

Is Paul Courtyard's ghost stalking me?

He did show up at my guest house unannounced the night he died, which was suspect in the first place. Maybe Paul escaped from rehab on a mission to find me and kill me, but he accidentally died, so his ghost attached itself to me from the afterlife and is following me around the world in an attempt to finish what Paul started, i.e., drag me to heaven/hell/wherever so that our spirits will be united forever.

The "Paul's Ghost as a Stalker" theory was actually terrifying, so I called Myrta, my psychic, to run it by her and see what she thought. She did a spirit reading over the phone and had a vision of Paul "swimming in a pool of wine," which she said confirmed that he had fully crossed over to the other side, thank God. Paul wasn't trying to kill me.

No, the person who was after me had to know me well enough to track my every move without my noticing. I'm usually on the lookout for creepy people driving or walking or talking or breathing too close to me anyway, so my stalker was stealthy. It had to be someone close to me. Someone who knew me well. But who? Who has known my whereabouts since I got out of rehab besides my dad?

And then it hit me. The only person who'd been in almost every city I was in when I got stalker notes was . . .

7. *Robert*

He'd picked me up at the guest house that day we went for a hike, he'd stayed at Chateau Marmont at the same time as me, that must've been him at Silencio in Paris, and he'd been living in NYC ever since. Robert was the perfect killer prototype: tall, dark, handsome, successful—a living, breathing Patrick Bateman. Only until recently had his slick facade started to crack. Maybe his feelings for me were reignited, causing him to abandon his relationship with Michelle, thus losing his grip on the perfect life he thought he'd have for himself. And now, after being unable to come to terms with the loss of Michelle and the loss of me, it's caused him to lose his mind.

I knew he was unraveling when I first saw him in NYC. It was so obvious. I mean, Crocs and a mock turtleneck? Roberto wasn't Robert's alter ego, à la Babette. There was no Roberto. There was Robert: The Killer. Driven to madness by love. He'd become utterly obsessed with me and needed to possess me, body and soul, in death. And now he could be anywhere. Lying in wait, ready to end my life. Fuck. I should have forced Felix to drive me upstate. This train was not safe.

I turned to look out the window. The world was flying by me, but I felt paralyzed.

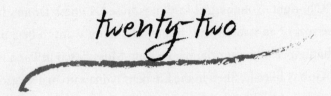

twenty-two

THE LEAST CHIC OUTFIT
IN THE HISTORY OF BABE.

When I got to Donna and Gina's front door, I stood there for a few seconds before knocking. I thought about all of the years that had passed without my having any idea who these people were. I didn't know that my mom was even alive until about a year ago, and here I was on the front steps of her house, wearing the least chic outfit in the history of Babe.

Gina, whom I hadn't seen since rehab, opened the door, cradling an enormous jug of water and wearing wellies.

"Babe!! How are you, mama?!" she squealed.

"I'm good. This place is so much cuter than I'd expected."

"Good, good, I'm so happy to see you! We just finished dinner, I'm going out to fill Carla's water bowl and pay the cabdriver." Gina kissed me on the cheek and walked past me toward a barn-ish building way in the distance.

"Who's Carla?"

"Carla Bruni, our pig. Your mom named her. She's French!" Gina laughed with a howl. She was in such a good mood. I wondered if being a lesbian and living on a farm made you a happier person.

"Oh, right. Your pig," I said, unamused. I guess Donna had some sort of an issue with Carla and I did not want to be a part of that, especially after the whole Kate Moss fiasco in Paris.

"Go say hi to D. She's in the kitchen," Gina said in a singsong voice as she disappeared into the darkness.

The house was really cozy. Tasteful, rustic; chic, even. I could hear Donna's voice as I approached the kitchen door, but she was clearly talking to someone. I prayed she was on the phone, because I couldn't deal with meeting someone new right now. I just wanted to take a long, hot shower and rid myself of all of the nasty train and cab residue that was residing on my hair. After everything I'd been through today, I just couldn't deal with pretending to be nice to some "local" friend of theirs.

Then I heard a recognizable voice laugh loudly and deeply, and terror shot through me like poisonous venom. I was mortified. I was dead.

Robert. Is. In. The. Kitchen.

It may have been over for me, but I couldn't let Robert hurt Donna and Gina. They were former supermodels, for God's sake. I had no choice but to go into the kitchen and pretend that I was happy to see him. If he knew that I knew, it could set him off and he was liable to murder-spree us all. I took three deep breaths, said one silent *ohm*, and quietly opened the door.

Donna and Robert were sitting at a long wooden table having

tea. Robert's back was facing me. This moment was crucial. If I displayed any emotion other than pure joy and surprise, he would know that something was up.

"Hi, Donna. Am I interrupting?" I asked. Robert stood and turned toward me and I did my best I'm-shocked-in-a-good-way face, which was hard to do because he was still wearing that hideous Banana Republic turtleneck. "Robert?! Oh my God, you're here?" I've always believed I was a great actress, but this was an Oscar-worthy performance.

"Hi, my love," he said, smiling warmly, and I knew the killer inside him was delighted that I'd fallen right into his trap.

I ran up to Robert and gave him a huge hug, because that seemed like the right move. My heart was pounding and my eyes filled with tears of terror, which I pretended were tears of joy.

"Robert was just telling me how much he adores you. How 'meant to be' he thinks you guys are," said Donna, giving me a slightly confused look. *What's going on?* she mouthed silently. I shook my head ever so slightly to signal that we couldn't address those issues, and broke free of Robert's hug. He put his hands on my shoulders, admiring me.

"I can see where you get your radiance from," Robert said, smiling at us both.

"Thank you, you're very sweet," Donna said, standing up from the table and walking over to the sink with her empty tea-cup, leaving me with Robert.

"And I think this outfit is just adorable," he said. "Always the fashionista!"

I almost puked in my mouth. I knew then and there that he was batshit insane.

"Do you want to go for a walk?" I asked Robert. I turned to Donna. "Is that cool?"

"Of course, darling. You two take all the time you need. There's a nice little bench out by the barn if you want to sit and chat."

"Great."

"It's getting pretty late anyway. Gina and I will leave the door unlocked for you guys. Oh . . . and there is a room right at the top of the stairs that's been made up for you, Babe. We'll see you in the morning?"

"Yeah, sounds good. Thank you."

"So nice to finally meet you, Donna," Robert said as we walked out. "Thanks for telling me all about the pasteurization process." He smiled.

How was he acting so normal? God, what a fucking psychopath.

Robert and I walked out into the black night air, toward the barn. He grabbed my arm and pulled me close.

"I've missed you." He tried to kiss my neck. I lingered for a moment and then pulled away.

"Robert, you just saw me, like, five minutes ago."

"I know, but every second away from you feels like an eternity. Did you end things with Charles?"

"Yes. He dumped me. Told me to get all my shit and get out, but in a nicer, more British way. How did you know I'd be coming here?"

"I have a way of knowing where you are. It must be our connection. Our story is written in the stars, lit by the moonlight. Do you see him? He's smiling at us."

"See who?"

"The man in the moon smiling down on us?"

I was definitely going to die tonight.

"Totally. Love him. Oh! Look, it's the barn. Wanna sit in there?" I said as I darted into the dark building without waiting for his response. I didn't really have a plan, per se, but I figured that I might be able to lock Robert in the barn, run back to the house, alert Donna and Gina, and call the police, thus evading death.

Robert followed me into the barn and flipped a switch that activated fluorescent lighting high above us. It was so fucking creepy. The horrible white light, the hum of the fixtures, the smell of animals, animal poop, and damp wood. Barns are legit disgusting and this one was no exception.

Now that I was in the barn, I didn't know exactly what to do. With Robert basically breathing down my neck, I walked in a quick circle around the entire barn and back toward the entrance we'd just come through. I started giggling, not really clear why, probably out of hysteria/fear of being murdered. I figured if I could get back to the door and lock it behind me with Robert still inside, I might have enough time to make it back to the house.

But Robert was right on my tail. He was gunning for me, and caught up to me right as I was about to be out the door.

"Where are you going, lover? You stone fox." He grabbed me and pinned me up against the wall. I was basically panting. This was it—if I didn't act now, I was 100 percent dead. When you get that close to death, you can just feel it. Robert started kissing my neck, giving me time to look down and locate a stray two-by-four. Without hesitation, I ducked Robert's embrace, grabbed the piece of lumber, then turned and whacked him in the head with it as hard as I possibly could.

Robert fell to the floor.

I blacked out.

When I came to, I was staring at a note on the wall right above Robert's limp body.

Blood is red, blood is blue.

You are me and I am you.

In my right hand was a black lipstick. I stared at the note and inspected every detail. I had no recollection of writing this fucking note, yet it looked exactly the same as every other one I'd gotten over the past year. My eyes began to lose focus. I had a vision of Robert kissing me, telling me he was engaged, and then finding a note on my bathroom mirror; then Robert and I making love at Chateau Marmont, and me finding the note on my iPad; then our fight over the intercom and the destroyed photo; then talking about Robert with Donna in Paris and the note on the bathroom door; then dinner with Robert at Koi and the next day getting the black lipsticks; and after that, a note on my compact; then finally the breakup with Charlie and the severed roses. Robert was never my stalker. He was just the catalyst. Being around him, or even thinking about him, had made me write these notes.

"It's me," I whispered. "Oh my God, I'm my own stalker."

But I wasn't my own stalker. Babette, that cunt-faced whore, had possessed me and caused me to stalk myself. She was my fucking stalker.

"Oh my god! Oh my god! Oh my god! Oh my fucking god! Robert!"

I looked down to see Robert lying lifeless in a pool of blood. My poor, beautiful, kind Robert. What had I done?

I screamed, terrified, until I heard Donna and Gina yelling from the direction of the house. I couldn't wrap my brain around what had just happened, but I did realize that they were about to walk into a murder scene. I just couldn't deal with that right now, so I ran over to the huge barn door and slid it shut. I found a leather horse bridle with reins that was hanging on the wall, looped it all through the door handles, and tied a thick knot, locking the two barn doors together.

Donna and Gina were now banging at the barn door and yelling for me to open it.

"Babe?! Are you okay? We heard screaming. Why is this door locked?" shouted Donna.

"I'm fine," I called back in the most normal voice I could muster. "We're fine. We're just talking."

"Babe, open this door right the fuck now!" Gina yelled.

"Please just leave us alone for a bit. We have a lot of stuff we need to figure out."

I could hear Donna and Gina whispering, but I was in too much shock to focus on what they were saying. I've had nightmares like this, but everything seemed too real to be a dream.

I grabbed a small bunch of straw from the stable floor and propped up Robert's head, kissed him on his forehead, and said my final good-bye. The stark truth was that Babette had to die in order for Robert's untimely death to be avenged. Unfortunately, the only way that I could kill her was to kill myself. Definitely not the best turn of events, but it was either that or spend the rest of my life in a New York State correctional facility. Suicide seemed to make a lot more sense in the context of my personal narrative than a life of wearing orange in prison.

I climbed up a twenty-foot ladder that led to a loft above the barn, but when I got to the top I realized it wasn't nearly high enough to jump off of if my endgame was death. I needed to get much higher if I was going to successfully *Black Swan* myself. I saw a small door on the roof that looked like it might provide access to the outside, but I had no way of getting up to it.

I heard screaming coming from below me. Donna and Gina must've gotten into the barn and discovered Robert's body. There was a crack of thunder. It had started to pour outside, and the raindrops sounded ominous on the barn's tin roof.

"Babe? What the hell are you doing up there? Are you okay?" Donna shouted as she noticed me struggling above.

"What happened to him? What's going on?" Gina pleaded.

I didn't answer them. I couldn't speak.

The end of a ladder was sticking out from underneath some hay on the far side of the loft, and I ran over and began uncovering it. It was massive, but I had so much adrenaline and power pumping through me that I was able to hoist it up and wedge it against the ceiling. As I climbed toward the roof hatch, Donna climbed the first ladder to the loft.

"Donna! Don't!" I screamed. "If you come any closer, I swear to God I'll jump."

Donna froze.

"I'm the stalker, Mom. I'm the monster. It was Babette all along." I started to cry.

"What are you talking about?" she asked. "We can fix this."

"But, like, we can't!"

"Babe, we'll figure this out! Just come down!"

"It's over. The only way to kill Babette is to kill Babe—don't you understand?!"

By the time I had reached the hatch on the ceiling of the barn, I was bawling, with hair in my face and sweating through my tank top.

I threw the hatch open, and rain started pouring down on me. I took one final glance at my mother and then lifted myself up and out onto the slick roof. The rain was so heavy that I could barely see two feet in front of me. I held on to some kind of steeple that had a weather vane on top. I tried to walk along the crest of the roof, but I couldn't get my balance, so I crouched back down, holding on for dear life. The wind, lightning, and thunder were tremendous. I was praying that I would get struck by a bolt of lightning, ending my misery. But I didn't have the time to wait for a miracle.

Donna and Gina had run outside of the barn and I could hear them shouting at me from below. All of a sudden there was a slight break in the wind. This was my chance. I stood quickly, kicked off my flats, and without another thought in my head started running. When I reached the end of the roof I just kept going, closed my eyes, and imagined Robert and me on a beach in St. Barths. As I fell to my death, I was smiling. Now we would be together, forever.

PART I

THE FUNERAL

The funeral was beautiful. The sun broke through the clouds, giving the entire outdoor service a glowing aura. The guests were all seated in a circular formation around a simple closed oak casket out on a lawn next to the barn where all the drama had gone down just a few weeks earlier.

The harpist, a local friend of Donna and Gina's, who was hired to play Radiohead songs during the service, was a delight. For someone who played a classical instrument, she was actually very chic. I mean, aren't the types of people who play violin and piano or whatever so awkward normally? It's like they never had a chance to learn how to make themselves cute because they've spent their entire lives behind an instrument with a fat instructor breathing down their necks. Not this woman. She had long black hair and wore all white everything, a very bold move for a day about death, but it totally worked. She was the perfect amount of chic for a perfectly chic funeral. It was like she knew that everyone there would be chic, so she chic'd herself for the occasion. Wherever you are, harpist, please know that I really appreciated you that day.

The harpist wasn't the only person who looked good that afternoon. In fact, everyone brought winning looks, as if they knew that the best way to honor me was to show up to this service looking fucking amazing. And everyone important was there.

Mabinty, in her favorite purple Diane von Furstenberg wrap dress, sat next to Donna and Gina, who were both wearing all black. Black sweaters, black pants, black boots. I guess they're traditionalists when it comes to deathwear, but nontraditionalists when it comes to being former-model lesbian farmers. Next to my lezzie moms sat Roman and then Genevieve. Roman was wearing a look that I'd never seen him try to pull off before. His silhouette is typically tailored, body-conscious, and inspired by motorcycle clothes, but on that day on a farm in upstate New York, he found it appropriate to show up and give us all witchy layered Rick Owens vibes, with a new bleached dye job. It was overwhelmingly major. I'll never forget how loved I felt when I saw him that day.

Genevieve wore her typical bandage dress situation (but in black) with some sort of bootish heels that only deserved a quick glance; a true examination of her shoes would have most likely upset me and spoiled the entire event, so I opted out. It was whatever. I was happy she was there.

Closing out the circle were my dad and Lizbeth, both of

whom were paying due tribute by arriving in the finest of forms. Okay, Lizbeth always looks "good," or whatever, but I'd never seen the two of them look so healthy and vibrant. My dad wore a pair of black Simon Miller jeans that fit him impeccably; a crisp, white Tom Ford button-down; a very handsome, very black Givenchy sport coat; and suede Alexandre Plokhov boots. Chicness. Lizbeth wore an appropriate below-the-knee black Fendi dress and was giving us legs and arms for days, as usual. It almost brought a tear to my eye to see how complete they looked as a couple sitting there hand in hand. They were truly obsessed with each other and no matter how much I wanted her to be a stepmonster and how much I wanted to hate her, I would never hate Lizbeth and there was nothing I could do about it. When my dad told me in London that love takes time because people need time to figure out the type of love that they require from each other, I wanted to slap him. But it finally made sense to me on the day of the funeral. They deserved each other. Ew, anyway . . .

The last guest, and maybe the most important guest, was, of course, Robert. I don't know if this is weird to say, but he looked so insanely Robert-ish that day that I would have fucked him right there in front of everybody if I could have. It would've been too much, though. Too much drama, too much skin, and my dad and Mabinty were there. So, no. But he was gorgeous and his welcome speech touched everyone's souls. I could see it on their faces. Despite the fact that it was a funeral, everyone there knew that the deceased was in a better place. It was almost a celebration. A cathartic energy lofted through the open, beautiful space. I really couldn't have asked for more.

"Hello, everyone, it's really nice to see those of you whom I haven't seen in a long, long time."

I saw Mabinty shed a single tear when he looked at her and smiled.

"And to be honest, I'm happy that these are the circumstances that have brought us back together. Only Babe could have pulled something like this off."

Having him up there made me so proud.

"So, Babe asked me to keep this short and sweet, and that's what I'll do. She wrote the words but wanted me to deliver the speech. Then we can all go relax and have a glass of wine and eat some organic greens grown right here on Gina and Donna's farm. Per Babe's request, obviously."

Everyone laughed together. I may have even smiled. I was so happy. It was weird.

"So here goes: Dearly beloved, we gather here to say our good-byes to the world's most terrifying, nauseating, tacky mess of a bitch, Babette Walker. May she stay dormant in Hades for ever and ever and ever and ever."

With that, I couldn't contain myself from running to him. I sprinted from my seat and threw my arms around Robert. Hearing him say those words was the final nail in Babette's literal coffin and it felt like someone had just shot adrenaline through my heart. I was free, I was alive, I was a Babette-less Babe sprinting from my dark past and toward the man who represented my solid, beautiful future.

But wait, I think I might be getting a bit ahead of myself . . .

PART II

THE PRE-FUNERAL

*T*he weeks after I jumped off the barn roof were strange and confusing days for everyone. I have hazy memories of the night itself, like the moment when I struck Robert across the head with that two-by-four and the way the rain felt pouring down on me on that tin roof. I can still feel the coldness on my skin if I let myself go back to that place emotionally, which I try not to do, ever.

The first real memory I have is waking up in a stark and clinical room that I thought was either a mental ward, a hospital, or heaven. I was still kind of a complete fucking mess. The thing that was most shocking to me in that moment when I woke up in the white room was seeing Robert in a doctor costume standing above me.

"I'm sorry, but what the fuck is going on?" I tried to sit up, but the pain was agonizing.

"We're at Saint Francis Hospital, near Poughkeepsie. You were in an accident," Robert said.

"I know I'm in a fucking hospital, but I thought I killed you. I thought I killed me too. What's going on?"

"You tried to do both of those things."

"Wait. So we're dead? Is this heaven? Tai Tai?" I called out for my dead grandmother.

"Babe, Babe. You're fine. We're both fine. You broke your wrist and we had to remove a couple ribs. But other than that—"

"I broke WHAT? You did WHAT?" I was stunned.

"You broke your *costae fluitantes,* aka your lowest ribs, in the fall, and after we discussed it, you said you'd rather have them removed. It was a simple procedure and you said you've always wanted fewer ribs. Do you not remember any of this?" He looked concerned; I probably looked ecstatic.

"No, I don't remember, but I'm obsessed—my god, yes. I've wanted those ribs gone forever. I guess this whole Babette-scapade wasn't all worthless. Every cloud . . ."

Robert just laughed at me, but in a cute way. He looked so proud of me, as if I'd just come home from the war or something actually scary. But you know what? I had just come home from war. War with myself, but still it was, like, a legit war.

"Also, why are you wearing scrubs? You're not still Roberto, are you?" The thought rushed through my bones like cold water.

"No! I'm pretty sure he died when you hit me."

"Oh, thank God."

"I've been taking care of you here."

"But why you? I don't get it. Where's my doctor?" Last time I checked Robert was a sports agent, so I was either high or I was high.

"I'm your doctor. I'm a sports doctor, Babe. You knew this." I could see that he could see that I had no idea what he was talking about. "Or didn't you?"

"Um . . ."

"Wowwwww. Really?" He smiled, shaking his head back and forth. He leaned in and kissed me on the forehead. "Nice to meet you. My name is Robert, I'm a doctor. Have been for the last seven years."

Why did I think Robert was a sports agent this entire time?

What? But then again, why wouldn't I have missed that? As soon as someone starts talking about sports, I immediately tune out.

"But wait, are you okay?" I asked him, grabbing his hand.

"I had a minor concussion. All the blood was coming from a small gash near my temple. Couple stitches, no biggie. You hit me hard as fuck, though. I'm actually impressed. Babette is a strong motherfu—"

"Let's not talk about her," I interrupted, cutting him off. It was too soon and I needed space from it all. "I'm sorry, Robert, I really am. I wasn't myself that night."

"I know, Babe, and we don't have to talk about it. We don't have to talk about it ever again if you'd like."

"Well . . . I was thinking that in order to bury her, I might need to literally bury her."

Robert shot me a confused glance, which quickly became a smirk, and that's how the idea for Babette's funeral was born.

PART III

THE NOW

*A*fter the funeral, etc., Robert and I decided that we'd been through everything that a couple should ever have to go through in order to be together, so the only thing left to do was move into a small beach house together in Malibu—Malibu was his idea, not mine. I told him that living with that much sand in the air can dry your skin and your hair to the point of no return, but he wouldn't back down. New Robert is all about telling Babe what to do, and New Babe is all about letting Robert make decisions. It sucks, but my therapists tell me it's good for me and for Robert. For us.

We are being soooo us. Waking up next to him each morning is all I've ever wanted, but I never knew how it would feel IRL. It feels so good. It feels too good to be true, actually, but I try not to let myself think that.

We adopted a pug with cancer and changed his name from Lucas to Lulu Guinness. I'm in the process of turning him gay by telling him he's gay every morning. It's not working, but it gives me a purpose.

Robert is working for the Lakers full-time as the team doctor.

We're happy, we're infatuated with each other more than ever, and we fuck every day. I'm happy to say that neither Babette nor Roberto has popped into our lives since that night in the barn, which makes me anxious to think about, but I carry a new hybrid of Xanax and molly with me at all times now, in case I need to extinguish the beast. Fingers crossed that she's eternally deceased.

The funny thing is, after the hellish ride that this year has been, I never thought that I'd find this level of happiness. I'm almost too happy and it scares me. But like Jackson always said, the universe delivers.

Maybe I should write a book about all this bullshit. Eh, probably not.

acknowledgments

I couldn't have made it through this insane period of my life without the continual love and support of the following psychos:

Dad, Lizbeth, Robert, Charlie Dean (sorry), Mabinty Jones, Donna Valeo & Gina, Genevieve Larson, Roman Di Fiore, Lara Schoenhals, Tanner Cohen, and David Oliver Cohen.

And the following psychos couldn't have made it through their insane lives without my continual love and support:

Byrd Leavell (my super hot agent who is basically responsible for everything good that's ever happened to me), Tricia Boczkowski (my brilliant editor), Elana Cohen, Alex Lewis, and the entire Gallery/Simon & Schuster Team.

Butch Schoenhals, Linda Schoenhals, Jake Schoenhals, Kurt Schoenhals, Sara Schoenhals, Jennie Hunnewell, Chandler Hunnewell, Marcia Cohen, Stewart Cohen, Cristiana Andrews Cohen, Penelope Ziggy Cohen, Hal Winter Cohen, Jessica Lindsey, Natalie Stevenson, Luce Amelia Stevenson-Cohen, Liz Newman, Frank Newman, Tristan Andrews, David Ludwig, Howie Sanders, Larry Salz, Jason Richman, Fred Tozcek, Chris

Abramson, Brian Agboh, Pellegrino, Wyatt Hough, Audrey Adams, Leonardo DiCaprio, William Reid, Ryan O'Connell, Green Juice, Jason Sellards, Chris Moukarbel, Toby Moukarbel-Sellards, Oliver Daly, Luke Gilford, Jenny Grier Craddock, Adam Schneider, Chloe Yellin, Elizabeth Banks, Max Handelman, The Leon Chopped Salad at La Scala, Olivia Wolfe, Stephanie Krasnoff, Tajli Siladi, Chris Macho, Fabrizio "Fat Jew" Goldstein, Christine Ronan, Amanda Bynes, Emma Roberts, Bill Bellingham, Francesca Eastwood, Skye Peters, Steve Jobs, Princesca, Gizmo, Babe, Catcher, Oscar, Moose, Big Pudy, Little Pudy, Milo, Pepper, Tiger, Socks, Pudy, Nancy, Neko, Toby, Sophie, Biscuit, Rockwell, Panda, Martha, Orangie, Emily, Red Sox, Little Kitty, Tabby, Butch Jr., Madison, Little Black Princess, Wolf Girl, Dirty Nose, Whiskers, Cleopatra, Sophie, Whitey, Lauren, Maxwell George, Maggi, and Samba.